ALIYA

TO THE
INFINITE CITY

Dust, heat and magic are in the air . . . I can almost smell the rich scents from Aliya's world! A fantastic journey awaits you; fly through time on a magic carpet, meet new friends (some of them not *quite* human) and uncover dark secrets and truly unexpected truths. This is an epic and so, so enjoyable! Climb aboard with the stunning new author Laila Rifaat and become a time-traveller yourself!

BARRY CUNNINGHAM
Publisher
Chicken House

ALIYA

TO THE
INFINITE CITY

Laila Rifaat

Chicken House

2 Palmer Street, Frome, Somerset BA11 1DS
www.chickenhousebooks.com

Text © Laila Rifaat 2024
Illustration © Gaia Alessi 2024

First published in Great Britain in 2024
Chicken House
2 Palmer Street
Frome, Somerset BA11 1DS
United Kingdom
www.chickenhousebooks.com

Chicken House/Scholastic Ireland, 89E Lagan Road, Dublin Industrial Estate,
Glasnevin, Dublin D11 HP5F, Republic of Ireland

Cover design by Helen Crawford-White
Cover illustration by Gaia Alessi
Typeset by Dorchester Typesetting Group Ltd
Printed in Great Britain by Clays, Elcograf S.p.A

FSC
www.fsc.org
MIX
Paper | Supporting
responsible forestry
FSC® C018072

1 3 5 7 9 10 8 6 4 2

British Library Cataloguing in Publication data available.

PB ISBN 978-1-915026-35-4
eISBN 978-1-915947-09-3

To my family

Chapter 1
THE SECRET ROOM

Aliya's grandfather had vanished again. She knew it the moment she put her ear to the keyhole of his study. Pressing it tight to the cold metal, she listened for newspaper pages rustling, tea being slurped, backgammon chips rattling or snoring, but there was only silence.

Today of all days, she had thought he might not vanish, but the silence through the keyhole offered no other explanation. Aliya gave the study door an angry shove. You only turned eleven once in your life. Yet here she was: cake- and present-less, standing like an idiot in front of a locked door.

She tried peeking through the keyhole again. It really was oddly quiet in there, as though the room had magically whisked her grandfather away. Most days, the keyhole let through nothing but silence and darkness, like now. But at other times she could swear she'd caught a glimpse of some faraway place – a billowing desert or a street full of people. There were smells too, sometimes, of spices or petrol or camel dung. It was as though the room couldn't make up its mind as to where it was leading – or was it just her loneliness creating fancies in her mind?

Aliya had done her best to think of plausible explanations that would dispel the mystery. Was there a secret exit in the study that Geddo used to escape somewhere? To a local coffee shop, perhaps, to read his paper in peace? Or for a glass of tea with mint and a game of backgammon with a worthy opponent? Aliya stuck her nose into the keyhole and sniffed. No odd fumes floated out of it today. Still, there was something strange going on. She just knew it.

Before his disappearances began, Geddo had been a fairly normal grandfather – the kind that lost his glasses, fell asleep in the armchair, and watched boring documentaries on the old television. They had done ordinary granddaughter–grandfather things, like take slow walks to the corner store and eat Geddo's old-man dinners, mostly spicy sausages and eggs. She had helped him hang the laundry (her socks were too fiddly for his fingers) and dry the dishes. They had fed the street cats together. Whenever a new one appeared to feast on their tuna and soaked-bread mix, they had thought of cat names. Aliya was partial to cool, American names – like the ones from the series she watched – but Geddo insisted on Arabic names that began in the back of the throat and shot over the tongue as if they were late for an appointment: *Kharboush*, *Zoronfil* and *Abu Samak*. Egyptian cats couldn't be called Phoebe or Chandler.

Then, one month ago, Geddo had gone into his study and come out . . . different. He had begun to look worried. He'd stopped talking to her. Things really got strange when he took her out of school and told her they had to move – urgently – no questions asked. But Aliya had asked a hundred questions. Where were they going? Was he feeling well? Should she call a doctor? What about the street cats? Who would feed them when they were gone?

Next thing she knew, they had left everything behind.

First, they had stayed with an old lady in a house on the edge of a desert, then a week in a crumbling hotel – under a false name – and now they were in a rented flat in a tumbledown house by the Mediterranean.

Aliya glanced around at the shabby place, water damage spread on the walls and ceilings like a rash. Dumped in an almighty heap were all their earthly belongings, looking like they were put up for a jumble sale.

What was even stranger was how her grandfather had begun to keep one room to himself wherever they went. A room that became *secret*, that only Geddo and Mr Kamel, the new butler – yes, *butler*! – were allowed into. Aliya ran her hand over the door and knew – knew with her whole being – that the answers to Geddo's strangeness were locked away in there, within this mystery that went with them everywhere.

Turning from the door, Aliya scanned the cluttered living room. If Geddo wasn't going to get her a gift, she'd find herself some money and go get herself one. She sniffed, eyes burning with dust and oncoming tears. She might not be worth celebrating, but at least she was going to have something other than leftovers for her birthday lunch.

Getting up, she picked her way through her grandfather's things, which lay in haphazard heaps since their last move. There was some of his gilded furniture, bum-shaped dents sagging their middles. The usual Cairo mix of sand and dust had been carried with them and lay like a thin shroud over everything.

An old suitcase full of books caught Aliya's eye. One title read *Sphinx Tutmos: An Interview*. Turning the book over, she studied a photo of a sceptical-eyed sphinx in knitwear. Weird. She had never seen these old tomes before. They had to belong in Geddo's study with the rest of the secrets. With each move, things from within the closed room had begun to spill out, feeding her clues, like a treasure chest springing a leak.

She picked up another sour-smelling book called *Raw Health – A Guide to Ghoulish Healing (No Cooking Required)*. Then there was *Carpet Care for the Expert Flyer*. The photo showed a carpet poised in mid-air, its rider, by the looks of it, holding on for dear life.

Geddo had always told Aliya bedtime stories about fantastical things – they were part of their bedtime routine – but these books looked so real, as if they had some actual, practical use.

The stories, which her grandfather told as if they were bona fide truths, featured everything from sphinxes with allergies, to Egyptian ghouls who were quite sensitive once you got to know them, provided you survived long enough. One of Aliya's favourites told of a naughty girl who got swept away by a flying carpet. It flew around most of the world before the girl could think of the magic word that made it land.

'What was the word?' Aliya would ask when the carpet had sped across the Andes with no sign of slowing down.

'"Please,"' Geddo would say. 'Please is a magic word.'

Politeness was the only kind of magic Geddo approved of. Many of his stories warned of another sort, that was dark and dangerous and fed on people's souls.

That would bring Geddo to the story of the beautiful prince with hair like gold and the bluest eyes, whose ambition knew no bounds. He wanted to rule over time itself, like a god, and sought out the beings of darkness to trade pieces of his humanity in exchange for powers such as no man should have. That story always ended with the prince making an awful mess of his kingdom, so one night Aliya thought up a new ending, starring a young girl much like herself fearlessly saving the day.

Now, as she sat staring at the closed door of the study, Aliya's heart pinched as she remembered the look Geddo had given her. He clearly didn't think she would be capable of such bravado – or of any kind of adventure, not in real life or even as part of a fairy tale.

She turned from the door again, resolving to find some money for a gift and a meal amid the mess.

Then, behind her, the door to the secret room suddenly thumped open.

A tall man in a tweed suit towered in the doorway, the door quickly swinging shut behind him – too fast for her to glimpse beyond its threshold. He looked a bit like a neatly ironed Sherlock Holmes, but with glasses. It was Mr Kamel, the new butler. He had appeared out of the study one day, about a month ago, as if Geddo had conjured him out of a wardrobe.

Aliya watched as he settled himself into one of the gilded armchairs and began polishing his pipe. Weren't butlers supposed to be some sort of servant? Were they really supposed to wear that much tweed? She had seen them in movies, where they always stood around looking sombre and dutiful. They would announce visitors or bring plates of food, that kind of thing. But Mr Kamel didn't check any of those boxes. He never did anything useful, and only ever polished things that belonged to himself. Most annoyingly, he wouldn't answer any of her questions about what was going on with Geddo, although *he* got to go into the study – a total stranger. She watched him light his pipe and send a small cloud of smoke adrift towards the ceiling, looking very much like an evil genie out of Geddo's fairy tales.

'What is it you put in that thing?' she asked, making a face. 'It smells like farts.'

Mr Kamel paused mid-puff.

'Pulverized girl bones.'

He turned to her with a frown that deepened as he noticed Aliya's dirty feet wagging in his direction. Aliya wiggled her toes challengingly at him.

'It's my birthday today,' she said. She waited for a moment, but Mr Kamel only blew another smoke ring. 'Do you know what it's like to celebrate your birthday alone?' she said. 'Your *birthday*. With nothing but old sandwiches to eat?' She gestured at the mess on the coffee table. 'And he missed my parents' memorial day. He never did that before. We always read some prayers.'

Ever since her parents passed away, she and Geddo had marked the anniversary by visiting their graves to recite some suras from the Quran. Then they had gone to the ice cream shop on the corner near the graveyard. It was *tradition*.

'Death-days and birthdays,' Mr Kamel said with a scoff. 'Your grandfather has important things to take care of. He certainly doesn't need a witless child to weigh him down.'

Aliya flinched. Her birthday wasn't important? The thought smarted, as if Mr Kamel had pinched her.

'What things?' she asked.

'If he wanted you to know, I guess he would have told you.'

Another smarting thought. Aliya pressed her lips into a line. Mr Kamel looked at her with raised eyebrows. He wore the same expression Geddo had when she proposed a new ending for the disastrous prince story. He was probably thinking about the tutor Geddo had hired to help her catch up with school – the one she'd managed to exasperate until he quit, leaving behind a letter for Geddo full of phrases like 'no aptness for academic studies', and 'fell asleep again'. Aliya had hidden the letter from Geddo, then turned it into an assortment of origami cranes that had been left behind to gather dust in their old flat. Maybe she should have studied more. Cared more. Shown him she was dependable?

Maybe then, Geddo would have confided in her? Was it too late now?

As Mr Kamel returned to his pipe, a cold feeling slithered around Aliya's heart, hissing terrible thoughts. What if Geddo was in trouble? Geddo had looked so unwell this past month, with all his pacing about and frowning, and his silence.

Fear bubbled up, fizzing in her chest.

She stood up.

'He's *my* grandfather,' she said. 'If he's in trouble I should help him!'

'You want to help?' Kamel pointed at her bedroom door with his pipe. 'Then stay out of the way. Beat it.'

Before Aliya quite knew what had happened, she had scraped up a handful of sandy dirt from under the rug and thrown it straight at Mr Kamel's chest. They both stared at his soiled shirtfront for a moment before he lunged at her, thin hands outstretched. She scuttled backwards across the floor like a panicking crab. Skidding through her bedroom door, she slammed it shut behind her. She fumbled with the latch. It slipped in her hands. Her heart throbbed in her throat. The door shook as Mr Kamel tried to open it.

Bam. Bam. Bam.

Clack. The latch slid into place.

She was safe.

She took a deep breath to steady herself, then crouched down and peeked through the keyhole, only to jerk back in fear. An eye, yellow and unblinking, was staring back at her.

The key turned on the other side. She waited until Mr Kamel's footsteps had died away and the front door had opened and closed.

He had locked her in.

Great. Now there were two doors between her and the mystery in the study. A feeling of defeat stole over her. And there was another feeling too. Being alone had never really scared her before. But now . . . Geddo was in trouble, and she had no idea how to help him. To start, she would have to find out what was going on, and to do that she needed to get into the study.

Chapter 2

THE NECKLACE

It was near midnight. Aliya had paced her room for hours, then finally dozed off, only to be awoken by a strange smell spreading through the bedroom. As she sniffed the air, her heart leapt into her throat. Something was burning!

Woozy with sleep, she tumbled out of bed and skidded to a stop in front of her now open door. A black envelope lay on the floor, smouldering in one corner. Flecks of burning paper glowed in the half-light. Aliya stood frozen, looking at a thin pillar of rising smoke. Beyond the door the living room lay dark and deserted.

She poked the corner of the envelope with her foot. Could it be a message from Geddo? But why would he be sending her a burning letter?

She stomped on the envelope but when she lifted her foot, it still bristled. In the kitchen she tried sprinkling it with water, but the smoke shot back into the air the moment she stopped. Even stranger, the black paper felt cool under her fingertips. As she tore it open, the blackness seeped away, like ink slipping off a plate. Left was a milk-white card. A few words spelt out a thrilling message:

Only for you . . . Aliya Sultan.

Then a golden chain dropped into her palm.

She stood looking at the gleaming thing in her hands. It was a necklace with a teardrop-shaped diamond. There was an engraving on the setting. Cursive letters spelt a name in the gold.

Nabila

Aliya stroked the word with her fingertips. That was her mother's name.

Searching the envelope for a clue as to its sender, she found a note.

My dear girl . . .

Aliya drew a shaky breath. No one had called her 'dear' for as long as she could remember. Geddo would sometimes pat her on the head, but he wasn't good at words, especially not caring ones.

Many years ago, your mother pledged something very special to my safe keeping – an item which it is now time to pass on to you. Let it help you find your calling. It will protect you against those who try to stop you, but you must keep it a secret!

Rub the diamond and ask for assistance . . .

The note was signed by an initial, an elegantly coiled letter. Was it a D or a Z? She quickly ran through Geddo's and her acquaintances: a couple of neighbours, a few tutors, the old grocer on the corner . . . none of them fitted the bill. This had to be someone else – someone she'd never met, someone from her mother's life.

She was about to slip the necklace around her neck when the oddest feeling made her drop it to the floor. For a moment it had felt alive in her hands!

As she picked the necklace up the gold felt comfortable again, resting on her warm skin.

Rub the diamond . . .

She gave the stone a tentative stroke.

It began glowing.

A red haze rose out of it, forming a cloud. Aliya stumbled backward and fell on her behind. A feeling like soda-pop bubbles fizzled through her. The cloud detached from the diamond and floated off like a dream taking shape.

Magic. This had to be *magic*!

Aliya felt like screaming in terror and laughing all at once. This was too much – this was *unreal*. But – the sensible side of her brain protested – what if it was a trick?

'Show me who this necklace belonged to.' Aliya rubbed the gem again. More haze collected into a shape, like a holographic image. A woman took form in mid-air. She had almond-shaped eyes and a round face framed by a cerise veil. There was a mole on the right side of her face, just above her eyebrow, and she was smiling as though she'd just heard some fantastic news.

Aliya's memories of her mother were all fuzzy — snapshots from too long ago to remember. Yet there she was, almost real, full of life and colour.

Her mother's face dissolved into thin air. Aliya's fingers combed the air where it had appeared. For some moments she stood still, staring into space.

Magic. Her heart hammered as she stared down at the diamond in her hands.

At certain angles she almost thought she could see something moving within its shimmering surface, as if it had captured a shadow.

Then, lifting it up for a closer look, she noticed that the letters on the setting were *moving*, flowing into a thin line then shaping a new name:

Aliya

She pressed the necklace to her chest. It had belonged to her mother and now it had become hers – her odd inheritance.

'Please bring my parents back. Bring them back from death. Unmake the accident.'

She waited with bated breath, but nothing happened.

'Please,' she tried again, rubbing the diamond harder. She had *magic*. She should use it to change everything – to get her family back, to start over!

But the gem lay dead in her hands. It wasn't complying – not with this wish.

A rosy haze still hung in the dark room, shedding glitter over the mounds of dusty books and leftover sandwiches – a whiff of something fantastic in her dreary world. She followed it with her eyes as it slid away along the floor before slipping under the door to the study. And then it was gone.

Aliya rushed across and tried the door. Locked. *Of course it is*. She slammed her palm against the wood.

She might not be able to magic her parents back, but she would find out what Geddo was hiding from her. She was tired of secrets.

For a moment, she hesitated. Geddo had said magic was evil, *haram*. But if her mother had owned a necklace like this, perhaps Geddo had got it wrong? Perhaps magic wasn't evil at all, just misunderstood?

Taking a deep breath, she squeezed the diamond. Whatever the truth was, she couldn't sit around and wait for it any longer. She'd have to go after it – come what may.

'Open this study,' she commanded.

The gem glowed red. A moment later, the heavy door in front of her clicked open.

Chapter 3
THE STUDY

The study door opened to darkness. Aliya fumbled for a light switch without success. After a moment's hesitation, she stepped inside, feeling her slippers sink into something soft – a Persian carpet.

The room was illuminated only by the soft glow of a fireplace. In front of it stood a large armchair, upholstered in green velvet. Rich carpets in reds and blues covered the dark parquet floor. There were bookcases full of old-looking tomes, a large globe on a wooden stand, and glass-fronted cabinets full of unfamiliar, gleaming things. An antique-looking desk stood in one corner, hardly visible under a spread of papers.

She went over and picked up a magazine. With

wide eyes she read an ad for *Habashy's Flying Carpets: Persian silk, camel, and goat hair. Handcrafted by the Nifty Chrononomers Needlepoint Society.* Another recommended *Mrs Dashing's haberdashery: everything for the time-travelling lady and gentleman.*

Time-travelling?

She flipped the pages in bewilderment, pausing at a photo of a man in a Victorian suit sitting in a hospital bed. With his sideburns and bushy eyebrows, he was clearly an adult, but seemed to have shrunk to the size of a baby. It made quite a peculiar image, since he was sucking on a pipe. The headline read:

ANOTHER COUNCIL MEMBER SHRINKS –

NEW POISONINGS SEND SHOCKWAVES

THROUGH THE TIME-TRAVELLING WORLD.

Under a photograph of a thin man in a shirt with lots of circles Aliya read:

Council member Neon Ticker dis-
misses rumours of magic entering
the Infinitum. 'Nothing but old
tales and superstition.'

She had expected the study to have something like a secret passage leading out into the city, one that Geddo had used to make his escape from her, but *time-travellers*?

Dropping the magazine, she walked over to the fireplace, feeling giddy.

The velvet armchair looked big and inviting. She sat down and watched the flames dancing. On the armrest lay one of Geddo's woollen cardigans. She picked it up and hugged it, breathing in the familiar smell of her grandfather: sandalwood and lemon aftershave. A strange mix of comfort and ill-ease came over her. Nothing was the same any more. Things had been so simple – boring and frustrating maybe, but simple. It had just been her and Geddo sharing everything, but now . . .

There was a photograph on the mantelshelf. Her mother again: soft, hazel eyes. Her round face in a white veil and the mole just above her right eyebrow. And her father – deep eyes, dimples, bushy hair, and the slightly crooked Sultan nose, just like hers and Geddo's. Aliya leant in and read the small text on a diploma her father was holding up:

This is to certify that Farid Farouk Sultan has successfully completed the course of studies and is hereby awarded the title of Traveller by the Infinitum Time Travel Society.

Aliya stared at the photo, grappling with the information.

'Time-travellers,' she whispered, as if pronouncing the words would give them more sense.

Maybe it wasn't literal – perhaps they were some sort of historians who travelled a lot? Academic types. Sort of like the students she sometimes spotted in the stationery shop on the corner, who were always using the photocopiers?

She had just put the photo back when someone seized her by the collar of her T-shirt and lifted her clean off the ground.

'*Infernal menace!*' Mr Kamel hissed in her ear. '*How did you get in here?*'

Aliya shook herself loose and ended up in a heap on the floor.

'Don't ever touch me again,' she hissed. 'If you do, you'll be sorry.'

As she spoke, Mr Kamel's eyes changed. Their

yellow sheen turned red as a pair of glowing coals, a pair of demon eyes. Aliya scrambled backwards until she couldn't get any further.

'That's enough,' a familiar voice said.

Geddo appeared behind her, windswept and frowning.

'He's not *human*!' Aliya shrieked into the folds of Geddo's coat as he scooped her up in a half-hug, half-shake. She tried to turn around, but Geddo held her still.

His grip tightened.

'You entering the study set off an alarm. That wasn't supposed to happen. How did you get the key?'

Aliya wriggled in his grasp, her thoughts tumbling over each other. She grasped at one. 'His eyes . . . He's a demon or something! Did he put some spell on you? Is he keeping us *captive*?'

'He's under my command,' Geddo muttered into the top of her head. 'Watch.' He turned to the butler. 'Kamel! Shrink.'

With a look of great indignation, the butler mysteriously began to shrink until he was no bigger than an apple. Then, with the same indignant expression, he slowly began swelling again. Just like the genies in Geddo's bedtime stories.

'W-what?' Aliya stammered. 'Is he actually a . . .'

'Genie.' Geddo sighed. 'There are things I haven't told you.'

Aliya untangled herself from Geddo's grasp. Her immediate shock was wearing off and another emotion was barging in.

'My parents were *time-travellers*? Is that even a real thing?' She shook her head wildly, then pointed accusingly at Mr Kamel. '*He* . . . or *it* knows. You told him and not me, even though I'm supposed to be your . . .' Her voice caught.

'If only you had done what you were told,' Geddo muttered. 'And stayed out of trouble in your room.'

'Stayed in my . . . You're joking, right?!'

Geddo glanced at his pocket watch, then straightened his red felt tarboosh hat, which sat like an exclamation mark on top of his stern face.

'I can't explain now,' he said. 'We must get you to safety.'

Geddo turned to Mr Kamel. 'My informant just

told me that the Council's on its way.' He nodded at Aliya. 'They mustn't find her. We'll head for the next hiding place.'

'Why?' Aliya cried. 'Who's coming? What've we got to *hide* for?'

Geddo waved her questions away.

'Go get the car,' he commanded the butler. 'We'll meet downstairs. Quickly now!'

Mr Kamel had just disappeared through the door to the living room when the study window slammed open, and a leg in a blood-red high-heeled shoe appeared through it.

Chapter 4
BETRAYAL

'*Hide*,' Geddo cried, dragging Aliya towards the writing desk. Pushing her down, he motioned for her to get behind it. She pulled the other way.

'Not until you tell me—'

'*Now!*'

She was about to gather herself for more resistance, but something in Geddo's face, an outrage she had never seen before, made her get down on her knees and crawl under it. Peeking out, she saw an elderly lady in a dress suit clamber through the window.

After a few ungraceful moments of prying her high heels from the window frame, the lady landed on the floor. Her hair was bobbed, and balanced atop it was a red hat that matched her sharp finger-nails. She reminded Aliya of the glamorous stars in the Egyptian black and white movies – only this lady was all in colour.

'Surprised to see me?' she asked Geddo.

'Gigi Hanem,' Geddo said, suddenly cool. 'I knew the Council was sending someone, but I didn't expect it to be you. I thought you never visited the twenty-first century?'

'It is a vulgar place.' The lady glanced around. 'But this is an emergency, as you very well know. We got an anonymous letter yesterday telling us where you were hiding. Inspector Prickly would have arrested you himself, but as a favour to me as your sister, I got the chance to bring you in quietly. His police robots have stun guns in their fingertips now. Did you know?'

Under the desk, Aliya froze. *Sister?* Geddo had always said they had no relatives. She felt his boot pressing her further into the cramped space. Her neck prickled. Why would her grandfather's sister be someone she needed to hide from?

'If this is about the family portal,' Geddo said,

'there's a perfectly reasonable explana—'

'Really?' Gigi cut him off. 'Could *blowing up* our family's portal ever be reasonable?' She shook her head, making the movie-star bob wobble. 'Thanks to your antics our family is under investigation! I had to use a *public* portal to get here. I needed *special permission* to use my own portal key. Can you even begin to imagine how humiliating that was?'

Aliya thought the way she said 'public' sounded like she'd described having grilled rats for lunch. What was a portal? Why had Geddo destroyed it? Her head felt light. Everything about this scene belonged in a dream, yet she felt very much awake.

'It's time our family cut their ties with the travelling world,' Geddo said. 'As I've told you in multiple letters. I was hoping blowing up the portal would get me exiled.'

'Cut our ties?! *Exiled?*' Gigi closed her eyes and pinched the bridge of her nose as if she had just got a massive headache. 'So, you really are mad after all. I've heard the rumours, but I didn't want to believe what they were telling me. That my brother, the esteemed Captain Sultan, head of the Infinitum

Brigade, would be skulking around dingy alleyways in Old Cairo looking for a mythical magic shop and some magician that you claim is *conspiring* against our family?'

As she spoke, Gigi's pencilled eyebrows had crept towards her hairline and disappeared under the brim of her hat.

'It's not just a myth,' Geddo said, doggedly. 'The Shop – The Old Evil – exists and is the centre of great wickedness. My genie is a first-hand witness to its workings. He lived in the Shop for a hundred and fifty-two years, trapped in a cookie tin.'

As Geddo spoke, his eyes widened into a mad stare. His nostrils flared.

'A genie in a cookie tin?' Gigi exhaled sharply. 'I can see it now. You really *are* in need of help. This is your grief acting up, creating fancies in your poor, tired mind. We mourn the loss of dear Farid and Nabila too, but it's been *six years*. You really must consider the counselling plan we had drawn up . . .'

'I'll be damned if I let some nitwit poke around in my brain!' Geddo barked. 'My son died, my daughter-in-law . . . and little Aliya. They're gone. No blasted treatment will change that.'

Aliya's head snapped up and smacked into the underside of the desk.

Had Geddo just told his sister that she had *died* with her parents?

'Please don't make this more difficult than it has to be.' Gigi shifted on her heels. 'We need to evaluate your . . . state of mind, don't you see?' Gigi's hands trembled as she took a letter from her handbag and waved it in front of his face. 'There was something else in the anonymous letter I received about this child you claim passed away with her parents – your granddaughter. Yet this informant asserts that she *didn't* die in the accident. That you, in fact, raised her – a girl presently eleven years of age. I was even sent a photograph.' She took out a glossy photo. 'Here the two of you are, playing backgammon.'

For some moments the room was perfectly silent. Aliya felt her pulse throbbing in her ears.

'Ah yes,' Geddo said finally. 'I might have failed to mention her.'

'Failed to mention her?' Gigi stared at him. '*Failed* to mention the survival of our only heir?'

'Well, that's just the thing.' Geddo cleared his throat. 'She's not fit for the task, you see. I've tried to teach her, but when I found she was . . . lacking, well, I didn't see the need of mentioning her to you. Get your hopes up and all that.'

'Are you saying that our only hope for the future is . . . unfit?' Gigi sniffed. 'You're bluffing.'

'I could show you the letter her last tutor left,' Geddo said. 'But we'll need some glue, and patience. She turned it into a couple of origami cranes. Very pretty. At least we know she's good at something—'

'*Stop!*'

Aliya crawled out of her hiding place and stood up, facing her grandfather. Dust from the floor hung off her knees. Her head still hurt from when she bumped it, but she didn't care.

'You . . . pretended I was *dead*?'

Geddo looked back at her, his face unreadable. In all her life, she'd never imagined that he was ashamed of her. So ashamed that he hadn't told their only relative that she was alive! She sought his eyes for the understanding that used to be there, but he wasn't looking at her. He was shaking his head and shrugging! Disbelief washed over her like a bucket of ice water.

'That really proves it, doesn't it?' she said, her voice catching. 'That you . . . and I . . . and this – home – was never . . .' She bit hard on her lip. 'You know what? I don't even *want* you to be my grand-father any more!'

For a moment, Aliya thought she saw pain in Geddo's face – the mask cracked and something of the old, gentle man she had known peeked through, but only for a moment.

Now Gigi tottered over to her, heels clicking against the parquet. She grabbed Aliya by the chin, turning her face towards her. Aliya saw recognition light up her eyes and, for a moment, her angular face softened.

'You've got the Sultan nose,' she said in a hoarse whisper. 'And your hair . . . just as wild as your father's. The Sultan family has an *heir*.' Gigi turned to Geddo, her eyes moist. Then her face hardened again.

'You knew the state we were in, with no one to carry on the legacy, and yet you chose to lie and to hide her.' Gigi shook her head. 'You haven't prepared her or trained her. Instead, you've been gallivanting across the country on some mad quest against an enemy that only exists in your mind! If you had *any* sense at all, you would be supporting her to do her duty, not hiding her away! That's what her parents would have wanted, and you know it!'

At the mention of her parents, Aliya saw Geddo flinch, as if he had been slapped.

'I don't really know what you're playing at hiding her away,' Gigi continued. 'But it's madness, one way or another. Suitable or not, the girl comes with me to the Infinitum. We'll evaluate what's to become of her.'

'Gigi, *just listen*.' Geddo stepped closer to his sister, eyes intent. 'I always knew there was something off about Farid's and Nabila's deaths. After the fire there were traces in their flat – unnatural residues of magic. The Council wouldn't hear of it, of course. They did what they do best and stuck their heads in the sand, so I investigated on my own. And finally – a month ago – my search led me straight to the magical shop, and to *him*, as alive as you and me. *He's* the one running it now.'

As Geddo spoke, his face began to change: it contorted, froth building at the corners of his mouth. His nostrils flared. Aliya cringed. What was happening to him? He looked *mad*. Not angry mad, but as if his mind had suddenly broken.

'Saw who?' Gigi's voice overlapped with Aliya's, who had blurted out the same question.

'Dorian Darke.' Geddo spat the name as if it tasted foul. 'He's the one who hexed me.' He gestured at his scrunched-up face. 'So that I wouldn't be able to speak of his schemes.'

'You are rambling!' Gigi looked rattled. 'We all attended Dorian's funeral years ago, don't you remember? He was a tenured professor and an esteemed member of our travelling community. He was your daughter-in-law's mentor, for goodness' sake!' A pleading note crept into her voice. 'You helped carry him to his grave! Are you saying you saw his *ghost*?'

Aliya finally understood what had kept her

grandfather away for the past month. He had been out hunting someone called Dorian Darke.

Someone who was dead.

'He's alive, Gigi!' Geddo grabbed his sister roughly by the arms. 'He's been alive all this time, plotting against us. He's collected an army of cursed teapots and porcelain figurines and cupboards. That's why we need to break with the travel world – at least for now. I don't have enough evidence to prove it yet, but once I get a team together, I can beat him at his own game. I can—'

'*Enough.*' Gigi shook herself free and backed away. She fished a small white box out of her handbag. Pointing it at Geddo like a weapon, she clicked a button. The atmosphere suddenly became electric. Outside the still-open window, a faint buzzing grew louder. A moment later, a multitude of sleek white drones zoomed into the room. In a symphony of whirrs and clicks, they unfolded into lanky robots that trained their attention on Gigi.

'Prickly sent them along,' she said. 'In case things got . . . difficult.'

But before Gigi could give the robots a command,

Geddo had pulled an egg-like orb from his pocket and thrown it with force on the ground. It cracked open, releasing a quickly expanding cloud that smelt of soiled nappies and enveloped everyone and everything in a pink fog.

Aliya felt her grandfather's strong arms around her, dragging her towards the study door leading back into the apartment.

'*Get him.*' Gigi's order to the police robots cut through the smoke.

Aliya struggled against her grandfather's embrace. She banged at him with her fists. In front of her, the door to the flat opened, and her grandfather tried to pull her through. She resisted, wedging herself against the doorframe, tears and snot and fog turning everything into a blur. Then she felt other arms, sleek and metallic, grasping at Geddo's heavy frame. He struggled against them like a wounded bear, but the robots soon had him overpowered. Within a matter of moments, they had captured him in a web of sleek lassos.

As the smoke cleared, Aliya found her grandfather in a helpless heap on the floor, unable to move. She was overcome by an impulse to help him get free. Instead, she stood frozen, watching as he was hoisted through the window by the robots, his legs swallowed by the darkness beyond.

'Child!' Geddo roared over his shoulder.

His eyes shone with something intangible that made Aliya's blood freeze. He was not the old man she had taken for granted. He was someone she didn't know, with a past she knew nothing about.

'He will come for you. *You're* the one he wants, but you mustn't listen, child, do you hear?' He clawed the air, reaching for her against the arms holding him back. 'You mustn't believe anything he—'

'Geddo!' Aliya lunged towards the window, but it was too late.

It closed with a click, blotting out all sound.

Chapter 5
AN UNEXPECTED OPENING

'I had no choice.' Gigi smoothed down her bob. Reaching out, she gave Aliya a quick pat on the cheek. 'Your grandfather isn't well, don't you see? He needs help.'

Aliya stood forlornly in the middle of the room, the image of the struggling Geddo still in her mind's eye. Her head throbbed. Nothing made sense. One moment he had denied her existence because he was ashamed of her. The next, he'd seemed desperate to protect her . . . but from someone who was dead? Who had raised an army of cursed teapots and cupboards?

'Pure madness.' Gigi sighed. 'Or a severe case of time-hopping fever, which usually amounts to the same thing if left untreated.'

'Where did they take him?' Aliya asked. 'What will they do to him?' She tried to swallow the painful lump in her throat and focused her eyes on a spot on the carpet. If she wasn't careful, she would burst into loud, ugly sobs.

'There's a great counselling service available at the Infinitum, and a range of first-class treatments. He'll be well taken care of.'

Gigi looked around the study, as though searching for something. 'It's high time we went. Now, where is that assistant with my key? *Esmat!*'

Aliya gasped as a pair of black-rimmed glasses materialized out of thin air, and after them a briefcase clasped by a pair of thin hands. A young woman appeared as a continuation of the items. She was delicate-looking, with brown hair that fell in soft curls around her face. Her whole figure emitted a slight radiance, as though an LED lamp powered her.

'I'm s-sorry,' she stammered, gesturing at her still-invisible legs. 'Witnessing your family drama rendered me quite invisible. It always happens when I get nervous.'

Gigi gestured towards the glowing woman. 'Aliya, this is Esmat, my genie assistant . . . *when* I can find her.'

Aliya managed to return Esmat's smile as she hugged herself to stop shaking.

'Now, let's have a look at you.' Gigi gave Aliya an appraising look. 'I guess she'll grow and look less . . . what's the word?'

'Befuddled?' Esmat offered. 'She looks a bit befuddled.'

'I mean *wild*. She looks like she stumbled straight out of the Wilderness. Just look at that hair, and those . . . ugh, nails.' Gigi fanned herself, as though the mere thought of Aliya's unkemptness would make her pass out. 'And what is it that she's wearing? I suddenly remember why I visit this time so seldomly.'

Aliya looked down at her skinny jeans and her T-shirt with a print of a falafel sandwich wearing sunglasses. Swathes of dust still hung off her in places, all the way down to her SpongeBob flip-flops.

'I think she's pretty,' said Esmat. 'Just look at those dark-brown eyes and wild curls. She looks a lot like her grandfather. I hear he was quite dashing in his youth, even dated Cleopatra—'

'Nonsense.' Gigi inspected a strand of Aliya's tangled hair with a look of disgust.

'She can't possibly enter the Infinitum looking like this. She's a Sultan and must look the part.' She turned to Esmat. 'Schedule an emergency appointment at the bathhouse and let the dressmaker meet you there.'

'Meet us where?' Aliya looked from Gigi to Esmat. 'What's the Infinitum?'

'The world's greatest time-travel hub,' Esmat said proudly. 'Not the only one perhaps, but the oldest and greatest.'

'So, it's true?' Aliya said, wide-eyed. 'You *are* all really time-travellers?'

'Naturally.' Gigi unrolled a lipstick. 'Esmat, explain!'

'Well,' Esmat said, 'the short and sweet of it is that you're terribly late and frightfully ill-prepared. The other students have already begun their academic year. There's hardly time to make you ready, but we've got to follow the protocol for initiates. *It's in the rules*.'

She whispered the last part, as though the rules were around somewhere and might jump out and bite them.

Aliya glanced back at the study and, beyond it, the desolate flat. If she stayed behind, she would be alone — truly alone this time. Even if Geddo came back, everything would be different. He wasn't who she'd thought he was. And how could she stay with someone who believed she was useless? Who had pretended she was *dead*? She suddenly felt hollow, as if any gust of wind might sweep her away. It was all too much. She glanced around at the chaotic mess of upturned chairs and porcelain fragments on the floor left in the wake of Geddo's struggle with the robots, her mind reeling like a spooked horse. What had become of her home?

Her gaze settled on her parents' photo on the mantelshelf. Would they have thought she was useless too? Or maybe she would discover that she didn't belong here with Geddo at all, but with them in their world?

As if in response to her thought, Esmat lay a glowing hand on her shoulder.

'Come on, dear. You belong with us now.'

Belonging. The word shimmered in Aliya's mind for a moment and, as she looked up, this angular relative, her great-aunt, suddenly seemed to her a beacon of hope. A very tall, frowning beacon, but still – compared to the gaping aloneness of the dark flat, she didn't look too bad.

'OK,' she said. 'I'll do it. I'll come with you.'

'Of course.' Gigi picked up her handbag. 'Suitable or not, you'll have to do your duty. It's all been decided.'

'My things,' Aliya said. 'Don't I need to pack?'

Gigi glanced at the falafel sandwich on Aliya's T-shirt. 'All you'll need is available at the Citadel and, as your great-aunt, I will personally be taking care of your expenses. Now, come along.'

Chapter 6
THE INFINITUM

Great-Aunt Gigi took out a silver key and turned it in the small lock of the window she'd arrived through. Aliya glimpsed a perfectly white stone lodged in the key's blade, suspended by filigree silverwork in the shape of an eagle.

The window swung open into blackness, but as they stepped through, Aliya was pulled into a tube of light. It felt like being sucked into a vacuum cleaner, and as though every particle in her body was on fire and coming apart while her mind was turning itself inside out. The remains of her scanty breakfast came right up and disappeared into the bright air. The light pulled at her clothes, as if inspecting them, but the golden necklace lay safe in her pocket.

Her feet touched ground. Her head felt light, and for some moments she didn't know which way was up.

A steadying arm held her.

'I should've warned you about the *Whoosh*,' Esmat said. 'It's a chamber between your world and the travelling world, sort of like the customs at an airport. It makes sure nothing from your side passes into this one – bacteria, foodstuffs, that sort of thing.'

Aliya clutched the outline of the necklace in her pocket – how had that made it through, in either direction? What world was it from?

Feeling nauseous and wobbly, Aliya slowly focused her eyes on Esmat, and behind her, the most glorious room she had ever seen. She was standing on a wall-to-wall carpet run through by patterns of gold and green. A grand hall stretched out around her, with wood-panelled walls, golden lanterns and ornate woodwork arches on top of passages that led to carpeted corridors. Huge crystal chandeliers hung suspended from a ceiling that seemed to recede forever upwards.

There was a bustle of people hurrying across the carpeted floor, opening side doors and emerging from the corridors. A man in flowing robes and a white turban passed by close to them, carrying a precarious stack of books. A group of ladies in large hats appeared out of a door in the wall and disappeared down one of the corridors, their wide, puffed-up skirts swinging into each other.

'Exciting, isn't it?' Esmat said next to her. 'Those are all time-travellers coming back from missions.'

Aliya nodded, breathless. The vast space, the lights, the colourful jumble of people . . . It was *true*. There really were time-travellers, and she was in a different *world*. She took a tentative step, her flip-flop sinking into the lush carpet.

'The Infinitum arrival hall is a work of art.' Esmat's voice dropped to a whisper. 'You're lucky to see it today. Normally, Gigi would be using her Council-approved shortcut, which would have landed us straight in her office. However, as the Sultan family's private portal was sabotaged, she has to use the main arrival hall for the time being, just like everybody else.'

Gigi gave them a narrow-eyed look before pointing to a row of small fountains at the other side of the hall.

'Let her drink while I go see about transportation,' she said to Esmat. She tottered off towards one of the corridors as fast as her high heels could carry her.

Esmat led Aliya up to the row of marble fountains, where jets of sparkling water fell into a bubbling pool.

'The Infinitum has one common language for all its travellers,' she explained. 'We just drink some "Wordy Drops" and – cheers – we all understand each other. It is necessary, with all these people from different times and places meeting. Changes every ten years. Before this we all spoke Sudanese, but for now it's British English.'

She handed Aliya a small cup full of sparkling water. Aliya looked at the crisp bubbles.

'Don't worry, it won't make you forget your Arabic, just improve your English.' Esmat took a sip herself. 'Mmm, gooseberry.' She smacked her lips with pleasure. 'My favourite.'

Following suit, Aliya felt the cool drink tickling her insides. Suddenly a rush of words flooded her mind. 'Blimey . . . bee's knees . . . Bob's your uncle.' She turned to Esmat in shock, clutching her head. The words kept coming: 'Chinwag . . . chock-a-block . . . codswallop.'

'That's it,' Esmat smiled. 'Your mind is being upgraded.'

Esmat took Aliya by the arm, and they hurried off in pursuit of Great-Aunt Gigi. Turning into the corridor, they found her hovering over a sleepy-looking man in a tight galabeyya, who was sitting on top of a stack of Persian carpets.

'Asleep on the job?' she was scolding. 'What have you to say for yourself?'

'I wasn't sleeping on my job,' the man said, yawning widely and revealing at least three golden teeth. 'I was sleeping on my carpets. It keeps them calm.'

The argument turned to money, with Gigi insisting that, as Dean of Student Affairs (with connections to the top tier of the Infinitum ruling elite), she shouldn't have to pay. Soon the carpet handler was no longer sleepy, but red with irritation.

The edges of his carpets were twitching beneath him. Aliya stood watching, nauseous and weak-kneed, her mind still flooded with the most peculiar expressions: *Geezer*, she thought. *Give us a tinkle on the blower . . . gobsmacked*.

'How long will this go on?' she asked Esmat in a breathless whisper, pointing to her head.

'Until you reach *zonk*.' Esmat gave her a reassuring pat. 'That's the last word, I believe.'

Meanwhile, the carpet handler was pulling a fiercely red carpet out of the pile.

'Don't worry, madame.' He glowered at Gigi. 'This one will get you where you want to go before you can say "tea with mint".'

Aliya thought the way he said it sounded like he meant: 'And hopefully all the bones in your body will break in the process.'

'This one was hand-woven by members of our Executioners' Guild from the Medieval Quarter,' he continued. 'They do it for relaxation. Works wonders for the equilibrium of the mind . . . apparently.'

The red carpet had scenes woven into it showing what, to Aliya, looked like bundles of people with broken limbs, screaming for help.

'An executioner, as in chopping people's heads off?' she asked Esmat.

'That's right,' Esmat nodded. 'Very common practice during the Middle Ages. Thankfully they only work in their own time, back in the Earthly Dimension.'

'I call it *The Fiend*.' The handler patted the carpet with an ugly grin.

Gigi waved at Aliya and Esmat to sit on the carpet. She had removed her high heels and was carrying them pinched under her armpits.

'Will you need assistance, or do you know how to fly?' the handler asked her.

'I will not be needing any assistance, thank you very much.'

'It's been a long time since we used one, ma'am,' Esmat said, looking worried. 'And with a nickname like "The Fiend"—'

'Nonsense. I am a certified carpet flyer. Haven't you seen the diploma on the wall in my office?'

'Yes, but I believe that was Speedy, our office carpet. He was woven by the Nifty Chrononomers

Needlepoint Society. Those carpets are known to be calm and friendly, but this is an entirely different—'

'Again, nonsense.' Gigi waved at the carpet handler. 'Just get it started. The rest will come back to me in a jiffy.'

The man pulled out a little black box and attached it to the front of the carpet.

'I'm throwing in a tour guide for free, seeing that it's the young lady's first visit.'

He winked at Aliya, then gave the carpet a few taps with a thin rod.

The carpet rose lightly into the air. Aliya, who had experienced so many strange things in such a short time, hardly felt surprised.

'Don't worry about returning her when you're done,' the man called from under them. 'She knows her way home.'

Another light tap sent the carpet shooting down the corridor, making everyone on board scream in fright.

'Just remember the secret word,' the handler shouted after them. 'Or you'll have trouble getting off!'

'*Now* he tells me!' Gigi cried, holding on to her hat.

To the passengers' relief, The Fiend slowed down and flew at a steady pace along the corridor, zigzagging between time-travellers on foot or on carpets like theirs. Aliya had a tickling, breathless feeling in the pit of her stomach as the carpet sped along, rising and falling through the air with wavelike movements. The wind whipped her face, making her eyes tear. She kept a pincer grip on Esmat's luminous arm.

'How does it actually work?' she asked, breathlessly, as they swooped over a group of men in dark suits, nearly knocking their tarbooshes off.

'Oh, it's all in the threads,' Esmat cried back at her over the rush of the wind. 'There are lots of mysteries here that you won't find in your world!'

'Like magic?' Aliya risked relaxing her grip and allowing one hand to gently stroke the silky carpet.

Esmat made a face.

'Not magic, no! Don't mention it! It's not allowed here.'

'But you . . . you can appear out of thin air, and the carpets are *flying*.'

'That's not magic!' Esmat looked scandalized. 'That's *Baraka*. We borrow it from the Sublimes.'

'The . . . sub-what?'

'They are a very special substance that make this place what it is. They animate our world with their energy. It's like electricity, but more mystical. Magic, by contrast, comes from a corrupted source, and always at a price.'

Aliya thought of her mother's necklace. Could it be vitalized by Baraka, and not magic? Maybe that explained how she could have kept it in the travelling world? But how would one tell the difference? And what price did magic ask? Her head was overflowing with questions, but now the carpet made a swift turn and staying on board became a more pressing matter.

The corridor suddenly turned into an arched passageway, which at regular intervals led to large marble staircases that spiralled downwards out of sight. Through the arches, a huge city was spreading out. It looked like a patchwork of parts, each with its distinct character. Marble-white domes and minarets, sand-coloured fortresses and striped archways stood next to temples and pyramids with golden tops. Other parts had stately clock towers, manicured squares, and red-brick buildings with pitched roofs. A bustling bazaar, complete with camels and donkey-carts, ran the whole length of the town like a jugular vein next to a glittering river. Beyond the city wall, palm-trees grew in groves, dotting stretches of farmland. Yet further away were the beginnings of a desert.

The little black box crackled and suddenly a voice cleared its throat.

'Welcome to the Infinitum,' said a deep male voice. 'My name is Battouta. We hope you will enjoy your flight with us today.'

Gigi grimaced and reached for the box.

'I recommend you do not touch me, as it would end in electrocution, terror, agony and death – most likely in that order.'

There was some more crackling.

'Below us we can see the main town of the Infinitum, known as the *Citadel*. It is made up of multiple quarters, each reflecting a time period in Egyptian history. To your right you can spot the outskirts of the town, and beyond, to the east, you can see the beginnings of the *Wilderness*.'

They continued along the passageway, only just missing the top hats of a group of European-looking men in suits and sideburns.

'Oh, those are British *Victorians*,' Esmat explained. 'They colonized Egypt for a long time, but that's all in the past. I guess most things are here.' She laughed. 'And those' – she pointed to another group of men with big moustaches and elaborate headgear – 'are *Ottomans*.'

'The Infinitum is an ever-expanding parallel universe,' Battouta continued. 'A world making time travel possible. The Citadel – nicknamed the *Infinite City* – has, since its inception in 48 BCE, served as a centre for scholars who seek to preserve the knowledge handed down to us through the passing of time. The Infinitum is the oldest time-travel hub in the world, with a timeline beginning about two thousand years ago, and has a great cocktail of people and cultures in it. Sister hubs exist in Morocco and Lebanon, as well as in the southern hemisphere. The Infinitum presently houses two and a half thousand scholars from different times in Egyptian history. It is also home to approximately two hundred endangered mythical creatures, many of whom provide invaluable service to our travelling community, provided of course that they have passed our Reform and Civilization programme. For mythicals and human travellers alike, severe breaches of our time-travel code will lead to banishment and forced treatment with a memory-blotting serum . . . other possibilities are agony and death.'

'It really likes repeating that thing about agony and death, doesn't it?' Aliya asked Esmat.

'Our rules are sacrosanct.' Esmat hugged her briefcase. 'So it's in all our interest to follow them to the letter.'

The carpet, which had been gaining speed, turned sharply at the next staircase, and whooshed downwards in a terrifying spiral.

'Slow down, you moth-eaten thing, or I'll have you shrunk and mangled!' Gigi bellowed, clasping her hat.

The carpet responded by making a movement much like a bucking horse, sending the party airborne for a second or two before they landed again.

The staircase opened on to a cobbled street lined with shops, and the carpet finally slowed down.

'We have just entered the Khedivial Quarter and the Fishawy Bazaar,' Battouta announced. 'This part of town reflects the era between 1867 and 1914, and the rule of Egypt's last royal dynasty. It also houses one of our student hostels.'

They zoomed through a gateway and into a large square, then headed for a huge white stone building with a spiked metal door.

'We have arrived at our destination,' Battouta announced. 'Matron Olfat's Scholastic Hostel.'

'Oh, good.' Gigi tapped the carpet. 'Just stop here, will you.'

But the carpet showed no sign of slowing down. Aliya held on for dear life as it zoomed relentlessly on, heading straight for the door that was guarded by – Aliya blinked – *sphinxes*?

Yes, a pair of lion-sized sphinxes were posted at either side of the massive door. One had a black Cleopatra hairdo and the other wore a golden turban on top of its curly locks. Their human faces watched in surprise as the carpet made a sharp turn to one side, like a roller-coaster carriage. Aliya shrieked as they swooped around the square. Through tearing eyes, she caught blurry snapshots of flowering trees and benches and buildings between which narrow alleys disappeared into the shadows.

'The Khedivial Quarter,' Battouta started up again, 'is home to one of our finest student hostels, hosting approximately fifty students at one time. The quarter has everything a young travel student might need. In addition to a bathhouse, there's a clinic and a shop for second-hand travel inventions—'

'Open the gate!' Gigi shouted down at the sphinxes as they approached again.

The sphinxes exchanged looks.

'We can't open this gate unless you've got your health certificates in order,' the sphinx in the golden turban called back. 'Blood pressure, rabies shots, defleaing, that sort of thing.'

'And your time-travel insurances,' added the sphinx with the Cleopatra hairdo. 'They've got to be valid.'

'Are you joking?' Gigi screeched, as the carpet circled back again. 'You mangy mythicals. Just wait until I get hold of the matron!'

At the mention of the hostel matron, the sphinxes paled.

'OK, we're not supposed to ask for any of that,' said the sphinx with the turban. 'But with all the diseases going around these days, who's to tell what these earthlings bring with them when they come? Hosneyya got a chill this morning, and I've inherited my mother's weak chest.'

Aliya had read in Geddo's book on Arabic folklore that sphinxes like to ask riddles – it hadn't mentioned anything about defleaing or their susceptibility to sniffles.

'Holy chronometers!' Gigi screeched as the carpet headed for the hostel again. 'Will you open that gate?!'

At the last moment, the heavy doors swung out of their way and they zoomed into a shaded courtyard. They just missed a pair of grinning stone gargoyles which decorated the central fountain, then nearly beheaded a group of maids in black carrying a tub of laundry.

'To get off, use the secret word,' Battouta crackled as the carpet made a swoop around the fountain and headed for the upper storeys. A group of students stopped on the stairs and stared at them.

'Secret word? What secret word?' Gigi cried, as they knocked down a large portrait of a hairy, big-nosed man. It landed with a massive crash on the flagstones below.

'Shazam!' Gigi cried. 'Simsalabim! Open sesame! Stop, you blasted thing!'

'I told you!' Esmat cried. 'You've forgotten how to fly!'

Gigi got up on all fours.

'That's it. I'm jumping.'

'Jumping off a flying carpet can lead to—' Battouta began, in the same droning monotone.

'Let me guess! Agony and death!'

'You are correct.'

'Please,' Aliya whimpered, nausea and exhilaration jostling her insides. By now she felt both sick and dizzy and unless the carpet slowed down soon, they were going to crash into a portrait of another hairy man. She clutched the carpet's fringe. 'Please stop!'

After another mind-tumbling swoop, the carpet began to slow down.

'Whatever you're doing, it's working!' Gigi screeched, nearly popping Aliya's eardrum. 'Say it again!'

'Please,' Aliya cried, suddenly remembering Geddo's story about the girl and the naughty carpet. 'Please is the magic— I mean, the secret word!'

She frantically stroked the velvety pattern.

'Would you *please* let us down?' She leant over to address the edge of the carpet. She had no idea where its thinking part was, but it heard her, because it made a smooth turn and began sinking. At last, it touched down right next to the fountain. With a last shuddering sigh, it finally lay still. They all tumbled off, grasping at each other for balance.

'A sensation of imbalance is common when stepping off a flying carpet,' Battouta crackled. 'Thank you for flying with us and we hope to see you again.'

In a red flash, the carpet zoomed across the courtyard and disappeared through the open gate.

'"Please" indeed,' Gigi said, smoothing her hair. She turned to Aliya. 'Well done, Sultan Junior.

Perhaps you are not as slow as your grandfather claims.'

She bent down to examine her right shoe, the heel of which was snapped off.

'That was a compliment,' Esmat said, and patted Aliya kindly on the arm.

Aliya, whose legs were jelly, sat down on the edge of the fountain, trying to decide if what had just happened had been terrifying or fantastically exciting. There *had* been some odd connection between her and the carpet, as though it had really listened to her. It was nice, for a change, even if it was just a piece of textile.

She had taken exactly two deep breaths to calm herself when someone behind her cried, in a voice that might freeze lakes:

'Whose liver am I going to chop up and fry for dinner?'

Chapter 7
THE GHOUL MATRON

'Whose brain am I going to boil and serve for afters?'

The voice behind them sounded like nails on blackboards doing a duet with a rusty chainsaw. On the winding staircase, a broad figure stood hunched over the fallen portrait of the hairy man. Aliya could make out a pair of very sharp heels, and a skirt full of sequins that sparkled in the dusty twilight. But most alarmingly, the person's hulking shape was as broad as the back of a bull.

'Nothing to worry about,' Esmat said next to her.

'Really?' Aliya whispered to the air where Esmat's voice had come from. 'So why have you gone invisible again?'

Above them, young people Aliya assumed were students were peeking over the banisters. Black-aproned maids glared at them from shadowy corners. The only one who seemed unconcerned was Gigi, who sat on the fountain ledge, fiddling with her broken shoe.

'She's a *civilized* ghoul,' Esmat said. 'So, all this talk about cooking and eating us is probably just her way of joking.'

'Wait, what? A *ghoul*?'

'Yes, but with an important distinction. Matron Olfat comes from a long line of ghouls that success-fully passed the Infinitum's Reform and Civilization programme. She should be quite safe to be around – if she wasn't, she would have been impaled and cremated long ago, so no worries.' Esmat smiled.

Aliya swallowed. The hostel matron was a ghoul? Images of slobbering monster-creatures in grave-yards swam through her mind. According to Geddo's book on Arabian folklore, ghouls liked to hide in remote places, luring travellers off their paths to feast on their flesh, not work as hostesses to students.

Great-Aunt Gigi staggered to her feet, then

limped forward on her one good heel.

'Matron!' she called to the ghoul. 'Sorry for the mess. We'll fix the painting, of course. Just have it sent to my office. Hamza, the janitor, can work wonders with genie-spit and carbonated water.'

The ghoul hauled up the enormous portrait as if it were feather-light and peeked at them through the hole where the ugly man's head had been. Aliya stifled a yelp as her face appeared. It was not much of an improvement to the original. The long chin-hair was the same, as were the bushy unibrow and wonky silver teeth. There were some sideburns too. Ghouls definitely weren't pretty.

'This is my great-niece, Aliya,' Gigi said as the matron reached them. 'We just discovered her existence. She's the inheritor of the Sultan legacy.'

Matron Olfat glared at Aliya through beady eyes.

'The academic year began a month ago,' she muttered. 'The successful students are already installed.'

'I'm aware of that,' Gigi smiled stiffly. 'This is an unusual situation, of course, but we'll do our utmost to get all the details sorted.'

'Details?' The matron grunted. Aliya wasn't sure if it was a laugh or an audible frown. She took a step backwards as the matron pointed a crooked finger at her.

'Your parents stayed here.'

Aliya snapped to attention.

'Really?'

'Bleeding menaces. Should've boiled their innards and made sausages, that's what I should've done. Flew their bleeding carpet inside the hostel. Knocked Great-Cousin Morbidus right off the wall in the upper gallery. Irreparable damage. Besides, we're out of rooms.'

Aliya heard only half of that. In her mind's eye she was seeing her parents on a carpet, making elegant swoops past the upper storeys. She would love it here, she decided, however many ghouls and gargoyles they threw at her. She'd make this her home and do something to make her parents proud.

'I'm sure you'd have one room to spare for an old friend?' Gigi said. She began rummaging through her bag. 'Look here, I've got something that I think would go very well with your . . . eh, chalky complexion.' She took out a golden capsule. The ghoul sniffed it before unrolling a fiery-red lipstick.

'Blood Bath Number Seven. Thought you'd like it.'

'We might have something.' The ghoul slipped the lipstick into a glittering pocket. 'But she'll have to share.'

They followed the matron into a mess hall. A girl about Aliya's age was loading a cart with dishes that a scary-looking kitchen maid was handing her out of an opening in the wall.

'There,' the ghoul matron said, with a laugh that sounded like pebbles being churned. 'Your menace can share with this menace.'

'Ah, Karima.' Gigi peered down at the girl over her sharp nose. 'I see you're on food-delivery duty again. What are you being punished for this time?'

'Accident with a strawberry cordial, ma'am.' Karima curtsied and nearly lost her balance. She stood up with a wobble. 'Someone sort of changed colour after drinking it.'

'I hope you are not teaching this young student to practise menacin?' Gigi asked the matron, suddenly serious. 'The Council agreed to let you keep your dungeon lab, but you're not to treat any patients without a written approval.'

'The matron has not taught me anything at all,' Karima blurted. 'Except to stay well out of her way *and* out of the dungeon lab.' She curtsied again, as if for good measure. 'If you ask me, it's awfully rotten of the Council to be so strict about menacin. It's their loss, really it is, and the whole of the Citadel's too. And now with these poisonings and everything—'

'Well, no one asked you,' the matron cut her off. She gave Gigi an icy smile. 'The Council has made it perfectly clear that they don't want my help. We ghouls are still a tad too *uncivilized* for their taste.'

Gigi shifted on her broken heel, looking uncomfortable.

'Her corpseweed plant is a miracle . . .' Karima started up again, then stopped. 'I mean, or so I've *heard*.'

There was a tense silence.

'Well,' Gigi said at last, turning to Aliya. 'Try to get some sleep. You'll be joining Karima tomorrow for a day of time-travel classes. You've got a lot to catch up on and very, *very* little time.'

Aliya gulped. *Catch up on what?* She hoped it had nothing to do with studying.

'And you.' Gigi fixed Karima in a stare. 'Try to be a *good* influence.'

She gave Aliya an awkward pat on the head before turning on her uneven heels and wobbling out after Matron Olfat and Esmat, who still hadn't completely materialized and looked like a floating head.

When they were gone, Karima wiped her brow with a *phew* which pretty much summed up Aliya's feelings too.

'Why did the weird matron call you a menace?' she asked Karima, who had started unloading plates of food on to the table.

'It's because of my accidents. I'm a medic. Trying to be, anyway. One of my patients sort of turned purple, and one got rabbit teeth.' Karima shrugged. 'I'm not supposed to be learning ghoulish medicine, you know. That's what menacin is, by the way. It's this really great way of healing, but the Council's hung-up on the past when it was mixed up with magic and mayhem . . . It was what the ghouls practised before they were civilized.'

Aliya blinked. There it was again. *Magic*. Wherever she turned she was met with some rule against it.

'But now it's only about rare plants and some, well, uncooked innards. I want to learn all about it, but it's hard without anyone to teach me.'

She sighed.

'But once I'm initiated into the Medic Department, I'll prove to them that menacin is safe. Trouble is, after the last accident my parents said they'd bring me right home to the thirties to work in our family bakery if I put so much as one toe out of line again . . . but I just can't spend my life baking buns! Do you see?' Karima gave a bread roll a petulant slap. 'Menacin is my *calling*. I'm made for something bigger, just like my brother. He's always up to his neck in trouble, but no one ever suggested that *he* go home. Not precious Fuad.'

For a moment Karima's eyes shot daggers.

'Thirties?' Aliya said. 'As in the 1930s?'

'You know about all us travellers coming from different times, don't you?' Karima asked, with a laugh. 'We've got a boy in our class from the

Mamluk times, and a girl from 2090! Here, look at this.'

She produced a photograph showing a smiling couple who looked like they belonged in the same black and white movie as Great-Aunt Gigi.

'That's Mum and Dad outside our bakery.' Karima pointed at the sign, which read MANDIL'S in large block letters.

Aliya took a deep breath. She was beginning to get a headache, but then her brain had been through a lot in a very short time and now, as she was trying to comprehend that Karima, in reality, was older than Geddo, it felt like there might be actual knots in there.

'You look all windswept and cross-eyed,' Karima said, looking at Aliya through narrowed eyes. 'But never fear. I'll fix you right up. Here, try this.'

She handed Aliya a hot pitta bread. 'I remember when I first came to the Infinitum. Made me ravenous. Something about the shift in gravity. Don't worry, I won't poison you. You can sit over there.'

Aliya sat down at the long dining table that ran

the length of the room. She glanced around at the cavernous hall. Heavy appliqués with waxy candles hung from the dark walls that stretched between two massive fireplaces, both lit with smouldering fires. The tall, arched windows were draped with shabby lace curtains that bore a remarkable resemblance to spiderwebs or— wait! They *were* spiderwebs! On the walls hung more portraits of ugly relatives with names like *Vongol the Flayer* and *Murkus the Uncooked*. It looked like the kind of hall Count Dracula might have his suppers in.

Aliya turned her attention from the uncanny interior to the warm pitta Karima had stuck into her hands. She sank her teeth into the bread, and it melted in her mouth. There was something comforting about hot bread and Karima's kind face, and for a moment she relaxed.

The image of her parents returned. Perhaps they'd had their dinners at this table too. The thought warmed her, and she squeezed the necklace that lay safely hidden in the inner pocket of her coat.

'Tasty, isn't it?' Karima nodded enthusiastically. 'Mrs Dickens makes it. That's our hostel cook. Even

Matron eats her food, even though it's cooked.'

Karima looked as though this was a particularly remarkable thing.

'I mean, she usually eats stuff raw cos she's, you know, a ghoul.'

Aliya nodded. She took another deep breath. If her parents had survived a ghoul matron, she could too.

'What's that?' she asked, pointing to a framed photograph on the wall between the kitchen door and the fireplace. It showed a moustachioed man in a turban next to a bald man in a toga. A lady in a wide skirt and a hat full of feathers took up most of the space on the right side. In front of them sat a young man in a silver suit, with hair the colour of blueberries.

'That's a travel pod.' Karima brightened. 'That's the dream, isn't it? To get selected for a pod and go on missions.'

Karima walked over to the photo and pointed at the turbaned man. 'He's an incognito specialist, see? His job is to take care that travellers blend in whatever different times they visit.' She pointed to the man in the toga. 'That's a travel-invention specialist. He's in charge of making sure all the gadgets work, you know, like the knowledge turbans and the rest of the information tech.'

'Knowledge turbans?'

'They whisper facts to you when you wear them.'

Aliya nodded in approval. If she'd had a turban like that back at school, she might not have fallen so far behind.

'And that's the medic.' Karima tapped the glass on top of the lady with the hat. 'Her job is to care for the travellers, in case of any sickness or emergencies.'

'Who's that?' Aliya pointed at the man in the silver suit.

'He's a locksmith. They usually work on making time keys and other mysterious things I wouldn't know about, but sometimes they go along on special missions when new portals need to be opened.'

'So, what exactly does a travel pod do?' Aliya asked, her eyes still on the photo.

'They go on missions to the past or the future to gather knowledge and spread wisdom, that kind of thing. Sometimes they save mythical creatures and give them refuge here. There's no space for them on Earth any more.'

Aliya took another bite of bread, feeling its warmth flow through her tired limbs. Only this morning she had thought that mythical creatures only existed in Geddo's books on Arabic folklore. No wonder her head felt like it had been through at least one cycle on their tumble-dryer. Her world had cracked open like a piñata, with secret after secret tumbling out – most of them good, but some, like Geddo's betrayal, salty and foul like stale liquorice sticks.

Karima had begun filling the space in front of Aliya with small dishes of salads, sauces, pastes, puddings and potatoes. She put a plate in front of Aliya, and kept spooning things on to it and crying '*This*, you've *got* to try this' until Aliya felt close to bursting.

'Nice to meet you, by the way,' Karima said finally, stretching out a sticky hand. Aliya shook it happily. 'You're a Sultan, am I right?'

'Yeah.' Aliya wiped her mouth. 'But I don't really know anything about them.'

'Oh, I heard about your grandpa. The whole Citadel's talking about him. Do you know why he destroyed it? Your family portal?'

Aliya shook her head.

'I didn't mean to pry,' Karima said, looking worried. 'That's me and my big mouth.'

Aliya slumped in her seat.

'My granddad doesn't want me anywhere near this place. If it was up to him, I'd still be locked up in my room.'

Karima looked surprised.

'But you've got to be here, being next in the traveller line and all.'

Aliya looked up at a family portrait, featuring Matron Olfat and a group of scary-looking ladies in glitzy hats.

'I want to stay,' she said. 'I've got no one back there. But my grandpa . . . maybe he's gone mad.' Aliya shrugged, her throat cramping painfully. 'I don't know. They've taken him somewhere to get treated.'

'Oh.' Karima fiddled with some plates. 'When my great-aunt Nariman got ill, she thought we were all chickens. It wasn't so bad, except when she tried to collect our eggs. She'd pinch our bums, looking for them. People can change, you know, without meaning to.'

Aliya shook her head. The change in Geddo had come like a thunderbolt, shattering all that came before. Aliya winced as his words surged up again, stinging like wasps. He had treated her like someone not worth believing in, a nobody best kept out of the way. Had it really been madness talking? What if he had meant it?

She pressed her eyelids with her palms until black and white patterns appeared. How could her wizened old Geddo, who fed street cats and told her bedtime stories, have turned into some insane criminal that sabotaged portals and raved about cursed teapots?

'Nerves and shock.' Karima gave Aliya an appraising look. 'Possibly a broken heart. I think I've got just the thing.' She rummaged around in her cart, pulling out a plate of something white and creamy, spotted with green, and put it down on the table. 'I'm not supposed to . . . but try this white cheese and mint salad. I made it myself and it has special properties. Don't be surprised if you suddenly feel very relaxed.'

Aliya tried a little.

'Do you feel it?' Karima asked after a moment. 'Sort of like balsam in your soul?'

Aliya reflected. The hurt in her chest felt better, like milk on a heartburn, but her ears were tingling or, if that was possible, *fizzing*. As she reached up to touch one, she felt it sticking out of her hair like a big, rubbery flap.

'Oh-oh.' Karima reached out and removed the cheese salad. 'I think it might need some adjustments.'

'What's happened to my ears?' Aliya cried, feeling the flaps.

'Don't worry. In a few hours they'll be back to normal . . . I think. Lemonade?'

Karima held out a glass with a hopeful smile.

From outside in the courtyard a growl cut through the air – Matron Olfat was shouting something about boiling livers.

Karima tugged at Aliya's sleeve. 'Come on, we've got to get you ready for bed.'

Chapter 8
TROUBLE IN THE NIGHT

Aliya lay still, feeling the light pressure of the feather-down blanket on her exhausted body. Her ears were thankfully back to normal – that side effect had worn off – but her mind was worked up and there was no way she could get to sleep. The hurt in her chest was just a faint throbbing now, perhaps thanks to Karima's strange remedy. She listened to the sounds around her – Karima's light snoring at the other end of the room, and the even lighter snoring of her bedpost guardians. Yes, there were little wrinkled, old-lady faces carved into the four posts of her wooden bed that, as she had climbed under the blanket, had suddenly said, 'Goodnight, miss', and scared her half to death.

According to Karima, they were supposed to guard them while they slept. Aliya smiled as she listened to their tiny, high-pitched snores. Some guardians . . .

She sat up a little as a soft thudding passed by outside. That had to be one of the sphinxes – Karima had told her that they patrolled the corridors at night.

Lying down again, she let the memories of the past day swirl through her mind in a great bitter-sweet mess. She had discovered a new world – the world her parents had belonged to. But she had also lost Geddo. Everything she'd thought they shared, had it been a lie? He didn't think she was capable of anything, yet her great-aunt was talking as if she was the saviour of the family. How did any of it make sense? She didn't even know what it was she was supposed to do.

Had her parents ever felt this lost? Their first night at the hostel might have been just like hers. Maybe they had slept in a four-poster bed too, with bedpost guardians snoring around them.

Slipping out of her bed, she knelt on the floor, pulled up a loose plank she'd found earlier and fished out the necklace from its new hiding place. Should she wear it? The intense gold colour and the sparkling gem were eye-catching to say the least. Wearing it would attract attention. But there was something else that made her hesitate. If she really listened, an odd sensation came over her whenever she touched the necklace. Something that scared her, that did not quite feel the way Esmat had said spiritual energy – Baraka – felt, which was all positive and sparkly. This feeling was deep and full of power, like an impatient ocean waiting for her to jump in so it could embrace her . . . or drown her. She didn't know which.

Still, she couldn't quite resist . . .

Rubbing the gem, she whispered: 'Tell me about my parents, please. Tell me who they were and what they were like.' She waited. Nothing happened. Maybe this wasn't how the necklace worked. It had refused her request before when she had asked it to bring her parents back. Perhaps it just didn't have the ability to do everything she asked?

'OK,' she whispered to it. 'Could you at least show them to me?'

That soda-pop feeling bubbled through her again as red haze snaked out of the gem. It crept towards the ceiling and solidified into the shape of a man and a woman sitting on a carpet. Aliya stood up. Her father, who sat in front, turned the carpet with a merry shout and swept around the room. Her mother was rosy-cheeked and giggling. They were so young! Teenagers – a couple of kids on a joy ride. Aliya ducked as the carpet suddenly dipped.

'Farid!' her mother screeched, clapping her arms around her father from behind. 'You did that on purpose!'

'Of course.' Her father turned to her with a wide grin. 'How else would I get you to hug me?'

Another swoop and a turn and her parents flew straight into the side of her bed and disappeared in a cascade of glitter.

Aliya stood frozen, looking at the place where they had disappeared. It had just been a memory. But they had been so real and so . . . wild.

A high-pitched sneeze snapped her out of her thoughts. Heart in throat, she looked over at Karima. Had she woken up and seen everything? But

Karima was still asleep, snoring lightly with her mouth open.

Aliya exhaled in relief. Karima seemed very nice, but the necklace was not to be shared with anyone, as the note had said.

She was about to get back into bed when she found herself staring into the eyes of one of the bedpost guardians. Some red glitter lay sprinkled on its little head like a turban. When Aliya reached out and wiped it away, it squeaked:

'Invaders! On a carpet! I saw them!' Its small eyes darted around the room.

'No, no, no,' Aliya said, panic pricking at her neck. 'That was nothing. You must've been dreaming.'

The little face scanned her for a moment, then took a breath and yelled:

'To arms, sisters! We are under attack!'

Soon the other guardians chimed in, their tiny but piercing voices cutting through the night. Aliya wondered what 'arms' they meant, but goodness, how could such small things make so much noise?

'Intruders!' they shrieked. 'Invaders! Marauders!'

Over in her bed, Karima moaned and turned

towards the wall. *Wow, she's a heavy sleeper!*

The door banged open, and Matron Olfat glared into the room. Aliya hardly recognized her in her black nightgown with puffed sleeves and nightcap trimmed with lace. Part of a knitting project trailed out of her pocket, and the matron was holding one of the needles in front of her like a weapon. Behind her came the sphinx with the golden turban.

Aliya tensed. This was not good. She hadn't even made it one night at the hostel without getting in trouble. She'd have to think fast. Shoving the necklace quickly into her pyjama pocket, she rubbed the diamond with her thumb. In the doorway, the sphinx gave a loud sneeze.

'Make the bedpost guardian forget what they saw,' Aliya whispered. The soda-pop feeling fizzled in her chest. A thin stream of red smoke emerged from her pocket, heading straight for the bedpost guardian. Aliya took a sideways step, blocking the smoke from view. *Let her not see it*, Aliya prayed. *Please, please.*

A moment later, Matron Olfat shoved her out of the way.

Her one thick eyebrow descended as she narrowed her eyes.

'What ho?' she grumbled to the guardian. 'What fiendish thing have you spotted? Bedwetting? Sleepwalking? Running around in the corridors? Or' – she fixed Aliya with a stare – 'visiting *other* rooms?'

The guardian yawned, its little eyes closing. Aliya spotted a thin ringlet of red smoke still hanging in the air over her pillow. To her relief, the other bedpost guardians were falling asleep too.

'Must have had a nightmare,' Aliya offered.

The matron sniffed the air.

'Something funny's going on here. I can smell it. Nitzi, get in here!'

The sphinx padded into the room. Behind it, a gaggle of maids in black nightgowns appeared.

'Do you sense that?' the matron asked the sphinx.

The sphinx threw an anxious glance around, then sneezed loudly. Its eyes widened and it began backing away.

'We should have asked for a health certificate before we let the earthling—'

'It's not that,' the matron snapped. 'There's something odd in the air. Is it Baraka?'

The sphinx lifted its pointy nose and sniffed. It was wearing a knitted blanket over its lion-body, and a scarf around its human-looking neck.

'That's not— *Achoo!*' It sprayed Aliya's legs with snot. 'That's not Baraka.' The sphinx retreated towards the door. 'My body's tingling all over.'

'Well, what is it then?' the matron barked.

The sphinx looked baffled.

'It's tickling the horizon of my memory, but I can't quite place it. That's the problem with being ancient – I can't seem to keep more than a hundred years' worth of memory at a time. It's been like that ever since they blotted me.'

The matron huffed. She grabbed Aliya by her pyjama front and pulled her close – close enough for Aliya to see every hair of her moustache.

'Whatever it is you're up to, I'll find out sooner or later.'

Aliya nodded and tried not to inhale the matron's breath, which smelt like the rotten, fermented fish that Geddo ate at Easter.

'I'll be keeping a close eye on you.' She let go of Aliya and tapped the side of her beady eye. For a moment, Aliya imagined she was going to pluck it out and leave it behind to keep watch over her.

'What is it?' Karima asked when they were alone again. She was sitting up in her bed, eyes shining with excitement. Aliya stared at her.

'What's what?'

She had just got back into bed and was trying to stop her mind from reeling off in panicked scenarios, all of which ended with her being hauled through a portal into her cold, desolate room back in Cairo, where Mr Kamel stood waiting for her in his tweeds, demon eyes blazing.

'Is it a spiritualized snack box?' Karima asked. 'The thing you're hiding? My brother got one from Mr Gouda's second-hand shop. Kept burping petits fours. Don't worry. Your secret's safe with me.'

Aliya sneaked her hand under her pillow where the necklace lay. Could it be the reason the sphinx got the allergic reaction? It had said it wasn't Baraka it felt, but something else . . . Maybe it *was* magic after all . . .

'What did the sphinx mean when she said they had blotted her?' Aliya asked.

'It means they wiped her memory of all things before she entered the Infinitum,' a scratchy voice spoke from the darkness.

Aliya and Karima jumped with fright. A shape moved towards them out of a shadowy corner.

'To make sure she broke her habit of using magic.'

'Sawsan,' Karima screeched as one of the matron's maids appeared. 'Pickled frogs . . . you scared us half to death! What are you doing in our room?!'

Like Matron, Sawsan was dressed in a black nightie with puffed sleeves. Her black hair hung like wet seaweed down her shoulders.

'I wasn't listening to your conversation,' she said, scratching her nose. 'Or maybe I was, but I forgot to keep quiet when the new girl was about to tell her secret. So, what is it?'

She trained her beady eyes on Aliya.

'I don't have any secret!' Aliya cried. 'Really, I don't.'

'And even if she did,' Karima said, 'which she

doesn't, it would be none of your ruddy business! What do you think Matron would say if she knew you'd been skulking again?'

The maid leered at them, her pasty face dim in the dark.

'I heard things that could make the blood freeze in your veins, rumours wafting around the place like unrestful spirits . . .'

'What?' Karima asked. 'Go on then, what do you know?'

'If you tell me your secrets, I'll tell you mine.'

'There's nothing to tell,' Aliya said, shrilly. At the corner of her pillow, traces of red dust still glittered through the gloom. She quickly swiped them under the blanket.

'Oh, go on then,' Karima said. 'Or maybe you've really got nothing to tell?'

The maid's leer faltered.

'Oh, I've got something to tell all right. People would say they're just old wives' tales, but there's something to them, the stories, or there wouldn't be so many whisperings. They tell about the Old Evil. The Black Market. That's where the magic comes from, see.'

Aliya tensed. The Old Evil: that was the magic shop Geddo had been raving about.

'Are you saying the Old Evil could really exist?' she asked. 'You mean, it could be real?'

'Of course not,' Karima scoffed. 'It's just some old tale that travellers tell their kids to scare them.'

'Please go on,' Aliya urged the maid. 'I want to hear.'

'The Black Market,' Sawsan nodded gravely, clearly pleased to have caught a listener. 'Some call it the Devil's Thrift Shop. Some, the Old Evil. Oh, it's a terrible place. Full of bad magic. The myth says that a traveller created it – a traveller gone bad. The Shop is a living, breathing thing, but its life is stolen. It feeds on the souls of men and mythicals, trapping them in its objects. It's a *predator*. And the demon who runs the Shop – the Collector – well, he travels around, doesn't he, collecting souls to trap. You could be turning in to buy a sugared bun at the baker's one morning – only, it's not the baker's that you step into, it's the Shop in *disguise*. And once you're inside, there's no turning back. The door closes behind you and – SNAP – you're trapped!'

'That's enough,' Karima cried. There was something shrill in her voice that told Aliya she was scared. 'You know it's just nonsense! Now get out of here before I call Matron.'

'Perhaps it's true . . . perhaps not.' Sawsan looked pleased as she backed towards the door. 'But the poisonings – something's causing them. Something dark and dangerous.' She wagged a long finger in the air. 'And everyone's a suspect, aren't they? The inspector and his constables will be like a scourge, going through even the tiniest corner of every place in this city. Everything will come to light.' She grinned. 'No one's secrets will be safe.'

She slid out and snapped the door closed behind her. Aliya and Karima could hear her ominous chuckle disappear down the corridor. Through the gloom, Aliya could see the reflection of her fear in Karima's face. The idea of the demonic Collector hovered between them like a ghost.

'Don't mind Sawsan,' Karima said finally. 'She always tries to scare us. Always turning up with those garbage ghost stories.' She tripped over to

Aliya's bed and curled up next to her. 'That thing Sawsan said about secrets, though. I have one. A big one.'

Karima hugged her knees.

'I wasn't planning on telling anyone, but if we're gonna share a room I think it's best you know. I think it'll be OK, because today when I accidentally supersized your ears, you could've told on me, but you didn't. No one's ever *not* told on me before. And now, I promise to keep your secret. I owe you. We could make a pact.'

She stuck out her hand.

'OK, but I don't really have a secret,' Aliya lied. She hated to leave Karima hanging, but the necklace had to remain hidden.

'No secret?' Karima looked a bit disappointed, but still grabbed Aliya's hand and squeezed it. 'We're still friends. Come on, I've got something to show you!'

Aliya scrambled out of bed again and followed Karima into the bathroom, suddenly excited. She'd never really had a friend before – she was too tongue-tied. By the time she'd thought of something to say, the kids at her old school had usually moved on and found someone else to talk to.

The bathroom was large, with pistachio-coloured tiles and a tub with golden lion feet. One wall was covered by a crimson drape. In front of it stood a chest of drawers.

'You have proved your worth,' Karima said solemnly, stopping by the chest. 'Which is why I'll show you my holiest of holies.'

Aliya helped move the chest of drawers to the side, then watched Karima pull back the curtain to reveal a large wooden cupboard. The doors creaked as she pulled them open. Inside were many shelves, all filled with bottles, jars and peculiar things in pots.

'Menacin?' Aliya guessed.

Karima nodded. 'My secret lab.'

She beamed as she pulled out an odd-looking plant. 'And this is what's going to save me from going home.'

She waved the plant in front of Aliya's face. It was light pink and looked like a cactus, but with tentacle arms that curled up at the ends. Aliya wrinkled her nose. It smelt worse than Matron Olfat's breath.

'Corpseweed,' Karima said reverently. 'I'm using it to develop an antidote. You've heard about the poisoned elders of the Council, haven't you?'

Aliya remembered the article she'd found in Geddo's study back home. It had said something about poisonings in the time-travel world. There had been an old man in a photo, no bigger than a baby.

'No one understands what kind of poison it is,' Karima explained. 'But it makes people *shrink*. Three Council members have been affected already – they just got smaller and smaller until they were helpless as babies! Thank God, they stop once they reach that size. Still, the Council won't let Matron Olfat help, even though she's the best menacist in the Infinitum.' Karima watered the plant using a dropper. 'But even she thinks corpseweed is just a *weed*. Ghouls use it to make compost for their subterranean gardens, and to make raw liver pâté. But I've been working on a theory that, fingers crossed, will blow everyone's minds.'

'But how is this . . . corpseweed gonna help?' Aliya asked. 'If you don't know anything about the poison?'

Karima's eyes lit up.

'Well, that's the beauty of it, see. I think if you feed this plant a little of the poison, it'll *develop* the antidote. That's why it smells so bad. It's transforming something vicious into a cure. It takes time, though.'

'But where'd you get the poison from?'

'I visited the police station with the food cart and got myself a sample. It's amazing how easy it is to get access to places when you've got a cart full of pastries.'

Karima gingerly put the corpseweed back in its place. She stroked one of the tentacles. 'I've got to help Matron, see. She's the one who saved me when I had TB. That's tuberculosis.' She laid a hand on her chest and coughed. 'It's an infection of the lungs that will kill you if you're not careful. Back in my time, they hadn't found a cure yet, but Matron fixed me right up. So, I owe her, see? Once I've come up with the antidote and saved the elders, everyone is going to believe in menacin and they'll leave Matron alone. Also, Mum and Dad will have to let me stay, cos I'll be a hero. Brilliant plan, right? I've just got to be quick and get it ready before they find me out.'

Karima closed the doors to the lab. Aliya helped pull back the heavy curtain.

'So how close are you – to finding the antidote?' she asked.

'Almost there, I think. Only, there are still some side effects, like the purple colour, and the . . .' She gestured at her nose. 'Gets bigger, unfortunately.'

'Well, I'm not trying it,' Aliya said. Having her body parts enlarged was not something she longed to repeat.

'Don't worry.' Karima gave the curtain a last tug. They pushed the heavy chest of drawers back into place. 'From now on I'm my own guinea pig. Besides, you can't afford to get in any more trouble, at least not until you've passed the assessments.'

Aliya let go of the cabinet.

'Assessments? What assessments?'

'The *Brain Freeze* and the *Shocker*. They're these

tests we have to pass to get to stay on as students. You really don't know much, do you?'

Aliya stared at her, wide-eyed. 'The *what* and the *what?*'

'Don't worry,' Karima said, in response to Aliya's horrified expression. 'Those are just the nicknames, obviously. They're not as bad as they sound. We all passed them at the beginning of the year. That's why we're here, you know. Cos we passed.'

'And if I don't?'

'You get sent home. But you've prepared, haven't you?' Karima asked. 'Like private carpet-flying lessons, history classes, that kind of thing?'

'You're meant to *prepare?*'

So *that's* what Aunt Gigi had meant earlier when she'd said there was a lot to catch up on and very, *very* little time.

Aliya took a deep, desolate breath. That was it. She would finally, painfully, wake up from this fanciful dream. She couldn't fit here. Maybe that was what Geddo had meant. The unfairness of it all shot up into her eyes, making them burn.

'But maybe they'll make an exception,' Karima

said, with an uncertain smile. 'Because you're late. Did your aunt say anything?'

Aliya shook her head.

'You'll be fine.' Karima patted her arm. 'You seem clever enough, and your grandpa, he used to be a great hero, right? My brother and his friend can't stop talking about him.'

Aliya bit down hard on her lip. Geddo, who *could* have begun preparing her for the assessments when she was old enough to walk, had preferred to keep her locked up and out of the way.

'He's not a hero,' she mumbled. 'Not even close.'

Chapter 9

BREAKFAST

Early next morning, Aliya opened her eyes to find Karima sitting on her bedside, already talking. There was no time to lose, she announced, if they were to remedy Aliya's *shocking* lack of knowledge about the travel world.

Aliya only managed to catch snippets of the information Karima sped through as they got ready for the day. It didn't help matters that the bedpost guardians got excited and began echoing random words at the top of their squeaky voices. Aliya did manage to pick up that there were time-portals hidden all over human history disguised as different kinds of openings. They could look like ordinary doors, or windows (like the one in Geddo's study), or like a changing room in a clothes shop, or a dusty mirror in some out-of-the-way storage facility. They were always kept very secret, though, to prevent non-travellers from discovering them. Some portals even had guards who made sure that no one used them, except authorized time-travellers with the right permits. And, while travellers arrived *to* the Infinitum from all over history, they could only travel to their non-native times using the glorious hall Aliya had arrived to the day before – the Grand Central Station.

As Aliya followed Karima through the murky corridors to breakfast, her head was crammed with jumbled information, mixed with worried thoughts about the assessments. Karima had also explained that the first test, nicknamed the Brain Freeze, focused on Egyptian history. Aliya had never really thought about the history of her own country. She had seen a couple of documentaries featuring Ancient Egyptians with funny hairdos and fake beards, but Egyptian history was so much more than that. It featured an intense mix of people, from Romans to Greeks to Persians. There were lots of Islamic empires too, and Turks called Ottomans, some of whom were slaves but became sultans. Even Napoleon had been in Egypt and poked around – 2,000 years' worth of facts! Unless she found a way to upgrade her brain to Einstein smartness, she was cooked . . .

She stopped to look at herself in a dim mirror in an alcove. An 'emergency' visit to the bathhouse had done wonders for her hair, which now hung down her shoulders in near-tame curls. They had given her new clothes too – a comfortable dark-green training suit with the Khedivial Quarter's golden crest and stars embroidered on the chest. But this was not the chic, charcoal-grey blazer with a knee-length pleated skirt that Karima wore – the first-year uniform. Her beret alone was a work of art, with its hand-stitched patterns in blue and green and sparkly silver tassel. Glancing down at her own, velvet suit, Aliya felt somewhat underwhelmed. As comfortable as it was, her outfit said: *You're not one of us – not yet at least*.

Attempting to shake the gloomy thoughts off, she gave herself a forced smile and hurried after Karima, who stood waiting at the top of the stairs.

'Don't touch the banister,' Karima warned, pointing to a vine-like growth that snaked around the wooden rail. 'The flowers will snap your fingers if they get a chance, and then you'll smell like a sausage all day. The sphinxes might even try to lick you.'

She made a face.

Aliya took a tentative step past one of the oblong flowers that hung between large, silvery leaves. They did look a bit like a sausage. She started as the petals opened to show a set of miniscule, glimmering teeth.

'But why?' she asked Karima's back. 'Why grow flowers with teeth?'

'The matron uses them for removing warts.'

Aliya shuddered as a flower snapped at her.

Illuminated by the morning light, the hostel turned out to be much larger than Aliya had realized the night before. Several stone staircases led from a large central courtyard to four corners of the building. The first floor belonged to the 'novices'. That meant the new students. As she gazed up towards the wood-beamed ceiling, Aliya discovered four more storeys bustling with activity. She spotted the heads and torsos of older students shuffling past in their uniforms.

'The colour of the tarboosh, or beret if you're a girl, shows which year you're in,' Karima explained. 'Grey for first years . . .' She indicated her own beret. 'Blue for second years, yellow for third years, black for fourth years, and so on, until you reach green. That's the final colour. Or red, for the adults.

'Each year has their own mess hall and sleeping quarters on their floor,' Karima continued. 'We don't mix much with the older students. It's not encouraged for novices.'

'Why not?' Aliya asked, watching as a group of students in blue berets and tarbooshes marched across the courtyard and disappeared out the gate.

'Something about the levels of knowledge, blah, blah, blah . . .. They learn more secrets about the past and the future, things like that – things our little novice heads simply couldn't contain.'

In the courtyard stood a girl in a first-year uniform next to a lady in steel-grey overalls.

'That's Aion Verge and her AI nanny,' Karima whispered. 'That stands for *Artifical Intelligence*. That girl's even further ahead in the future than you, and from a new travelling family. Sometimes old families die out, you know, so the Council decides to add new ones.'

Die out, Aliya thought. That was what Great-Aunt Gigi was afraid would happen to their family, the Sultans. She took in the girl's neon-green glasses and long silver hair slashed with zebra-stripes. She did look like a character out of a sci-fi movie.

'Aion's been here the whole summer,' Karima whispered to Aliya, 'but still has trouble relating to real humans. Future families aren't big on quality time, at least not IRL.'

'I can't believe he's not coming!' Aion stomped the ground in frustration. 'It's not like I'm initiated to a time-travel academy every day!'

'Your father will be attending holographically,' the robot said in a soothing voice. 'You won't tell the difference.'

'Of course I will, and so will everyone else. Last time he came as a hologram – that was on my *birthday*, by the way – he ended up in the middle of the algae snacks and everyone laughed. Then Dad had his space-yoga class appear to sing the birthday song

'. . . in non-gravity headstands! It was, like, the most mortifying experience of my life.'

'Hey Aion.' Karima stepped up to her. 'This is Aliya. She's new and from the future, like you.'

Seeing them, Aion shrunk into an awkward pose.

'Aion's still practising the antiquated art of real-life conversation,' the nanny explained. 'Please don't take offence if she tries to swipe you or give you voice commands. She's spent her childhood surrounded by the likes of me.'

Turning back to Aion, she said: 'Now, remember what we rehearsed. You've had a whole summer to practise this. Step one: Listen. Step two: Speak. And if all else fails . . . deep breaths.'

Aion gave the girls a furtive look.

'I'm from 2024,' Aliya tried.

Aion snort-laughed, turning to her nanny. 'That's like when *Granny* was born.'

'The girls are standing right there, dear.' The nanny gave a metallic smile.

'It's OK,' Aliya said. 'I'm not very good at talking to people either.'

Aion acknowledged this with a grunt.

'Good morning, my plums,' a voice called out as the girls entered the novices' mess hall. A buxom lady in an apron and a frilly cap was waving at them with a butter knife. Aliya inhaled the sumptuous smell of freshly baked bread and felt her spirits lift.

The hall looked more cheerful in the morning light than it had the night before. The spiderwebs were glittering in the windows. Even the matron's relatives looked a little less bloodthirsty as they peered down from their portraits. A group of students sat around the table tucking into the breakfast food.

'This is Aliya,' Karima announced, pushing Aliya towards the table. 'She's a bit late, they only just discovered her.'

As Aliya took a seat, she felt all eyes on her.

'It's the Sultan girl,' said a blonde girl with corkscrew curls, turning to the others. 'I do hope whatever her grandfather's suffering from doesn't run in the family.' She traced a circle next to her temple. Aliya felt her cheeks flush.

'That's enough, Victoria,' the lady said. She turned to Aliya with a smile. She looked like somebody's aunt – the kind that likes to crochet doilies and has a tin box of candies in her purse, and Aliya instantly liked her.

Aliya surveyed the fantastic breakfast spread: piles of still-warm pitta bread fought for space with pans of sizzling pastirma with eggs. There were dishes of milky labneh, and white cheese with chopped tomatoes and mint, olives as black as night and tameyya, crispy and green. Finally, there was fuul – a thick, creamy bean stew. Aliya inhaled the aroma of cumin mixed with strongly brewed tea – that dark-red, comforting smell.

'My dear,' the lady said. 'Welcome to the Infinitum School of Time Travel and Related Subjects. My name is Dorothy Dickens and I'm really the hostel cook, but I usually serve at mealtimes. It's meant to be our matron's job, but she finds the emotional interaction a bit . . . challenging.'

'She's too busy trying not to eat us,' an old man next to Aliya muttered. Surprisingly, he was dressed in a first-year outfit. The end of his silver beard hung into his tea glass. Aliya watched in fascination as he wolfed down a piece of tameyya, spraying his beard with crumbs.

'I hope you'll all do your best to make Aliya feel at home,' Mrs Dickens continued. 'And help her understand how we do things around here. First days can be quite confusing, especially at a time-travel hub. How are you getting on so far? Any pressing questions?'

'She's not a student yet,' Victoria remarked. 'Not until she passes the assessments.'

'We *know* that!' Karima snapped at her. 'Come on, Aliya. Go ahead and ask anything.'

'Well.' Aliya looked around at the expectant faces. Her head was full of questions, but she didn't know where to start. She glanced at Victoria. 'Why are there British people here? I mean, if it's an Egyptian time-travel hub?'

Mrs Dickens lit up.

'Excellent question!'

Victoria's hand shot up.

'Yes, dear?'

'Because in 1882 the British came to Egypt to help civilize the country.'

'You mean occupy,' Karima muttered.

'Now, now girls.' Mrs Dickens turned to Victoria.

'What have we practised, dear? We mustn't forget it, or we might run into trouble. Say it please, so everyone can hear.'

'The British nation is not superior,' Victoria grumbled.

Mrs Dickens reached over and patted her hand.

'We British are a proud people,' she said, 'although we sometimes forget ourselves and . . . well, try to take over the world. Molasses, anyone?'

The molasses dish was passed around. Mrs Dickens looked around at the students like a proud mother hen.

'We must remember,' she continued, 'that we, unlike the people living out there in history, are travellers, and that makes us all sisters and brothers. Victorians and Ottomans, Ancients and Mamluks, even the odd Mongol – all of us are travelling kin.' Her eyes sparkled. 'We are a secret society of scholars and adventurers, bound together by trust and mutual respect. What is our motto, students?'

She raised her hands like a conductor.

'*Witness. Record. Reflect*,' the children chanted.

'Exactly so. And what must we never do?'

'*Interfere with the past.*'

'Fuad dear, I wish you wouldn't wear disguises at the breakfast table.' Mrs Dickens was addressing the old man next to Aliya. 'Just look at the state of your beard!'

Aliya stiffened in surprise when the man reached up and pulled his beard off. As he removed his turban, his white hair followed. He stuffed them unceremoniously into his jacket pocket. Without them, he became a thin boy with floppy curtains of dark hair.

Karima gave him a dead-eyed stare.

'I'm not washing that ruddy beard again.'

Fuad shrugged.

'Mum said you'd have to take care of me. That was part of the coming-here deal, remember?' He smirked into his toast. 'Or would you like to go back and make puff pastry?'

Karima ripped a piece of pancake and stuffed it into her mouth, eyes on fire.

'My twin brother,' she told Aliya when she had swallowed. 'Twin *bother*, more like.'

'*Haw, haw*,' Fuad fake-laughed. 'That was almost funny.'

Someone tapped Aliya lightly on her shoulder.

'I'm Mustafa Sirry, Cairo. Fifteenth century. That's the Mamluk era.' A neat-looking boy offered her a shy smile. 'I've read all about your family. Especially your grandfather's adventures with his SWAT team. The Brigade? My favourite part is when your grandfather knocked a rabid camel out cold – with one punch!' He took a sip of tea. 'Just imagine that! One punch!'

Aliya blinked into her own tea, trying to imagine Geddo boxing with a camel. Geddo, who wouldn't even let her use the kitchen knife alone or cross the street without holding his hand. Should she be sorry for him? Or angry because he was trying to destroy her life? But was he mad, or just pretending?

'I would love to have an adventure myself,' Mustafa continued, looking at her with very green, very earnest eyes. 'I have a bit of an, um, issue in that department. Dad's a professional soldier with the Sultan's royal guard. But I'm nothing like him. I don't think he's frightened of anything.' He sighed again and seemed to shrink a little in the process. 'I can't stop thinking and just *do*, you know? But if I join the SWAT team like your grandfather, if I just push myself, I might be cured.'

'Cured of what?'

'Cowardice,' Mustafa said, as if it were obvious. 'Mamluks can't be cowards. It's not right. But you, the granddaughter of the famous Captain Sultan – you must have courage in your blood!'

He didn't wait long enough for Aliya to contradict him.

'That's Victoria Prickly.' Mustafa chin-pointed across the table at the blonde with the corkscrews. 'Her father's head of Infinitum Security, which makes Victoria think she's all that and some extra on the side.'

Aliya looked over at Victoria, who was stirring her tea with a superior smile as she chatted to Mrs Dickens.

'. . . and, naturally, as the most promising navigator of this generation, I'm sure I won't have any difficulty with my classes . . .'

Aliya remembered that it was Inspector Prickly

who had ordered Geddo's arrest; he must be Victoria's father.

'Um, could I—' she began, quietly, feeling the weight of the necklace in her pocket.

'And that's Aion,' Mustafa continued, not hearing her as he nodded at the girl with the zebra-striped hair. 'I saw you met her already. Her mother apparently went on a time-trip and never came back. I heard her father tried to replace her with an AI nanny. Not so sure that would work, though. Replacing a human with a thing.'

Aliya's hand found the necklace in her pocket – the only thing that connected her to her own lost mother.

'Could I . . . I mean,' she began again, 'would it be possible to time-travel back and meet someone that's—'

'Lost loved ones?' Mustafa shook his head. 'Sorry. All the newbies ask that question. You might see them, but you won't be able to change anything of what happened to them. The past is fixed, you know. Can't be changed.'

'Oh . . .' Aliya fiddled with her plate, her appetite

gone. Ever since she'd learnt about time-travelling, the idea of going back to see her parents had hovered at the back of her mind. That, and perhaps stopping the fire . . . perhaps saving them and bringing them back. But there it was: the past was fixed. The realization brought a sting of disappointment.

She was snapped out of her thoughts when Mrs Dickens tapped her teacup with a spoon.

'As the rest of you already know, this term will be devoted to giving you a recap of Egyptian history, along with the rest of your subjects.' She looked at Aliya. 'You, my dear, will be attending the classes that help you prepare for your upcoming assessments.'

'I hope you like studying,' Mustafa whispered. 'It is rather intense.'

Aliya thought of the dusty cranes on top of Geddo's television back in their old flat. They were a pretty good summary of her academic aptness.

'I heard she had no idea about this place until yesterday.' Victoria pointed her fork at Aliya. 'So, how's attending a few classes going to help?' Her eyes drifted to Aion. 'In two years, we will need to qualify as a pod, but as it stands, I'm stuck with the mean scraps no one else wanted. With all of you who just *barely* passed the assessments!'

'What does she mean about the pod?' Aliya whispered to Mustafa.

'We were put together by the Council for a reason. They have experts who can gauge the students' talents, even before they know about them themselves. You're supposedly placed with novices who complement you somehow. Hopefully, the six of us novices can qualify together and form a time-travel pod in due course. It doesn't always work out, but that's the dream, isn't it? *Everyone* wants to be part of one. Then you get to go on real missions.'

'So, what's your talent?' Aliya asked him.

Mustafa shrugged.

'We're supposed to find that out for ourselves. It's good for the development not to be spoon-fed answers. That's what they say, anyway.'

Aliya stared into her teacup. If someone would spoon-feed her just one talent so she could be sure she belonged . . .

Across the table Victoria was still speaking. 'I could have joined any one of the other hostels, they were *dying* to have me. Mehmet Nazim's Scholastic Hostel in the Ottoman Quarter sent me an invitation, as did Madame Hippolyta's Hostel, both *begging* me to stay. But Papa thought it best for me to be here with the likes of you, to give you a fighting chance.'

'Don't mind her,' Fuad said into Aliya's other ear. 'Her *papa* put her here because he wants her to *fail*. He thinks she should stay home and wear corsets. Only us near-failures stay at the ghoul hostel, you know – ever since Matron got into trouble with the Council for practising menacin. The novices from the other hostels don't even want to take classes with us,' Fuad told Aliya with a grin.

'Not true,' Karima said. 'We've got some novices from Mehmet's Hostel in our Etiquette of Ancient Egypt class, and from Madame Hippolyta's in Chronology.'

'Yes, but they never speak to us,' insisted Fuad. 'And always sit at the back of the class.'

'We do have something of a reputation,' Mustafa said. 'Or the hostel does. There was a story about some girl being eaten by a cupboard in the downstairs dungeons last year. They say there are monsters in some of them. The year before that a second-grader fell through a trapdoor in the laundry room and ended up in medieval Iraq. He worked in a market trading race-camels for a year before they could find him and bring him back.'

They were interrupted by the sound of a television turning on. At the furthest end of the hall, Matron Olfat had switched on a large LED screen. A genie newscaster, a distinctly green lady whose hair seemed to be floating, was speaking:

'*A traveller by the name of Nortia Zenith was found unconscious next to her family portal, located in their antique shop, Fatimid era.*' A picture of a key shaped like a peacock appeared on screen. '*Zenith's key – as shown here – was found to be missing and it is believed that—*'

'I know all about that!' Victoria stood up, knocking over a sugar bowl. 'I overheard Papa talking about it this morning. They believe Zenith's key was stolen and that someone, a stranger, has broken into the Infinitum.' Her eyes widened as she looked around the table. The students exchanged worried glances. Even Mrs Dickens paled.

'Now, now,' she said, dabbing at her neck with a napkin. 'Before we get carried away—'

'QUIET,' Matron Olfat barked, making everyone shrink in their chairs. Victoria sat down with pursed lips. Matron grunted and turned back to the TV, where a man with algae-coloured hair and a shirt with a pattern of circles was holding a press conference.

'That's Neon Ticker,' Mrs Dickens said. 'He'll know what to do.'

'*On behalf of the Council, I urge you to stay calm,*' Neon said, raising a thin hand in a placating gesture. '*We've got the situation perfectly under control.*'

'*What about the rumours of magic entering the Infinitum?*' a sphinx in glasses asked.

'*Poppycock,*' Neon answered. '*Nothing but old wives' tales. Some of our . . . older travellers have been spreading rumours.*'

As he smiled, a sliver of ice entered Aliya's heart. He was speaking about Geddo. She remembered the magic market he had been raving about – the Devil's Thrift Shop. The Old Evil. The same myth that

Sawsan, the ghoul maid, had talked about last night.

'But you can't deny that magic once was a threat to the Infinitum,' the journalist sphinx continued.

'That's all in the past!' Neon said, with a dismissive wave. 'We've upgraded our security protocol to the point of infallibility. We've got Whooshes installed on all portals, and mythicals bearing the slightest trace of magic are reformed and blotted before they are allowed to pass into this world.'

Aliya thought of how confused the sphinxes had been when they entered her room the night before. If the necklace was magic, they had not recognized it because they had been blotted and made to forget. And what was more, the necklace had passed through the Whoosh . . .

'So how do you explain the cracks in the atmosphere?' the reporter asked Neon. 'If they have nothing to do with magic?'

There was a brief pause while a clip played of what looked like a rift in the very air above some rooftops.

'We're seeing a clip here of the crack by Qahira Square,' the sphinx said. 'Care to comment, Neon?'

'*Temporal irregularities, Samiha. In other words, absolutely nothing to worry about.*'

Matron switched off the TV, and the children returned to the business of eating their breakfast.

Aliya stuck her hand into her pocket where the necklace lay. She squeezed the chain, careful not to touch the diamond. Since the near-catastrophe the night before, she didn't dare leave it in her room. Comfort and worry blended in her chest. The necklace still made her feel . . . odd. Yet knowing that it had been her mother's made it a link between them – something that connected them across time and space, even in death.

'Sultan,' someone barked in her ear. She looked up into Matron Olfat's unsightly face. 'In my office. *Now.*' The ghoul marched off.

'Don't worry,' Karima said, with a squeeze on Aliya's arm as she stood to follow Matron. 'It's probably nothing. I mean, you haven't even had time to do anything wrong yet, have you?'

Aliya shrugged. She *had* brought a possibly magic necklace into the Infinitum . . .

'Oh, have you finally managed to make a friend,'

Victoria said to Karima, stopping next to them. 'Clueless Sultan.' She tilted her head as if she was thinking. 'It suits you.' As Victoria leant in closer, Aliya could see the symphony of freckles on her nose. 'You and disaster girl' – she nodded at Karima – 'better not ruin our chances as a pod. If you do, I'll—'

'You'll what?' Karima butted in. 'Embroider us to death? Strangle us with your corsets?'

'Don't think I don't know what you're up to.' Victoria smiled. 'It's just a matter of time before you get caught again. What will it be this time? Turning someone yellow? Giving them rabbit teeth or donkey ears?'

Karima and Aliya exchanged a quick glance.

'I don't know what you're talking about,' Karima said.

'Oh really? Well, I'll be watching . . . both of you. You know that your beloved Matron would get it bad if you were caught experimenting with menacin. They might even exile her. Or drive a stake through her heart. And as for you . . .' She looked at Aliya. 'The best you can hope for is to end up minding some portal in the earthly realm, if you're *lucky*.'

Victoria bounced away, as if she hadn't just sprinkled death threats.

'She's saying you'll become a *dud*,' Karima explained. 'Those are failed students that end up minding portals.'

'But at least they get to stay,' Aliya said, thinking of the horror of being sent back to the nothingness of her Cairo life.

'No. They're not allowed in. They're just there, on the other side, making sure the portal isn't discovered. It's like being a doorkeeper at a brilliant party you're not allowed to enter – ever. But you are constantly reminded of what you've lost.'

'Then why do they do it?' Aliya asked. 'Stay there, I mean, and watch the portal?'

'It's either that or blotting. But most people don't choose having their memories of the travelling world erased.'

Yes, Aliya thought. Once you had seen a place as brilliant as this, it would be hard to *want* to forget it.

'*Sultan!*' Matron had stopped at the kitchen door. A steel comb in her hair glinted like a knife.

As Aliya hurried after her, Mrs Dickens pressed a brown paper bag into her hands.

'Sugared buns,' she said, smiling. 'Karima mentioned it was your birthday yesterday. Now go.'

As Aliya hurried after Matron, she pushed her nose inside the bag: the buns smelt of sunshine, smiles and warm hugs.

Beyond the kitchen, a door led down through a narrow, dimly lit passage that opened on to a larger corridor, all the while sloping downwards. Aliya anxiously followed the matron, whose heavy footsteps bounced off the stone walls and made the dust dance in the corners. In a murky alcove a group of maids were hovering, sharing something slobbery out of a pot. Aliya noticed Sawsan, who flashed her an eerie smile. Matron barked something in passing that made them fish out some cutlery and napkins.

'We didn't come all this way to behave like beasts,' the matron muttered as she hauled open a thick door at the end of the corridor. 'Wait here.' She pointed to a velvet armchair just inside the door. 'And don't move.'

She disappeared into an adjacent room.

Aliya looked around at the overwhelmingly burgundy sitting room, remembering the stories she had heard of students getting eaten by cupboards down here in the dungeons, or falling through trap-doors and ending up in medieval camel markets. She decided to stay very still. The air smelt faintly of mothballs. On the walls hung more portraits of ugly relatives. Aliya's eyes slid over a stack of books with titles like *Ghoul Confessions: I Ate My Gym-Trainer and Other Stories* and *20 Steps to Healing Your Undead Heart*. Golden ornaments glittered from the side tables, making the dim room look like a treasure cave. Aliya remembered Geddo telling her that ghouls liked shiny things – that they used to steal coins from the pockets of the witless victims they had devoured.

Against the furthest wall was a large table covered with lab equipment, odd plants, and bottles full of differently coloured liquids. *Menacin*, she thought. Just like Karima's bathroom lab! The moment the thought took shape in her mind, a hazy streak shot out of the necklace in her pocket and slid across the room. It was as if it wanted her to sneak a peek. Part of her wanted to stay motionless and safe, but her curiosity was quickly getting the better of her. *Well, a look wouldn't hurt*, she decided.

The lab area offered a strange cocktail of smells and – Aliya scowled – bowls of raw innards. In a corner, a burlap cloth was covering something. Lifting it, she found a collection of petri dishes, each with a different-coloured liquid. '*Poison 1*', the first one read. '*Poison 2*', read the second and, towards the end of the row: '*Most effective. Instant results.*'

Aliya hurried back to the armchair on wobbly legs and sat down, heart throbbing. The poisonings! It was there in black and white: Matron was developing poison! Unless . . . she was trying to find an antidote too, like Karima. Karima *had* said Matron was the best menacist in the Infinitum . . .

Aliya jumped as the matron came back in from the next room, carrying a calendar. The ghoul sat down at a writing table, and Aliya's heart pinched with yet another worry. Was this it? Was she going to be expelled before she had even spent twenty-four hours in the travelling world?

'So,' Matron looked up with narrowed eyes. 'You've hardly any time at all to prepare for the assessments.'

Aliya exhaled. So, this wasn't about last night, or the necklace. That was something, at least.

'How little?' She watched the ghoul's finger move across the month of November and stop on a Saturday towards the end.

'One month to the first assessment.'

'Wait, what?' Aliya sat up. 'The Brain Freeze is in *one month*?'

Matron Olfat nodded. The golden pince-nez she was using to read magnified her eyes, making them look like huge pieces of coal beneath her thick eyebrow.

'You should be thankful that the Council gave you a chance to try out at all,' she said. 'The rest of the students did their assessments during the first week of the school year. But you, arriving late – it's most irregular. It's lucky your great-aunt works in the administration and can pull a few strings. Now, as for the second assessment . . .'

'The Shocker,' Aliya breathed.

Matron held up the calendar and pointed a claw-like nail to where a big red cross marked the tenth of December.

'The Initiation Ceremony for first-year students takes place on the hundredth day of the school year. It's tradition. Your second assessment is scheduled on the day before it. If you pass, you'll attend the ceremony and become a student at the Infinitum Time-Travel Academy. If not, you're out.'

'But that's impossible!' Aliya cried. 'The Brain Freeze will test me on two thousand years of history! And the Shocker . . . Karima says they had to ride lame camels through battles. They had to dodge arrows!'

Matron huffed.

'They don't use the arrows any more.'

'Wow, that's a comfort then.'

'Switched to cannons.'

Aliya stood up and took a few agitated steps around the room. 'Couldn't I just skip the history one?' she asked. 'I'm pretty good at thinking on my feet.'

The ghoul's lips twitched, showing glimpses of

her silver teeth. She seemed to be enjoying this.

'The Council won't listen to excuses,' she grumbled. 'It's the Sultans' problem you're not prepared, not theirs. The other students' families have been preparing them for the assessments since they were old enough to walk. Also, your classmates spent the whole summer here getting to know each other and taking preparatory classes.'

Aliya crashed down into the armchair. This was it. This was what it felt like to be cooked, no, fried – like one of her grandfather's sausages.

'If you're planning to give up, you might just as well leave immediately,' Matron grunted. 'Can't abide students who waste my time.'

She leant forward and put a thin tablet in Aliya's hands.

'It's an interactive guide for students. It has your schedule programmed and a GPS so you don't get lost.'

The tablet lit up to show a photograph of a bearded man in a tunic doing a thumbs up.

'That's Cletus,' Matron said. 'One of our Ancients, Ptolemaic era. He's from 20 BCE but has a knack for technology. Upgrades the students' tablets. Must have been testing the camera.'

Aliya swiped the screen and now Greek-style letters appeared that read: *Welcome to the Infinitum: Where All Time Meets.*

'Now, get out of here.' Matron ushered her out of the chair. 'Your first lesson starts outside the hostel. Walk down to the waterfront. Don't stray. Keep out of trouble, or I'll—'

'Chop my liver, feed me to the rats – got it.'

'That's right.'

Clutching her tablet, Aliya set off down the dim corridor, towards her first ever time-travel lesson.

Chapter 10

THE ORIENTATION

The way to the waterfront led through a darkened passage, branching off to narrow dead-end alleys to the right and left. Aliya was just passing by one of them when a movement in the corner of her eye made her stop.

A dark shape had shifted through the air. Had she imagined it?

She was about to hurry on when a musical note floated towards her. It was a flute – plaintive and a little hoarse. At once the necklace grew warm, glowing through her trouser pocket. She touched it through the thin material.

Wear it, the note seemed to say.

The necklace pulsed against her hand.

Your destiny is waiting.

In front of her, a patch of air began to thin until it looked like a stretched soap bubble about to pop. Through it, Aliya saw nothing but blackness.

Then the music stopped.

The alley around her grew quiet again. The air thickened and returned to normal; the street was brighter, all shadows gone. What had just happened? The mysterious music lingered in her mind like the residue of a dream.

She shrieked as something tugged at her arm.

Karima stood behind her, panting, cheeks blooming red, but too out of breath to speak.

'I just heard the strangest—'

'Where were you?' Karima panted, pulling her along. They set off towards the gate. 'We're all waiting!'

'A tour carpet?' Aliya blinked in the bright morning light. She and Karima had reached the river promenade to discover an enormous flying carpet hovering a metre above ground. On top were worn seats on which the other students were already sitting.

At the helm sat an old man in a toga, clutching a microphone, his white beard flapping in the breeze.

'If you would be seated!' he hollered into the mic. The air rang with feedback from the ancient speakers that were rigged up, front and back. Swathes of dust belched from their cones as the sound blasted.

'Lower the mic, Mr Philadelphus!' Victoria shouted from the back. 'You don't have to make us deaf, just because *you* are!'

'Always a ray of sunshine, aren't you, my dear?' said a man in a top hat and heavy sideburns seated across the aisle from Victoria.

'You're fooling no one, Fuad.' Victoria reached out and knocked off the man's hat. 'I'd recognize your stupid grin anywhere.'

The man began peeling off his sideburns. It was Fuad again, playing dress-up.

'My brother wants to work for the Incognito Department,' Karima explained as she and Aliya sank into two battered seats. 'He says showing up in disguise is practising. But I think he does it cos he loves pranks.'

Aliya watched as Fuad experimentally attached his sideburns to his upper lip.

'Do you all know what you want to be?' she asked.

Karima shrugged. 'Most of us, I guess. Travellers usually know what they have a talent for from a young age.'

Aliya sighed. *So, it wasn't just about passing assessments, one had to have a talent too?*

'What about you?' She turned to Aion, on her other side. 'What do you wanna be?'

Aion stuck a thin rod into Aliya's hand.

'Press that.' She pointed at a small yellow button.

Aliya pressed it and a holographic cat zapped out and jumped on to the back of Mustafa's chair.

'Get it off!' he shrieked, covering his head with his arms. The cat, who was fat and ginger, coiled its tail around Mustafa's forehead with a coy purr.

Aliya hit the button again, and the cat blinked out of existence.

'Travel inventions,' Aion mumbled, stroking her silver hair out of her eyes. 'I-I like old-school things. I want to upgrade them to things that pods can use on missions. Here—' She stuck her tablet into

Aliya's hands. *List of upgradable items*, Aliya read. *Shoes. Steaks. Toothbrushes. Toilets.*

'Like these.' Aion stuck her foot out to reveal a pair of sleek silver sandals. 'It's my own design. Biodegradable smart-shooz. The chip goes in the heel. I call them Achilles Air.'

'Wow!' said Aliya, genuinely impressed.

Aion looked pleased.

'You can keep that.' She indicated the cat-producing stick. 'I've got lots. They're good for company.'

'Buckle up!' Mr Philadelphus's voice blasted through the air.

Aliya quickly tightened her threadbare seat belt.

'I think the carpet is asleep,' she said, leaning down and touching it with her fingertips. Yes, the old thing was shuddering with snores. Yet when the old man at the helm tapped it with a rod like the one the carpet handler had used the day before, it stirred and rose upwards in a tired swoop.

Aliya's stomach dropped as the ground fell away. The wind whipped her face and filled her eyes with tears. The feeling returned from the wild carpet ride the day before: exhilaration with a sprinkling of panic.

'First stop – the Ancient Quarters,' Philadelphus declared. He had thankfully lowered the volume, but now the rushing wind made it almost impossible to hear what he was saying.

Around them the air was full of traffic. Carpets and flying pod-vehicles zoomed past in all directions. Aliya even saw a flying elevator.

'A whizzcalator,' Karima shouted over the wind. 'Only Council members use them. They don't like losing their hats in the wind or getting their fancy suits splattered with bird poo.'

'Or *hieracosphinx* poo if you're unlucky!' Mustafa cried, pointing upwards.

Above them, gliding gracefully through the air, was a creature straight out of Geddo's books on Arabian folklore – a great beast with a sleek falcon head merged with a brawny lion's body. There were wings, too, that spread out like grey-dappled sails, shadowing them from the sun. Aliya yelped as a great blob of white goo whooshed past her, just missing her head.

Mustafa nodded knowingly. 'Told you.'

Several times the carpet dipped precariously, as though it had nodded off to sleep. They made slow progress and got beeped at more than once by other airborne vehicles. With carpets and pods vying for space and overtaking each other, honking freely, Aliya felt quite at home. It was just like rush hour back in Cairo.

Under them, the Citadel's river, the Salsabil, snaked its way through the city, a band of rippling silver. On either side lay the quarters where the time-travellers lived, arranged chronologically, with the futuristic ones at one end and the ancient ones at the other. Pyramids and massive stone temples appeared as they approached the old parts of the city.

Behind them the speakers crackled. Philadelphus laboriously stood up and pointed downwards.

'Below us you can now see the ancient quarters, reflecting the periods between 3000 BCE to 641 CE—' He wobbled dangerously as the carpet dipped, his toga catching in the wind. Aliya pinched her eyes closed as his bloomers winked into sight.

'It was a scholar from the ancient Alexandria

library that found the first Fortuna grain and opened the portal to this parallel universe, the Infinitum. It was also in this distinguished world that . . .'

Twenty minutes later, Aliya had learnt much more than she cared to about what types of stones had been used to build various pyramids and monuments. When Philadelphus launched into another droning monologue about the archways in the Medieval Quarter, Fuad whipped around in his seat to face Aliya and Karima.

'Enough! I can't believe we got the morning off for *this*. Matron wanted the new girl' – he pointed at Aliya – 'to have an orientation, not to be bored to tears learning about archways and ruddy pillars.'

'So?' Karima asked.

'*So*, we're going to hijack the carpet and do a tour of our own.'

'I think I'm going to be sick.' Mustafa bent over and breathed into a paper bag.

'Well, I think you're daft,' Victoria told Fuad, crossing her arms. 'Are you asking the daughter of the head of Infinitum Security to do something *illegal*?'

'I hate to say it,' Karima said, 'but I'll have to

agree with bouncy curls.'

'Who said anything about illegal?' Fuad said. 'We're just going to give the old man a break. Look at him. He's falling asleep too, just like his carpet. It'll be an act of charity.'

They all turned to see Philadelphus drooping in his seat, mumbling something about marble. The carpet was sagging too and narrowly missed an oncoming whizzcalator.

'I'm not doing it.' Victoria whipped out her tablet. 'And if you do anything stupid, I'll record it and send it to Papa.'

'Too bad, then,' Fuad said. 'I had hoped you would help navigate the carpet.'

Victoria's eyes widened. She clicked her tablet off and shoved it back into her satchel.

'All right then. I guess a little extra practice wouldn't hurt.'

'That's more like it, Vicky.' Fuad grinned.

'Don't call me Vicky, ever, and don't grin. And your plan had better work, or I'll tell Papa you kidnapped us.'

Fuad shrugged. 'Fair enough.'

'Fair enough?' Karima hissed when Fuad turned to her and Aliya again.

'Keep your hair on!' Fuad chin-pointed at Victoria, who was already making her way to the front of the carpet. 'She's in her element. But you've got to help if this is going to work. So?' He pawed at Karima's satchel. 'What have you got?'

She hugged her bag tighter to her chest.

'No way. And – *I can't.*' She glanced at Victoria, who was slapping dust off the driver's seat. 'If she finds out I'm still experimenting, she'll tell her father and then I'm cooked.'

'Don't you want to give your new friend a real tour?' Fuad asked. 'Or do you want to sit through another hour of this?'

Aliya returned Karima's look with a bright smile. Despite all the talk about marble, she was anything but bored. How could she be? She was on a *flying carpet*, soaring through a *time-travel city*.

'I'm fine!' she cried, her stomach exploding with butterflies as the carpet swerved to miss an oncoming party of airborne Ottomans in the basket of a great balloon.

'But she's not even seen the departments,' Fuad whined. 'Or Qahira Square.'

'Well, all right.' Karima rummaged through her bag and drew out a box of pink macarons. 'These are for power naps. I made them for Pa, for his insomnia.' She nodded at Philadelphus. 'But he's already half asleep, isn't he?'

'So, it won't be suspicious,' Fuad beamed. 'Perfect.'

'But you know you're being reckless again. Mum said that if you started behaving recklessly I should—'

'What's going on over there!' Philadelphus was bumbling down the path towards them. 'You're meant to be listening, not chattering among yourselves! And you, young lady –' he turned back towards Victoria, who had sat down in the driver's seat – 'get back to your place!'

'Quick!' Karima shoved the box into Aliya's hands. 'I can't put one toe out of line, remember?'

Philadelphus stood swaying in their midst, his long hair flowing in the wind like white seaweed.

'W-we were just taking a snack break.' Aliya offered the macarons. 'Would you like one?'

Philadelphus examined them.

'They are pink.' He sniffed. 'Ridiculous colour for a refreshment. Must be modern, yes?'

Karima shrugged. The old man popped the macaron into his mouth and chewed. 'And the texture, firm yet soggy . . . odd combination.'

'It's a macaron,' Karima said. 'It's French.'

'Well, that explains it. First, a revolution and now . . . *macarons*.'

Philadelphus blinked once and swayed a little, then gave a great yawn. A few moments later he was lying stretched out across a couple of seats, snoring gently, looking like a slumbering Poseidon.

'It's one of my latest recipes,' Karima said. 'Pretty effective, but . . . oh no.' She pointed to Philadelphus's beard, which had turned decidedly pink. Karima looked up at the others, then nodded at Victoria. 'What about her? She'll tell her father we poisoned him!'

Victoria was already seated at the helm, her blonde corkscrews trailing in the wind.

Fuad bounded forwards through the seats until he reached her.

'Mr Philly sent me to tell you that he's taking a short nap!' Fuad shouted at her over the wind. 'He said for you to take over.'

'Naturally.' Victoria gave the carpet a stern tap with the rod. 'Where to now?'

'The departments.' Fuad grabbed the mic. Victoria tapped the carpet expertly and it descended with an elegant dip.

'Keep them, please,' Karima said when Aliya tried to give the macarons back. 'Just in case Victoria suspects something. She won't search you.'

Aliya had just stuffed the macarons in her satchel when Karima tugged at her sleeve and pointed. Right at the centre of the city, the dense quarters opened on to a wide square.

'That's the centre of town. Qahira Square.'

As they flew on, they saw a group of men and women on tall stepladders, examining a thin crack in the air – the one they had seen on the news that morning. It ran like a lightning bolt through the atmosphere and pointed down at a golden door that stood to the side of the square, unattached to any building.

'That leads to the Smithy, where the locksmiths are based.' Karima pointed at the golden door, a sudden awe in her voice. 'It's a very mysterious place. Do you know their department moves in space and time to keep itself safe from intruders?'

'Are they locksmiths, like the man in the photo?' asked Aliya, pointing at the people on the ladders. Aliya remembered that they were the ones who opened the time-portals.

Karima nodded.

They watched the locksmiths paste the rift with light that, Aliya realized, *emanated* from their hands. A tall man with a short beard and a large green turban was perched at the top of the ladder, wielding a silver pipe. Aliya marvelled at the glittering smoke that billowed out of it before seeping away towards the rift. Was he using the smoke to heal it?

'You said locksmiths make time keys?' Aliya asked when the carpet began drifting away.

'That's right,' Karima said. 'Time keys are what we use to travel – but that will all be explained in class.'

'They use Baraka to enliven stuff,' Aion mumbled.

'I saw this locksmith vitalize a carpet once. His hands were *fizzing*.' She held up her palms to demonstrate. 'The carpet woke up and started sweeping round the lab like a wild horse. It even *growled*.'

Aliya looked back at the golden door that stood glowing in the sunlight. A locksmith . . . Imagine having such a talent!

'There! That's the Department of Travel Inventions,' Aion cried. 'There's where I want to study.'

She pointed to a large brown-brick building with turrets, glimmering mazes of cogwheels, winding steps and spheres covering its facade. It looked like a clock had been turned inside out and made into a building.

'To your immediate left you can now see the Incognito Department,' Fuad boomed through the mic. 'Pay attention or you might miss it!'

'Which one?' Aliya looked in the direction Karima pointed, but all she could make out was a street leading off between two elegant mansions.

'Try squinting,' Karima said. 'And focus on the shadows.'

Aliya looked again, and to her surprise a building

made entirely of black bricks appeared out of the shadows.

'Bit hard to get in sometimes!' Fuad thundered. 'Especially at night! Look out, Vicky!'

A fearsome *caw* cut through the air. Aliya looked up just in time to see them nearly colliding with . . .

'The hieracosphinx!' Mustafa cried, curling into a ball on his seat. 'It came back!'

Hovering menacingly in the air before them was the great beast they had seen earlier – the one that had nearly hit them with a poo-bomb. Aliya gulped as it turned its great falcon head to look at them. The size of the beak alone looked like it could chop down a tree.

'He's a guard, patrolling the inner city on *my* papa's orders,' Victoria shouted from the front. 'Do you have any idea whom you are cawing at, beast? My papa is *head* inspector at the—'

'CAAW!'

'I don't think it cares who your papa is,' Fuad, who was ducking behind an amplifier, cried. 'Let it pass or we'll be bird food!'

Victoria had hauled out her tablet.

'When my papa sees this, you're going to be in so much—'

'CAW!'

The carpet quaked as the winged sphinx snapped at it. Despite her terror, Aliya couldn't help but admire Victoria's gumption. She might be a self-important snob, but she had guts.

The seat under her jerked. The sphinx had nipped the corner of the carpet and was whipping them from side to side.

'Somebody *do* something!' Karima squealed.

For a moment, Aliya was convinced she was going to die, that her short, inglorious life would come to an end right here in this unlikely but deadly traffic jam. She pinched her eyes closed and prayed.

A moment later, the air around her filled with a most familiar tune featuring pompous trumpets and a choir. Was it over already? But if this was the after-life, why were they playing the Egyptian national anthem?

She opened her eyes to see the hieracosphinx transfixed in a hovering pose, wings flapping in time to the music. Its falcon face looked stiffly into the distance.

'It's the anthem!' Mustafa was holding up his tablet, from which the grandiose music was streaming on full volume.

'Hieracosphinxes love pomp and circumstance,' he shouted, shrilly. 'Look, it's standing in salute.'

The sphinx remained engrossed in its triumphant affirmation of Egypt's glory until Victoria had steered them to safety.

'You saved us,' Aliya said to Mustafa when they were zooming back along the tree-lined walkway that ran along the river.

Mustafa looked flustered.

'He just pushed a button,' Victoria cried from the front. 'What's brave about that? *I* was the one who faced the beast!'

'Don't listen to her,' Karima said. 'You're a natural. You should be working with mythical creatures!'

Mustafa nodded, somewhat doubtfully.

'I guess. But I need to qualify for the SWAT team, you know. I hear some of them get churned to particles in the space-time glitch. That should impress my father and my brothers.'

Aliya exchanged a glance with Karima. Mustafa might be clueless about his real talent, but at least he had one.

Aliya looked around at her classmates. They were so sure about what they wanted. It had to be a nice feeling. For her it was just one more thing she lacked.

Chapter 11

ANOTHER SMOULDERING LETTER

The students were dropped off at the hostel by a refreshed, though somewhat pink, Mr Philadelphus, who woke up from his power nap just as the carpet steered into the Khedivial Quarter. Fortunately, he seemed too embarrassed about having fallen asleep to ask them any questions about what had happened.

'*Lunch break*,' Aliya's tablet announced from inside her satchel. A sprightly Greek melody followed. Aliya clicked it off and had a look at her schedule. *Culture and Etiquette of Ancient Egypt* was followed by *Incognito Studies*. Next came *Introduction to Time-Travel Devices*. The school day ended with *Chronology*.

'The classes sound really difficult,' Aliya told Karima as they clambered off the carpet. 'I'm not really good at school stuff.'

'Just do your darnedest,' Karima said. 'You're a Sultan, remember?'

Aliya shrugged. She really wasn't so sure that was an asset. If it was, how come she had only two living relatives?

She was following the others to the mess hall for lunch when the matron's hoarse voice called out her name. Making her way across the courtyard, she reached the dark corner where the matron sat behind a reception desk. She was knitting, or rather, stabbing the yarn as if it had just called her relatives ugly. A woolly meat-red shape hung down her knees like a giant tongue. For a moment, Aliya imagined it was going to come alive and lick her.

'A letter came for you,' Matron Olfat said. 'Flame paper. Burns the hands of anyone who tries to open it, except for the one it's meant for.' She narrowed her eyes at Aliya. 'I left it in your room. You haven't been up to anything funny, have you?'

Aliya blinked in shock. Another burning letter –

whoever had sent her the necklace had clearly followed up!

'N-no. Nothing funny.' She hoped the necklace wasn't sending any tingling magical vibes from her pocket. 'Thank you.'

Matron Olfat's eyes remained narrowed as Aliya backed out of reception.

After lunch – she'd barely been able to focus enough to eat – Aliya grabbed the smouldering letter from her bedside table and locked herself in her bathroom where the bedpost guardians couldn't see her.

There, she ripped open the envelope.

Dear Aliya,

I'm happy to see you settled at the Citadel. Life here suits you. And why shouldn't it? It's the life you were meant for. I see that you're still trying to play by the rules, though. Remember, your parents weren't tied down by what was 'allowed'. Use the necklace – let it help you! But, to unlock its full potential, you must wear it.

Aliya examined the signature. The single letter was doing that same strange thing again – it was moving. She watched as it slid across the page with a serpentine movement, how it formed, teasingly, into a letter – was it a Z? – only to twist into another a moment later – a D?

She gave up and studied the envelope. Still no address. Who did she know whose name began with a D or a Z? And how could this person know that she wasn't wearing the necklace? Was it someone right here at the hostel? Her neck pricked at the thought.

Taking out a paper and pen, she wrote:

Persons I know whose names begin with D:
Mrs Dickens (I think her first name is Dorothy).
Dolores (the kitchen maid with the scary laugh).
Persons I know whose names begin with Z:
No one.

Aliya went over to the window and looked out over the patchwork of roofs. Whoever the sender was, they were watching her.

She drew the necklace out of her pocket and watched the chain slip like liquid between her

153

fingers, so bright and sheer. The diamond glinted up at her.

'Show me who sent these letters.'

She rubbed the gem. Nothing happened. She tried again – still nothing. There was power in the gem. She could feel it. Should she use it to help her pass the assessments? If she didn't pass, she'd have to leave – and she'd be letting her parents and Great-Aunt Gigi down.

She thought of Geddo. He would have thought using the necklace was cheating, but that had been the old him. The new Geddo had told lots of lies – to her, and to others, even about her being alive! Everything she had thought was right had turned on its head now, as if green suddenly had become red.

She brought the necklace closer to her neck again but . . . no, she didn't dare. Using it to ask for sweets or to get out of trouble was one thing, but to use it to change her life, that was different.

Chapter 12
THE FORTUNA GRAIN

The afternoon's classes passed in a blur. Unlike students in ordinary schools, Aliya and her classmates traversed the city on shuttle carpets to reach their classes. Manners and Customs of Ancient Egypt was held in the Ancient Quarter, in the History Department, located in the shadow of a great golden pyramid. For their Incognito Studies class, they took a carpet back to Qahira Square where they spent a good half an hour trying to find the entrance to the building which, to Fuad's great delight, had disguised itself as a hardware store. By the time they were heading for their last class, Aliya felt both time-lagged and carpet-sick. She had desperately tried to follow what was happening in Manners and

Customs but couldn't bring herself to touch the lizard blood they had to mix into a healing paste. Writing hieroglyphics was even harder: she ripped her papyrus scroll twice, then accidentally wrote something rude by mixing up a heron with a monkey glyph. Her failures were followed with interest by the students from Mehmet's Hostel who shared their class – a clever and haughty bunch who seemed to expect nothing but bumbling failure from the 'ghoulies'.

She didn't fare much better in Introduction to Incognito Studies. Aliya managed to douse herself with too much invisibility cream, which left parts of her legs invisible for the rest of the afternoon.

The final mishap occurred in Introduction to Time-Travel Inventions, when Aliya agitated a knowledge turban by asking too many questions.

'You're not supposed to talk much when you wear them,' Karima explained on the shuttle carpet en route to their last class. 'You just touch or point to a thing, and it gives you the info about it. Turbans don't like being interrupted.'

'It was snooty and rude.' Aliya prodded the still-invisible parts of her legs. 'It told me I had no chance of passing the assessments, then it pinched my ear.'

Despite her failures in the classes, one afternoon in the Citadel had convinced her: she wanted nothing more than to be a time-travel student.

Perhaps the sweet shop in the Greek Quarter was what really won her over. After their Time-Travel Devices lesson, the class took a detour to Pastroudis Sweets, where every surface behind the shiny counter was filled with jars of delectable historical treats: from Ancient Egyptian candied dates to Victorian jelly babies. There were at least 200 different flavours of wobbly Turkish delight, and mouthpieces for inhalable chocolate (a favourite with the ultra-modern travellers). Aliya got a paper bag full of fusion space-paste that popped and fizzed in her mouth and nearly refused to be swallowed.

'I love it here,' she told Karima, as the carpet sped along the glittering river. She made a sweeping gesture that encompassed everything in sight. 'The food, the surprises, the carpets . . . I don't want to leave.'

'We won't,' Karima said, squeezing her hand. 'You'll see.'

For a moment, with the warm sun on her face and

the speed of the carpet sending tingles up her spine, Aliya almost believed Karima was right.

It was late afternoon when the shuttle carpet arrived at the site of the day's last class. Zooming through a striped stone arch, the children entered a world of slow-moving camels, colourful kaftans, turbans and face veils.

'The Ottoman Quarter,' Karima explained as they dismounted outside a white building with wooden mashrabeyya windows. 'This is where we study Chronology. We're discussing time keys today. First lesson on the subject!'

Inside the building was a wood-panelled foyer. A group of children Aliya hadn't seen before stood waiting at some distance. They wore the same uniform as her classmates but looked decidedly smarter. Their uniforms were pressed and starched, and their hair carefully coiffed under their berets and tarbooshes.

'They're from Madame Hippolyta's Hostel,' Karima explained, in a whisper. 'The poshest hostel in the Citadel. They've got lady's maids and butlers to help dress them in the mornings.'

Aliya watched as a group of Hippolyta girls swerved out of the way of Fuad, who came charging into the foyer, hair on end. Just like the students from Mehmet's, they looked anything but pleased to share a class with the near-failures from the ghoul hostel.

Aliya looked up to where a glass cylinder hung from the ceiling, golden sand rotating inside it in hypnotic swirls.

'A symbolic representation of the movement of time,' Karima said. 'And that's Professor Nigm.'

Aliya turned to see a tall bearded man enter through a door. He was middle-aged with an aquiline nose and dressed in a white turban and striped coat. He was puffing on a thin silver pipe with a long handle. As he exhaled, light-orange smoke snaked through the air. Reaching the children, it curled around their legs as if in greeting. Aliya realized that she had seen him before. He had been one of the locksmiths on the high ladder at Qahira Square, working to heal the strange crack in the air.

'He's an Ottoman,' Karima whispered to Aliya, a

little too loudly. Aliya felt her face heat up as the professor looked at her.

'So, you are the new student?' he asked. A smoke tentacle wafted past Aliya. To her surprise it did not smell bad, but zesty and citrusy.

'Yeah,' she said. 'But I'm not a real student yet.'

'You've got that right,' Victoria said behind her.

'My name is Nabil Nigm,' the professor said, 'and you are just in time for our first class about time keys. Now, if you would follow me to today's classroom.'

The students trailed after the professor through a door and into a high-ceilinged room. Aliya looked up into a dome, framed by woodwork shaped in geometric patterns of differently sized stars. Under it hung another spiralling gold mass in a cylinder, illuminating the room in a soft glow.

The children sat down on cushions that lined the niches along the walls, the Hippolyta students keeping a safe distance.

'Who do they think they are?' Victoria hissed behind Aliya, loud enough for everyone to hear. 'I could have gone to any hostel I wanted, and I've got a lady's maid too . . . from *France*.' At this, a blonde girl from Hippolyta's burst out laughing. But before Victoria could say anything more than 'How dare you!' Professor Nigm turned to face them, and the class fell quiet.

'How is time travel possible?' Professor Nigm began. 'Is it science? Baraka energy? Or a bit of both?'

He held up a glass tube. Inside it was a luminous pearl. Aliya felt a rush of excitement. For the first time today, she didn't feel helplessly behind. This matter of time keys was new to everyone.

'This is a Fortuna grain. This small piece comes from a mother-substance so powerful and dangerous that only the elect few can handle it without getting killed.'

'The locksmiths,' someone whispered.

Aliya got up on her knees to get a better look. How could something so small be so powerful? She recalled the golden door in the square. Everything the locksmiths handled seemed precious and mysterious.

Professor Nigm put the grain away and drew a box out of his pocket. Inside was a silver key with a filigree handle in the shape of a jackal's head. A Fortuna grain sat lodged between the animal's teeth.

Great-Aunt Gigi had used a key just like that to exit her grandfather's study and reach the Infinitum, only hers had been in the shape of an eagle.

'Once a Fortuna grain is tamed, it is lodged in a time key like this one,' Professor Nigm said. 'Only certified travellers own them.'

He walked up to Mustafa, pulling the tube with the loose grain from his pocket.

'Here, try holding the grain. Don't worry, this one's relatively tame.'

'Yes, go on,' Fuad said. 'What's the worst thing that can happen?'

Mustafa turned his pale face on him. 'Do you want a list?'

He winced as the professor emptied the grain into his palm. And he had every reason to, because when he touched it, a terrible noise erupted. It sounded like the grain was crying out with the voice of a living being, screeching in horror. Around him the others crouched on the floor, shielding their ears, their faces contorted – all except Aliya.

To her, the awful screeching was a cover on top of another sound – a sound that called to her, like a magnetic force. *Pick me up*, it called, tugging at her heart just like the flute had done. But this sound was familiar. It did not make her feel odd, and she wanted to obey. She *wanted* to hold it.

Opening Mustafa's hand, she tipped the grain into her own. It quieted, then lay there glowing contentedly in the groove of her palm. It was the strangest thing, the way the grain felt against her skin – as if it had always known her, and she it.

Looking up, she realized that everyone was staring.

'How did she do that?' Victoria blurted. 'It's impossible!'

Aliya looked at Nigm, but the professor's face was unreadable.

'Give it back, please, Aliya.' He stretched his palm out. Aliya handed the grain back with a mumbled apology, cheeks burning. Around her the class erupted in chatter.

'Maybe you're a *locksmith*,' Karima whispered to her, eyes wide. Aliya shook her head dismissively.

Professor Nigm was standing, frowning into his pipe, his smoke making odd patterns in the air. It was a cheerful periwinkle blue now – a stark contrast to his grim expression. Was he angry at her for touching the grain?

Around her, the chatter was growing in volume. Her hostel-mates were grabbing her hands and examining them. The Hippolyta's students were staring at her as if she had transformed into one of the monsters in the ghoul matron's cupboards. She was thankful when Professor Nigm rapped his hands together, making everyone fall silent.

'Enough,' he muttered. 'We're in the middle of a class.'

'But sir,' Victoria started, 'how could she touch the grain? She's not even a real student. She hasn't even passed the assessments!'

Professor Nigm stared at her for a moment.

'It would be foolish, Miss Prickly, for either of us to pretend we understand the workings of the Sublimes.' He held up the grain again to show them. 'They are a mystery, far beyond our comprehension. Let's leave it at that, shall we?'

He turned on his heel and walked out of the room, gesturing for the class to follow.

'Yes, that's exactly what it is,' Victoria hissed to Aliya as she passed her. 'A dratted mystery.'

A locksmith . . . The word echoed around as the class scrambled after the professor. Aliya fell back to the rear to avoid attention. Nigm had looked so stern when she'd touched the grain, almost as if he was angry. Had she done something forbidden? She sighed. What a great impression to make on her first day.

Professor Nigm stopped outside a large door with a brass sign that read:

THE INFINITUM EXHIBIT OF UNFORGIVABLE CRIMES AGAINST THE CODE OF TIME-TRAVELLING.

'Cheerful,' Fuad muttered.

'To help you understand the dangers of time travel, I thought you should visit this exhibition,' Nigm said, pushing the door open and ushering them in. 'Feel free to move about.'

Glancing around, Aliya saw Karima engrossed in a conversation with Mustafa, and decided to make her own way around the room.

'*Tutmos the Terrible*,' she read under a mugshot of an Ancient Egyptian youth in a black wig. '*Tutmos was exiled for trying to travel back to redo his assessment exams. He was also charged with vandalism after scribbling hieroglyphs on the walls of a public toilet.*'

Other displays showed travellers who had been exiled for travelling without permits, or for 'future harvesting', which involved selling information about the future to fellow travellers from further in the past than themselves.

Aliya stopped in front of a glass cabinet showing a large photograph of the most magnificent time key she had yet seen. Its Fortuna grain was far bigger than the ones in both Nigm's and Great-Aunt Gigi's keys. The handle was shaped like a black snake biting its own tail. A photograph showed the owner – a thin man in an elegant suit. His golden hair flowed down his shoulders. There, in the descriptive text, was a name she was sure she'd heard before: Dorian Darke.

'The Darkling,' a voice said next to her. Professor Nigm stood there, looking down at her over his pipe. 'The most powerful and most dangerous time key ever to be created.'

Aliya nodded in awe.

'Why dangerous?'

'Our history is made up of a series of fixed points that must remain unchanged. This has allowed us to travel back without worrying about upsetting past events. But the Darkling . . .' He paused, taking a puff on his pipe. 'The Darkling is different. When you travel with it, it *upsets* things. That's why it must be locked away. That, and the fact that it has left a string of locksmiths lifeless after trying to study it. Breathing, but blank. A mysterious affliction.'

Aliya looked back at the picture of the key. It was hard to believe that something so beautiful could be dangerous.

Suddenly Aliya remembered where she had heard the name written on the plaque under the exhibit.

'Dorian Darke,' she said. 'My grandfather thinks he's still alive.'

She glanced up at Nigm, instantly regretting bringing it up. It was one thing when thoughts of Geddo's madness whirled like daytime nightmares in her head, another to speak of them openly to a stranger.

'I know,' Nigm nodded. His smoke, now green, curled around her shoulders as if to comfort her. 'But I'm afraid he can't be. We all attended Dorian's funeral, even your grandfather. We helped put him in his grave.'

Aliya shuffled her feet. There was an awkward pause.

'Why did he make it?' she said, to change the subject. 'A key like that?'

'He was a genius. They tend to push boundaries. I believe he intended to create something great, and he did in a way, but changing the timeline has terrible consequences. So, in the end, he was left with a difficult choice: destroy his masterpiece or choose exile. Dorian died before he could decide.' Nigm gestured at his heart. 'Some say it was the stress.'

The professor gave her a nod and walked off, his smoke trailing after him like a tail.

'Did you ask him?' Karima said. She and Mustafa were suddenly at her side. 'About being a locksmith? Mustafa and I are almost certain.'

Aliya frowned.

'No, I didn't ask,' she said. 'I couldn't. He'd think I was daft. Besides, I don't even know what they do. How could I be one if I don't even know that?'

'I told you before,' Karima huffed with impatience. 'They make time keys. They open portals. They're mysterious and there are hardly any of them. They're like a super-secret society.' She grabbed Aliya by the hands. 'What if that's *your* thing, like mine is menacin? If you are one, they couldn't exile you. They *wouldn't*, even if you don't pass the assessments. Locksmiths are chosen. They're *rare*.'

Aliya looked at her. Geddo had spoken about her as if she was someone that didn't belong in the time-travelling world. If she was a locksmith, she'd be at the very heart of it. It was a delicious thought. Perhaps too good to be—

'A locksmith? Really?'

Aliya turned to find Victoria. 'Just one class and you're already the teacher's pet. Incredible.'

'I thought you wanted me to do well,' Aliya said. 'For the sake of the pod.'

'Yes,' Karima said. 'You know we'd have a real edge with our own locksmith! You know there's only a handful of those in the whole Infinitum!'

'You call that working together?' Victoria scowled. 'You just took the first opportunity to *show off*.'

'I wasn't showing off,' Aliya said. 'I was just—'

'You think you're so special, don't you?' continued Victoria. 'But just cos your mother was a locksmith doesn't mean you're one. Papa said it can skip generations.'

Turning on her heel, she stomped away towards the exit.

Aliya stood frozen, looking after her. *Her mother had been a locksmith?*

'I told you,' Karima said, tugging at her sleeve. 'It's your thing. Why else would Nigm talk to you? He never talks to anyone.'

'I don't know . . .' Aliya was doubtful, pushing down the hopeful fizzing feeling in her chest. But how could her mother have been a locksmith *and* owned a magic necklace?

Chapter 13
THE SULTAN LEGACY

That evening, Great-Aunt Gigi swept into Aliya and Karima's bedroom, followed by Esmat and a flying carpet heaped with thick books. Karima was out doing food deliveries, as penance for past experiment disasters.

Aliya had made use of her time alone by sampling the many snacks Mrs Dickens always left on a cart in the common room, and watching a show called *Historic Time-Travel Blunders*. As Great-Aunt Gigi entered, she was watching a very muddy travel student trying to re-enter a portal that, accidentally, had launched him into the middle of a rainy all-girls lacrosse tournament. Aliya clicked off the TV with a sigh.

'Sultan Junior.' Gigi removed a pair of diamond-studded sunglasses and looked down at her, eyes narrowing at her dishevelled appearance. 'Your evaluation was terrible. Continuing to attend classes with the others won't work.'

'I was being evaluated?' Aliya looked from Gigi to Esmat. 'No one told me.'

'Professor Ramses says you refused to touch the lizard blood!' Gigi spluttered. 'And in Travel Devices class, you traumatized a knowledge turban!'

'I think it was the other way around.' Aliya rubbed the top of her ear where the turban had pinched her.

'You're simply not learning as much as we had hoped,' Esmat said.

'I've only been in classes for a day! How much *could* I have learnt?'

Esmat laid a soothing hand on Aliya's arm. 'Never fear. You will be studying with me.' She indicated the towering book heaps on the carpet behind her. 'It will be intense, but we'll manage.'

Gigi sank down in the window niche, knocking over one of Karima's ornamental cacti with her lacquered handbag.

'*Time is of the essence*, Sultan Junior.' She pointed at Aliya with a sharp red nail. 'As you know, the Council has been very generous. Your first assessment is still a month away, which gives us some chance to prepare. And if you pass, you'll do the second assessment on the day before the Initiation Ceremony.'

'That stupid Initiation,' Aliya muttered. As far as she was concerned, it was the worst thing she had come across in the travel world, apart from blotting and angry ghouls. Not only did it dictate how impossibly little time she had to get ready for passing the assessments, but – provided she did make it to the ceremony at all – this was the moment when your special talent would be proclaimed to the world. And what if she had none? What if her dream of being a locksmith like her mother was precisely nothing but that – a dream?

'Yes,' Esmat said. 'It is part of our Infinitum tradition that the new students are initiated on the hundredth day of the school year. This is to commemorate the hundred days it took our founder,

Philadelphus the Intrepid, to open the first ever time-portal into the Infinitum, using the Fortuna grain he found in a cave.'

'I know,' Aliya said. 'Karima told me. But first he ended up sending most of his family, and his friends, and *their* friends, and various *pets*, to unknown destinations in the space-time glitch, never to be found again. That seems pretty stupid to me.'

'Stupid?' Gigi sat up, eyes widening. 'Traditions are never stupid! *Especially* not those of the Sultan family!'

'Your family has a great legacy,' Esmat said, hurriedly, steering Aliya away from her aunt. 'See here.'

She hauled a thick album out of the heap of books on the floating carpet and flipped it open to reveal an assortment of heavy-bearded men in turbans and a couple of ladies with haughty eyes and complicated hats.

'That's Faridun Sultan.' Esmat pointed to a tall man with a crooked nose, sitting cross-legged on a flying carpet. 'He founded the Great Race. That's the Infinitum's yearly flying carpet race where the students finally get their chance to qualify and join a real travel pod. Very important.' She flipped a page. 'And that's your great-great-aunt, Ferial Sultan. She *nearly* civilized a one-eyed marid. That's a kind of water genie. Very nasty.'

A newspaper clipping showed a stout lady playing backgammon with a dripping monster.

'They write *nearly* because the marid ate the backgammon pieces afterwards.'

Aliya flipped through the pages, where more clippings told her of her family's swashbuckling feats. When they weren't inventing or discovering things, they were busy winning medals. If Mustafa was right, Geddo had been exactly like this when he was young. So why hadn't he wanted her to be part of his amazing family?

'I have some news about your grandfather.' Gigi took a couple of agitated steps around the room. One of the bedpost guardians cracked open an eye to give her a sleepy look. 'Well, there's no point in mincing my words.'

'What?' Aliya whispered, tensing. 'What's happened to him?'

'He escaped from his treatment facility this morning. They found his room empty, as if he had gone up in a puff of smoke. Probably had some mythical help him.'

Aliya sank into her chair. *Mr Kamel*. That was who had helped him. That pesky butler-genie.

'So, what happens now?' she asked. 'Will they be searching for him, or . . .?' She wanted to say: will he be searching for *me*?

'You must focus on the task ahead.' Gigi grabbed Aliya under the chin, red nails poking her skin.

'Listen to me . . . dear. I know what it is like to have the family's fate riding on your shoulders. I also know what it's like to be – a failure.'

She blinked, and for a moment there was a crack in her cool veneer. Through it, Aliya saw something soft and desperate – a person on the verge.

'Believe me,' Gigi croaked. 'You don't want to carry that.'

She let go and smoothed down her bob, her usual composure slipping back in place. Aliya looked up at her, confused. Had Gigi just sympathized with or threatened her?

'*She* was the Sultan inheritor,' Esmat whispered, as Gigi headed for the door. 'But she failed. The family's connections saved her from getting blotted and gave her a job in the administration. It's not always easy. Everyone wants to be a proper traveller, you know. It has such great status.'

Aliya blinked. As Geddo's younger sister, Gigi had been the next in line to be a real traveller, and to carry on the Sultan legacy – but she had blown it!

'This is your time to shine.' Esmat brushed a piece of dinner off Aliya's lapel. 'As your great-aunt says, you just have to focus on the task ahead.'

Aliya swallowed, a fluttering in her stomach like a swarm of frantic butterflies. Maybe she was just the disappointing finish to a line of great adventurers?

'Shining isn't really my thing,' she said.

Esmat shook her head and squeezed Aliya's hand, gently but firmly. Her body emitted even more light today, as if she was fuelled by some mysterious, optimistic power.

'We don't have much choice, do we?'

Gigi turned in the doorway.

'You start studying at sunrise tomorrow. Esmat

will leave these books here. Read as many as you can tonight.' She slid her sunglasses back on. 'I'm off to the Pan-Asian travel hub for a conference. Last year they made us visit a samurai village and attend an actual battle. I broke a pair of very fine stiletto heels in the mud.'

Gigi pointed at Aliya and then again at the books.

'Sultan Junior. *Read*.'

'And don't skip the footnotes,' Esmat added with a wink.

After a good hour of trying to concentrate on her books, Aliya was just climbing into bed when the door slammed open, and Karima burst into the room.

'It's happened again!'

'What?' Aliya blinked.

Karima rushed into the bathroom. Aliya scrambled out of bed and helped push aside the cabinet that hid Karima's secret lab.

'Another one of the elders has been poisoned.' Karima's hands trembled as she opened the cabinet door. 'They were carrying elder Lydia Lumos out of the Council building on a stretcher. She'd already started shrinking. And I had just seen her when I served late afternoon tea at the meeting room lounge. She . . . she likes the creampuffs best.' She sniffed. 'It was almost as if . . . as if it was my food that did it.'

She looked at Aliya, eyes wide, as if something had just dawned on her.

'Come on,' Aliya said. 'Are you saying the poison came from the *hostel*?'

They stared at each other in silence.

'But who?' Karima breathed. 'Mrs Dickens?'

They both shook their heads. They had both seen Mrs Dickens get teary-eyed when a moth drowned in her teacup.

'The matron?' Aliya suggested. 'Or one of the maids? The maids are creepy. They could've done it. Especially that Sawsan. She's dodgy.'

She stroked her belly, thinking of the sour-faced maids that had served lunch earlier. Hopefully there had been no shrinking poison in the casserole.

'I don't particularly like the maids, and Matron is a bit rough,' Karima said. 'But she's the best menacist there is. It just doesn't make sense that she should poison anyone!'

'She's always threatening to eat us, and . . . I saw something in her office.'

Aliya told her of the poison samples she had seen lined up on the matron's desk.

'She saved my life,' Karima said when Aliya had finished, but there was a new uncertainty in her eyes. 'Poisoners don't help little girls get well, do they? Especially when they get nothing but a thanks for their trouble. Well, I promised her a lifetime's supply of pastries too, but she doesn't even *like* pastries.' Karima shook her head. 'I just can't believe it.'

But somehow, Aliya knew, they both thought the matron was the most likely culprit. Karima admitted that, more than once, she'd seen Matron slink down to her subterranean lab, carrying odd parcels, leaving dribbles of blood on the flagstones. She was always hiding away, doing God knows what down in the dungeons, always scowling at them and flashing her uncanny silver teeth. And the maids . . . skulking around in the shadows, whispering, as if they were plotting something, muttering about the

Council – how unfairly the ghouls were treated, how the hostel always got the worst students . . .

A foul stench wafted out at them from the corpse-weed plant, but Karima scooped it up in her arms as if it were a baby.

'He's not ready yet.' She stretched it out to show Aliya. 'The police have done all kinds of tests to identify the poison, but nothing comes of it. Only Corpsy knows.' She stroked one of the tentacles. 'The plant will smell like boiled cabbage when it's ready.' She stuck the plant under Aliya's nose. 'Does that smell like boiled cabbage to you?'

'It smells like something that died a long time ago.'

Karima nodded.

'That's cos we're in the middle of the transform-ation.'

She put the plant back with a sigh.

'There's nothing we can do but wait. Only, I hope it won't take too long. Some of the elders are no bigger than Thumbelina. We're running out of time.'

'Yes,' Aliya said, thinking of how fast the first assessment was approaching. 'You can say that again.'

Chapter 14
VOLATILE VOLUMES

For the next couple of weeks, Aliya watched the other children go off to classes while she stayed behind at the hostel for private tutoring with Esmat. As expected, their sessions quickly turned disastrous. Esmat transformed the girls' room into a chaotic library, with notes pasted all over the walls, even on the ceiling. If Esmat had a gift for droning, Aliya was an expert at confusing facts. Not even sitting on the floor without a backrest helped her focus. In Aliya's mind, Egyptian history became a chaotic stew full of odd, mismatched flavours. The more she tried, the more confused she became. Did the Ottomans come before the Fatimids? The facts bounced off her mind like water drops off rubber. Esmat never let her frustration show, but Aliya could still tell: she always turned invisible when she was agitated.

Aliya sometimes managed to distract her by asking about the Sultan curse. This was a guilty pleasure for Esmat, who loved to haul out the glorious Sultans' clipbook and recount all the disasters that had befallen Aliya's ancestors. They were indeed a terribly accident-prone bunch. There was Great-Great-Uncle Fadel Sultan, who had got knocked off his flying carpet, and Faaris Sultan, the fighter, whose silver sword had been swiped out of his hands in the middle of a battle with a particularly wicked genie. The list went on.

'And every one of their disasters tells of the same thing,' Esmat would say, her eyes widening behind her thick glasses. 'The curse of the black snake.'

The black snake was a mythical monster that the Sultans blamed for all their misfortunes. It would appear out of nowhere, at the cusp of their luck, to knock them off their carpets, or steal their scimitars just when they were about to slice a genie's head off. Sounded like a pretty lame excuse, Aliya thought. But maybe Sultans weren't the best at admitting their shortcomings. Gigi and Geddo hadn't exactly been open about theirs, although they had no problem pointing out *her* failings. And Geddo – he had raved about being cursed too, by Dorian Darke. Was he also using the old Sultan curse as an excuse for . . . what exactly? Or maybe he had really gone mad and believed it was true? He hadn't said anything about black snakes though . . . not yet, anyway.

'You don't really believe all that, do you?' Aliya asked Esmat as they studied photos and clippings of the unfortunate Sultans. 'About the curse, I mean? Great-Aunt Gigi doesn't.'

Esmat looked slightly taken aback, as if Aliya had accused her of cheating.

'I believe there are a great many things in the time-travel universe we have very little knowledge about,' Esmat said, snapping the album shut. 'But enough of this. We've got a lot of work to do, and very little time to do it in!'

As the days passed, the other students moved in and out of Aliya's day, relating all the exciting things they'd learnt during classes. And in the evenings, when Aliya was still poring over important events and dress styles, she could hear them living it up in the common room. Ever since she had questioned the reality of the Sultan curse, Esmat refused to tell more stories about the unfortunate family – now there wasn't even *that* to look forward to. Karima came and sat with her when she could, but she was sent out on food delivery duty most nights, and was terrified of more poisonings happening. Thankfully, none did. The girls tried to keep their eyes peeled to catch the poisoner, but no one at the hostel was acting suspiciously, or rather, *more* suspiciously than usual. But, as Aliya was discovering, it was difficult to play detective when you had 2,000 years of history to get through.

Mrs Dickens tried to make things better by sending Aliya trays of goodies to nibble during her study sessions, but Esmat wouldn't let her touch them while they were working.

In this way, the first assessment steadily drew nearer, until it was only two days away.

'I can't do it,' Aliya said to Karima as they were lying in their beds. That day's study session for the Brain Freeze had ended in disaster when Aliya had mixed up most of the medieval empires . . . again. Tears stung in her eyes. Her tutor back in Cairo had probably been right about her. It was just a question of time before Esmat cracked too.

'I don't remember anything!' she cried into the dark. 'I'm a blockhead!'

'It's really difficult,' Karima said, turning over to face her. 'We learnt all that stuff over years and years.'

Aliya sank deeper into her pillow. Tonight, not even the rhythmic snoring of the bedpost guardians was comforting.

'But if you're a locksmith you might not need to study after all.' Karima yawned. 'They'd never throw you out if you could prove it.'

Aliya got up on one elbow and looked over to where the moonlight spilt in and silver-streaked Karima's curly hair.

'But how would I find out if I am a locksmith? I tried asking my tablet. It says the information is *classified*.'

'I don't know. Maybe there would be a book about it at the library. Or ask Professor Nigm. He would know.'

Aliya lay back on her pillow. She couldn't ask Professor Nigm. She'd only met him once, that first day when the Fortuna grain had quieted in her palm. That was a hopeful sign, but how could she go up to him and ask if she happened to be the rarest form of traveller there was? No, she would try the library.

Tomorrow. As soon as she could escape from Esmat.

The moment the study session was over the following evening, Aliya slipped out into the cold night and headed for the library. Karima – who was on food delivery again – had told her that the library lay in the Victorian Quarter, where most British travellers lived. It wasn't far. The quarters were lined up chronologically along the river, and as the Victorian and Khedivial ages overlapped historically, they lay next to each other. Aliya gave herself a pat on the shoulder for remembering that.

After a short walk along the river promenade she reached a park where big oaks and weeping willows cast wide, trailing shadows across the walkway. She hurried on, her steps echoing against the stone, the mist swallowing everything around her.

A feeling slipped over her like a shadow, and she suddenly knew that someone was watching her.

She stopped. There – out of the corner of her eye, she saw a dark shape appear from behind a tree. She whipped around, her pulse hammering in her ears, but it was gone.

Her mouth tasted of iron. The thought of the Citadel poisoner swam up in her mind. Someone was attacking the elders . . . could they be after the students too? Another, more irrational fear surfaced, of the Collector and the Old Evil. Since the ghoul maid Sawsan had told Aliya and Karima the story on that first night, the nightmarish idea of the demonic shopkeeper had lurked in the back of her mind, along with his horrible shop. Was it real? Or just a story? Geddo had said that he had found a shop – a place full of magic that had cursed him. It had to be nonsense, of course. Every sane person in the Citadel thought of it as nothing more than some leftover folk tale! Still, the idea of the lurking Shop and its keeper was hard to shake, especially in a gloomy place like this.

She began jogging, avoiding the darkest shadows – trying to stay where the Victorian-style street lights illuminated the road. She squeezed the necklace in her pocket. If anything happened, she could always ask it for help. It was a comfort, but not enough to drive the fear away.

She had just reached the middle of the park when she heard it – the thin note of a flute floating towards her through the night air. She stopped, transfixed, and let it caress her ears. In her pocket the necklace was heating up. It glowed against her thigh, just like it had done before.

Go on, the note seemed to sing in its soft, plaintive voice.

Hurry up and wear it.

Before her, the air thinned as if it was being stretched . . . then the music died away. The necklace stopped glowing and grew cool. Aliya blinked, feeling as if she'd woken from a dream. She looked around, trying to discern someone in the shadows.

'Who's there?' she called into the darkness. The

trees stood still, the wind rustling their branches, but nothing moved.

Fear began creeping up on her again. It was so odd, so unreal, the feeling that had come over her. And the music, where had it come from? This was the second time she'd heard it. *Hurry up and wear it.* Had she imagined the words or had the flute really spoken to her? And why did whoever was playing it want her to wear the necklace?

Were they the same person who had sent her the necklace in the first place?

She set off at a brisk pace, the darkness nipping at her heels, then exhaled in relief as the illuminated facade of the library loomed into view – a grand white building with marble columns and a wide staircase. Groups of travellers were milling about outside the entrance. Aliya spotted a couple of ladies in wide skirts and hats, and some bearded men in togas.

Her tension gradually fizzled out as she stepped into the wide atrium with its high, domed ceiling. The light from the heavy chandeliers felt too bright after the murky atmosphere in the park, but at least she was safe. She stopped and took a few deep breaths, reminding herself of why she had come. Glancing around, she realized the library was humongous, with several storeys receding upwards towards the central dome. How would she find a book about how to be a locksmith in this maze?

There was a desk in the middle of the reception hall with a brass calling bell. A note read: *Ring for assistance.* Aliya pressed it and sent a high note echoing against the expanse of the ceiling. A few book browsers looked up and stared at her in disapproval. Aliya gestured at the bell. Why put it there if you weren't allowed to use it?

She jumped in fright as a semi-transparent bespectacled head and pair of shoulders emerged out of the nearest bookshelf, releasing a cloud of shelf-dust into the air. The head glanced at Aliya quizzically, then shifted through the bookshelf and turned into the full figure of a lady. She was quite short and had the kind of hair you get if you sleep with hair curlers, and clothes that reminded Aliya of her late grandmother – nylon stockings, knitwear and comfortable loafers, only there was little need for shoes since she was floating a metre above ground. As she came drifting towards Aliya, she brushed her sleeves off and enveloped herself in a cloud of dust from which she emerged, coughing.

'Don't worry, dear,' she said with a genial smile. 'I'm not a ghost. The closest we've got is a sila who works in the section for Volatile Volumes. I'm a genie librarian.'

Aliya nodded, speechless.

'My name is Margaret,' the librarian said. 'How can I help you?'

'I need a book on how to be a locksmith,' Aliya mumbled.

Margaret looked surprised.

'Did you say a book about locksmiths? My dear, why ever would you need a book like that?'

'Oh, just . . .' *Why hadn't she thought up a good story?* 'Just for research.'

'I'm afraid such books are stored in the Volatile Volumes section. No one's allowed there except with a special permit.' Margaret peered at Aliya over her half-moon glasses. 'But maybe you have one?'

Aliya shuffled where she stood. This was just typical.

'Locksmiths have a lot of secrets,' Margaret continued. 'Their occupation is full of hazards. I think they keep their knowledge hidden for our sake, not theirs.'

'OK,' Aliya said. 'Could you maybe just tell me where the right section is? I wouldn't want to wander in there by mistake.' That could have been the worst excuse ever, but Margaret nodded.

'It's over on that side.' She pointed right through a stack of books, her arm disappearing up until the elbow. 'Not that there's any reason to worry. The Volatile Volumes section is kept quite safe from trespassers. Now, would you like me to show you a holographic version of *Mary Poppins*? Future tech, and such great fun, especially when they jump through the chalk drawings on the pavement.'

'Um, no thank you.' Aliya began backing away. 'I think I'll just go home now. Bye.'

She turned and walked as fast as she could towards the exit, but once she was out of Margaret's sight she darted between two stacks and began looping her way back towards the Volatile Volumes.

The Volatile Volumes section was separated from the rest of the library by a black metal wall with a spiked door set into it. They looked like they belonged in a bank vault or, better: guarding subterranean treasure in a goblin's castle. Squeezing the necklace, Aliya hesitated. Should she ask it to help her open the door? Conjuring just enough of the red haze to make the lock open couldn't be bad, could it? It was just dealing with a practicality.

Making sure that no one was around, she pulled out the necklace and whispered:

'Please open this door. But just enough for me to get through, and quietly.' She rubbed the gem. The red haze appeared. It snaked its way into the door's hinges. A moment later the heavy door creaked open. Aliya stepped through it, quickly pushing it closed behind her.

Here, no lamps were lit. The only light came from the big windows at the other end of the hall, where the moonlight spilt in and bathed the bookshelves in an eerie glow. Despite the creepiness of the surroundings, Aliya smiled to herself. She'd done it.

She was inside.

She was just about to ask the necklace to find her the right book when a wafer-thin voice wafted towards her through the dark.

'*What goes there?*'

It was the kind of voice that turns blood to ice, that makes the hairs on the back of the neck stand up, and now it was making Aliya's brain scream with fear. Gliding towards her through the dark was a beige . . . *thing*. With it came a rushing sound, as if a strong wind was approaching. It pelted the books as it passed through the stacks, and Aliya suddenly realized what it was.

It was sand. Or, actually, a sandstorm with omnious glowing eyes. It came to a stop and hovered in front of Aliya, about a metre off the ground. She'd thought that Margaret was joking when she'd said that there was a sila in the restricted section. How wrong she had been. Her grandfather's stories had figured the odd sila. They were ominous spirits that lived in the desert, and whose sole purpose seemed to be luring lone travellers off their path.

'*Does it have a special permit?*' the sila whispered,

its voice carried on the undertow of the rushing sand that pelted Aliya's face like a thousand needles. She had to close her eyes.

'Yes,' Aliya croaked, the sand getting into her mouth. She tried spitting it out. 'Just a minute. I've got it right here in my pocket.'

She fished for the necklace, her fingers cramping. The sila moved closer, its sand circling Aliya, tugging at her clothes, looking for ways to get in. The bright, ominous eyes stared at her.

It's got to be civilized, Aliya thought. *Or they wouldn't have let it into the Citadel.*

'Please make this thing go away,' she whispered to the necklace. 'And show me the right book . . . and quick!' She rubbed the diamond.

At the sight of the red haze the sila began to scream. It was a mind-piercing, heart-stopping scream that shocked the whipping sand into an even more furious spin. For a few seconds it circled like a twister, then it was gone. Aliya drew a relieved breath. She hoped the necklace had disposed of the sila in a safe way. Could a being like that get hurt? She hoped not, anyway.

She froze as more red haze began enveloping her legs. Lifting her into the air, it carried her in a red cloud through the darkness between the bookshelves.

An odd feeling was creeping up on her. It had begun when she'd asked the necklace to help her open the door to the restricted section – a feeling of exhilaration, of *power*. She'd felt the feeling increase when she'd got rid of the sila – she'd just disposed of a mythical desert spirit! *Her!*

The cloud put her down in the middle of a dark section.

'Give me light,' Aliya commanded the necklace, which immediately responded with a beam that shone out of the diamond. Aliya trained it on the books – but these were not about locksmiths. *Magic through the Ages*, she read on one dusty book spine. *The Glory Days of Magic* and *Magic – Misunderstood*. Aliya's gaze fell on one book called: *The Surreptitious Power of Magic Objects*. She pulled it out and turned it over. The pages were old and yellowed. Why had the necklace brought her here? Did it want her to read about magic?

She stuck the book into her coat.

'Bring me a book about becoming a locksmith,' she told the necklace. Seconds later, she was holding a leatherbound volume in her hands. Glimmering, golden letters read: *The Apprentice Locksmith*. She opened it and gazed, wide-eyed, at the intricate drawings and golden cursive that ran, like some elvish language, up and down the pages.

A rushing sound brought her to attention. Something was moving towards her between the stacks, dumping a carpet of sand before it.

'*No special permit,*' a voice hissed through the dark. '*It deserves the touch of death.*'

Aliya clutched the locksmith book to her chest and whispered to the necklace.

'Get me out of here – quick!'

Chapter 15
FLYING KNIVES

Back in her room, Aliya sat cross-legged on her bed, flipping through *The Apprentice Locksmith*. The exhilaration she'd felt in the library was wearing thin. Stealing back through the park with her booty of stolen books, she had begun to feel guilty. She'd lied to Margaret, the nice genie librarian, and used magic to break into the Volatile Volumes section. Then she'd used it again to get rid of the creepy sila, before using magic to escape. She wondered if guilt could feel like a fuzzy headache – if so, it was catching up with her and squeezing her head like a clamp. The feeling of power that she'd relished in the library – it was frightening now that she was sober. And the way the magic kept pulling her in, as if it wanted her to use it . . .

She looked down at the book in her lap. If she could just use this book to prove that she was a locksmith, she would be allowed to stay without having to pass the assessments, without having to use the magic again. It would be a win–win. Then she'd keep the necklace safely stored in her room, as a treasured family heirloom. She'd take it out at times, perhaps, to conjure herself some sweets, but that would be it.

She listened to Karima's light snoring coming from the other end of the room. There was so much she wanted to tell her, but everything she was doing led back to the necklace. If she opened her mouth there would be more and more lies. At least saying nothing wasn't technically dishonest.

Flipping back to the first chapter of *The Apprentice Locksmith*, she struggled through the sophisticated cursive all the way down to where it said *Exercise for novices: How to influence metals.*

Once you have received the essential touch of initiation and read through the introduction with your master – Yeah, yeah, Aliya thought, get to the good stuff – *you will perform the following exercise to activate your innate power for influencing common metals. Step One: Find a metal object.*

Aliya remembered what Aion had told her about locksmiths. They could influence things by channelling the Baraka energy they took from the Sublimes – that mysterious power that powered the travel world.

Aliya looked around, then got up and got a hairpin from the dresser.

Step Two: Place your object in front of you and place your palm directly over it, then slowly attract the object until it touches your skin.

She held her hand over the hairpin and concentrated. Nothing happened. She tried again, then huffed in frustration. How did one *attract* a hairpin?

If you possess the innate powers of a locksmith, this exercise should be easy for you. Aliya hauled the book across the bed, then pulled the necklace out of her pocket.

'Just make metal objects react to me!' she whispered to the diamond. 'Like the book wants.'

A thin stream of red haze snaked out of the diamond and took a turn around the room before slipping under the door and disappearing. Aliya watched it in irritation. What good was that supposed to do?

When she got up to brush her teeth, she realized that the hairpin was sticking to her skin as if she were a magnet. As she made her way through the room, more metal things – pencil sharpeners, keys, the tops of Karima's perfume bottles – all came flying and stuck to her like brooches.

'It's working,' Aliya whispered under her breath.

Something was happening outside. There was a commotion downstairs.

Both Karima's and Aliya's bedpost guardians had woken up and were chattering agitatedly.

'What's going on?' Karima was sitting up and looking around sleepily. 'What's with the guardians? Wait, I hear something!'

And so did Aliya. There was a howl that grew steadily louder until it was right outside their door. Something heavy thumped against it, followed by a series of lesser thumps.

A hoarse voice roared:

'Whose guts am I turning into sausage?'

There were more thumps, more outraged roars. Aliya quickly turned her back to Karima and whispered to the necklace:

'Stop making metal attracted to me, *right now*.'

The hairpin and the other metal objects that had been stuck to her clattered to the floor. Thankfully, Karima caught none of that. She had got out of bed and was opening the door. Both she and Aliya shrieked when they saw what was outside. Matron Olfat sat pinned to the wood of the door by several large steak knives. At her feet lay a small mountain of metal objects.

'Pickled frogs,' Karima whispered. Around them, white-faced maids and sleepy-eyed students from the upper floors were appearing to watch the goings-on.

'They chased me all the way from the kitchen,' Matron Olfat spluttered just as a flushed and panting Mrs Dickens appeared on the landing.

'My goodness!' Mrs Dickens began tugging at the knives. 'My pretty knives. Whatever made you misbehave like this? Oh dear, oh dear.'

Two maids came to Matron Olfat's aid and got her off the door, but she was still frothing at the mouth.

'*You.*' She whipped around to face Karima. 'What do you know about this?'

Karima raised her hands in the air.

'I was asleep. I have nothing to do with this, Matron. Promise.'

Matron Olfat's black eyes scanned the girls' room, then landed on Aliya.

'And you?'

Aliya shrugged. She dared not open her mouth for fear that some horrible lie would tumble out.

'Could it be one of the mythical beings?' said Victoria, who had appeared in a long nightie and matching nightcap. 'Perhaps one of the sphinxes? Everyone knows they used to know magic in the old days before they became civilized.'

'Magic?' Mrs Dickens looked shocked. 'Not possible. No one uses magic at the Citadel. No one has for thousands of years!'

Aliya kept her expression firmly neutral.

'A mythical?' Matron Olfat grumbled. She cast a glance at the maids, who were giving Victoria dirty looks.

'Discrimination,' Aliya heard one of them whisper.

'Whatever it is, it will come to light,' the matron declared. 'You mark my words. And when I sniff this festering menace out, it won't be pretty.'

She stomped down the stairs again. The maids began gathering the metal objects, pulling the knives out of the door and carrying them back down the stairs, muttering about bias and prejudice.

'Whatever it is, it will come to right, my dears,' Mrs Dickens said, waving for the students to get back to their rooms. 'Do try to get some sleep.' She patted Aliya on the hand. 'You've got to be fresh for the assessment tomorrow.'

When the girls had closed their bruised door behind them, Aliya collapsed on her bed.

'Are you OK?' Karima was behind her, touching her gently on the shoulder.

Aliya nodded into her pillow. She turned away, tears stinging her eyes, and thought about what she couldn't tell Karima: it was the necklace that had made the metal react, not her. She wasn't a locksmith after all.

Half an hour later, Aliya lay in bed, totally unable to sleep. The assessment was in a few short hours, and now everything would depend on her brain's capacity to remember facts, which it couldn't. Or else, she would be sent home to Cairo, to her mad grandfather – *if* she could find him – and Mr Kamel, a demonic beast of a genie. She'd never find out the truth about her parents, or about herself, for that matter – but who they had been *mattered*. It *defined* her.

Sitting up in bed, she felt for the necklace under her pillow. Should she ignore the doubts and just use it?

'Can't you sleep either?' Karima was sitting up in her bed, too, her hair like a messy halo around her face.

Aliya nodded.

'Are you still thinking about it?' Karima asked.

Aliya nodded again. Karima thought she was worrying about the assessment, but she could just as well have been talking about the necklace. Neither the assessment, her failure at being a locksmith, nor the necklace was giving her any sleep.

Karima scuttled quickly across the floor and jumped in next to Aliya.

'My parents wrote,' she said. 'They're still not convinced about me staying here. Some of my past experimentees are still writing to them with complaints. But I've been working so hard to change their minds. It's just so *unfair*.'

'What about Corpsy? If you can cure the elders, everyone would think you're a hero.'

'He's not ready yet.' Karima sighed. 'I don't know if he'll ever be. Look.'

She lifted the covers and showed Aliya her naked feet. They were an odd shade of purple and the toes were longer than they should be. They also looked floppy, like overcooked macaroni.

'I tried a bit last night. It's been really difficult to walk all day.'

'That looks dangerous! Are you sure you should be—'

'You can't tell anyone!' Karima stuck her pinky out and hooked Aliya's with her own. 'Promise! Even if I turn green or start to shrink.'

Aliya nodded.

'But you have to stop testing the antidote on yourself!'

'I can't give up now.' Karima gave her an earnest look. 'Neither can you.'

Aliya looked down at their knotted hands. Maybe the two of them were just stupid for trying.

'I know it'll be all right,' Karima said. 'Because we belong here. I know we do. We're travellers.' She squeezed Aliya's hand. 'We're *meant* to be here.'

'I'm not,' Aliya said. 'I'm not a locksmith. Don't ask how I know. I just do.'

'Then you've got to pass the assessments!' She grabbed Aliya by the hand again. 'Let's make a pact. We, the misfits, swear to do our absolute darnedest to stay here and be real travellers.'

'OK.' Aliya winced from Karima's squeeze. 'I guess we'll do our darnedest.'

'You've got to say it with more *umphh*. You've got to believe it!' Karima's eyes were shining through the gloom. 'We'll do everything in our power to succeed. We might even bend the rules a little.' She nodded at her purple feet. 'But all in the name of science and time-travelling, because this is our home now and we can't go back!'

Above them, one of the bedpost guardians

hiccuped in its sleep.

'OK!' Aliya whispered. 'We will do our darnedest.'

Karima nodded, satisfied, then slipped off to her own bed, her floppy toes smacking the stone floor.

Bend the rules a little, Aliya thought as she drifted off to sleep. *That might be the best solution after all*.

Chapter 16

THE BRAIN FREEZE

On the morning of the assessment, Aliya woke in a cold sweat. She had dreamt of Mr Kamel chasing her through her old flat while Geddo had sat in an armchair, looking on with interest, but not lifting a finger to stop him.

She heaved a heavy sigh and got out of bed. As she brushed her teeth, random facts skittered about in her brain, refusing to come to order. On the way down to breakfast, she was so distracted trying to remember important Mamluk battles that the snapping, sausage-smelling flowers on the banister almost made a feast of her right thumb.

'Our darnedest,' Karima whispered conspiratorially as they entered the dining hall, where breakfast was already in full swing.

'Best of luck today,' Mustafa said as she sat down between him and Fuad. He gave her a genial smile.

'I've already told Papa all about what happened here last night,' Victoria said, slapping butter on her toast. 'I had to mention, of course, that the flying knives chose to attack *your* door.' She gave Aliya and Karima a pointed look. 'He sounded most concerned. I wouldn't be surprised if he launched a full-scale search of the place, starting with your room.'

Next to Aliya, Karima tensed.

'And then, of course, there's the question of the mythicals,' Victoria went on. 'I mean, how do we really know that they can be trusted?' She glanced at a maid who was busy licking the used cutlery she had collected in a basket. 'Until now, Papa has insisted on me staying here with you, even though it's a bother to have my lady's maid come in every morning to dress me, but now he might ask me to move back home with him. I've already decided what I'll tell him: *Papa, they need me there. How else will they even have a fighting chance at becoming a passable pod?* So there, I'm not going anywhere.'

She looked triumphantly at Fuad, who groaned into his omelette.

'We can't let anyone into our room,' Karima whispered to Aliya, eyes wide. 'It would be a disaster!'

'That's quite enough of that, Victoria.' Mrs Dickens set down her teacup with a clatter. 'Now, why don't we all wish Aliya the best of luck on her assessment today? Could we manage that, do you think?'

'She's going to need more than luck,' Victoria added, then shrugged at the others' scandalized expressions. 'Oh, you know I'm right!'

As Aliya passed Mrs Dickens on the way out, the cook laid a plump hand on her arm.

'Just do your best, dear. That's all anyone can ask.'

Aliya nodded, biting back her panic. Victoria might be horrid, but she wasn't wrong. Her chances at passing were smaller than an ant's kidney . . . and she wasn't even sure they *had* kidneys.

'And should you stretch the rules a little, it's not the end of the world.'

Aliya froze.

'What do you mean?' She looked up into Mrs

Dickens's flushed face. 'About stretching the rules?'

Mrs Dickens had begun making a chaotic arrangement of the used cups and saucers on a tray.

'What was that dear?'

'You said I could stretch the rules.'

'I'm sure I said no such thing.' Mrs Dickens dropped a saucer with a crash on the tray. 'Now, take care and I do hope I see you here this afternoon. If you'll excuse me, I've, er, a pot of jam on the stove.'

'But—?' Aliya watched her walk off towards the servants' quarters. 'The kitchen's not that way!'

'And best of luck!' Mrs Dickens cried over her shoulder. Aliya stood looking after her – Mrs Dickens seemed flustered, nervous even. What was that all about?

Perhaps she really was her secret benefactor? Stretch the rules . . . Was Mrs Dickens hinting that Aliya should use the necklace to help her pass?

The Brain Freeze assessment would commence at Grand Central Station, the main embarkation point for all the Citadel's travellers – at least those without family portals that allowed them to reach their destination with minimal fuss. Aliya remembered how put out Aunt Gigi had been about having to use public transportation, after Geddo had sabotaged theirs. But family portals were the last thing on her mind as she jumped off the shuttle carpet outside the brilliantly golden doors of the Grand Central Station, where Gigi and Esmat stood waiting for her. She expected a speech about the Sultan family honour and the importance of passing the assessment, but her great-aunt, who looked quite green, just gave her a stiff nod by way of greeting.

'Now remember,' Esmat began, hooking Aliya's arm as they walked. 'This assessment focuses on the historical knowledge we studied. There'll be at least two different periods to identify. Take your time but don't think too long.'

Aliya blinked.

'OK, but—'

'They might throw in a part about the time-travel code. Remember what we practised. *Witness. Record. Reflect.* That's our motto. We never interfere in the timeline . . .'

Aliya stopped listening and gazed breathlessly

around Grand Central Station's main concourse, which was even more spectacular than the arrival hall where she'd first entered the Infinitum. She marvelled at the many marble-floored passages full of luggage-carrying robots and hurrying travellers. Above them was a gigantic dome, like a great stone sky. Under it flying carpets criss-crossed, burdened with passengers and bags.

After nearly colliding with a luggage-loaded carpet, they sped down a long corridor and under a golden sign reading 'DEPARTURE HALL 5'. They went down some stairs and arrived at what looked like a train platform, but instead of a track there was a long row of doors made of polished wood, each with a large golden number. In front of one stood a short lady in a grey suit, hair pulled tight into a slick ballerina bun. She gave Aliya a curt nod.

'A minder,' Esmat explained. 'She'll tail you during the trial.'

Aliya nodded, then took a deep breath and, after receiving a pat on the head from Gigi and a quick hug from Esmat, she walked up to the minder.

'I'm Miss Prim,' the lady said. 'I'll be accompanying you during today's assessment.'

Aliya nodded. Miss Prim looked like an embodiment of effectiveness, down to the last shiny button on her shirt, and for a moment Aliya wondered if she might be a robot. But no, there was something definitely human about the disapproving look she was giving her, and the way she said: 'So you're the Sultan child?'

Aliya nodded and tried to look agreeable.

'Your grandfather's an old friend.'

'Oh.'

They stood silently. Aliya wondered when the door would open. Behind her, at some distance, Gigi and Esmat still stood. Esmat waved every time Aliya glanced their way.

'Excuse me,' Aliya said, 'but what does a minder do?'

'We make sure the students behave correctly, and that they don't get hurt.' Miss Prim emphasized 'behave' by arching her eyebrows. 'And should they not pass the assessment, we deliver them to their final destinations, back in their own times.'

She tapped the screen of a sleek tablet.

'Just a couple of clicks and you're out.'

'Just like that?' Aliya said, horrified. 'Right away?'

'You would have to drink some memory-blotting potion first.' Miss Prim produced a small vial of pink liquid and held it up for Aliya to look at.

'Those are the rules.' She gave Aliya a stern look. 'I hope that won't be a problem?'

Aliya shook her head.

'No . . . no problem.'

Miss Prim turned around and typed something on the tablet. Next to them the door opened with a click.

They stepped into a small windowless room. The floor was velvety red, with shelves along the walls holding an assortment of jars and spray cans.

'This is the equipment chamber,' Miss Prim explained. 'It's an anteroom where we prepare the students for their entry into the past. Today, we will only need a light coat of chameleon mist and an anti-bumper spray – they will keep us invisible and stop people from bumping into us.'

She picked out two spray cans and before Aliya knew it, she was enveloped in a two-coloured mist. It smelt a little like a mixture of wet dog and rotten potato.

Even Miss Prim coughed. Aliya looked down at herself.

'Didn't you say this stuff would make us invisible?'

'We will be, to all of them out there.'

Miss Prim pointed to a door at the end of the room. It looked surprisingly ordinary for a portal, Aliya reflected. Just plain, dark wood and a curved metal handle. It could have been the kitchen door back home in Cairo. But that was probably the point. Portals were not meant to be discovered or noticed, except by the initiated. Despite her nervousness, a tingle went through her at the thought of being one of the select few who got to *do* this – to traverse time.

'Now remember,' Prim said. 'Keep close, and the moment you recognize which time you are in, you tell me. If your answer is correct, we will move through to the next era. There are three, all in all.'

She pointed to the ground where a line of red arrows had appeared.

'That's your trail.'

Aliya followed Miss Prim to the door, then watched as she punched a code on the tablet. A flash of light appeared from under the door. The portal was opening! Miss Prim reached out and pulled the door open, flooding the room with blindingly bright light.

'In you go. I'll be right behind. Keep close, and don't mind the *Whoosh*.'

'The Whoosh? Wait, you said nothing about a Whoo—'

A firm shove between the shoulder-blades sent Aliya through the doorway and – *whoosh* – she was again being sucked through a vacuum-cleaner hose of light. The remains of her breakfast left her in a long, excruciating burp.

Then, nauseous and wobbly, she found herself outside, standing in a field of golden wheat. There were tall date palms to one side, and the sun was high. Some way off were square whitewashed houses, beyond which were more fields and thin canals edged by muddy banks.

Aliya looked around, desperation creeping up on her. This could be anywhere in the Egyptian countryside. How was she supposed to know *when* this was? Things looked pretty much the same in her own age. There were mud paths, the glittering Nile, and some water buffaloes milling around.

She needed to see some people. That might make things clearer. As she took a step, a path of red arrows appeared on the ground in front of her.

'How did that . . .?'

'Hurry,' Miss Prim announced, tapping her watch. 'We haven't got much time.'

Aliya set off at a sprint along the red arrows, jumped over a canal and landed next to one of the white houses. Rounding the corner, she nearly collided with a water buffalo, but just managed to swerve to the side where she caught sight of a bald man in nothing but a loincloth.

'Oops!' Aliya cried. 'Coming through!' She ran down a path towards a bigger building. Behind her Miss Prim panted, trying to keep up.

Aliya stopped, a stitch in her side. On one of the building's walls was a painting of a sun disc with rays extending towards a group of long-faced people dressed like pharaohs.

She pointed, breathlessly, at the image.

'I know who this is! It's that rebel pharaoh who

began worshipping the sun god, Aton, instead of all the other Egyptian gods. I've read about him with Esmat.'

Miss Prim stopped behind her, flushed from running and with mud on her shoes. She stroked a wandering hair back into place.

'Akhenaten!' Aliya cried at her. 'That's my answer. This is the reign of Pharaoh Akhenaten!'

Without a word, Miss Prim typed in the answer on her tablet. Aliya held her breath as it processed. There was a little fanfare and Miss Prim looked up.

'Congratulations, you are through to the next round.'

'Yes!' Aliya bounced with joy. She was about to hug Miss Prim but changed her mind as the minder tapped her watch.

Killjoy. But no matter. Who cared what a stuck-up minder thought? She had *passed.* And what was more, this thing was *easy.* Her attempts at studying were apparently paying off. Or had it been a stroke of luck? Either way, things were not nearly as bad as she had expected.

'Come along, if you please.' Miss Prim waved for

her to follow. 'Believe it or not, I have other times to be today.'

Leading the way towards one of the houses, she stopped at a door and aimed her tablet at it. Miss Prim cast a glance at Aliya over her shoulder.

'Ready?'

Aliya nodded. She would sail through this assessment in record time and make sure the Sultans' legacy continued at the Infinitum. She, Aliya Sultan, was the next great traveller in her family's line – she was a tamer of out-of-control flying carpets, a pacifier of Fortuna grains, and a proper history buff too. She was actually going to pass— *Wait. What?!*

Miss Prim had pulled the door open. Through a haze of dust and broken sunlight, she saw the person that was more familiar to her than anyone else in the world: was she dreaming, or was Geddo sitting there in a worn armchair, looking straight at her?

She blinked. Yes, it was him. And behind him, hovering like a shadow, fixing her with his yellow eyes, was Mr Kamel.

'Thank you, Prim.' Geddo heaved himself out of the chair. 'You've done me a great favour.'

Miss Prim dipped her head in acknowledgement, then pushed Aliya towards the doorway. 'The fun ends here.'

'No, wait!' Aliya cried, looking from Miss Prim to Geddo. 'What are you doing? I haven't finished my assessment! I didn't fail!'

Geddo stretched his arms out to receive her. 'You need to come with me now. I've got a whole plan laid out for how we can disappear. They won't ever be able to find us. Trust me.'

'Trust you?' Aliya took a step backwards, against the pressure of Miss Prim's hand. 'Let go of me!' She shook herself free, then turned to her grandfather again. '*Trust* you? After you lied about the travel world? You told everyone I was dead!'

'I did what I had to, to keep you safe.'

'Safe from *what*? The imaginary dead people you rant about?'

'Don't speak to your grandfather like that,' Miss Prim butted in. 'He's not mad.'

'I smell magic on her.' Mr Kamel skulked closer, white face tight behind his glasses.

'Stubborn child!' Geddo lunged at her, his fingers

grazing her shirtfront. 'You're not safe here because of what you are.'

Because of what she was? Aliya shook her head. There it was – again. He wouldn't even let her try.

'You won't have to explain anything once we blot her, sir,' Mr Kamel said. 'Much simpler, I say.'

'Blot me?' Aliya whispered. 'This is a trap. You're going to make it look like I failed. Then you're going to blot me, so I don't remember anything.'

'We'll go back to the way things used to be,' Geddo said, his voice softer now. 'Before any of this happened—'

'Never,' Aliya cut him off. 'I know you think I'm a disappointment, but I'm *through* listening to you. I'm done living in your old flat and never speaking about anything that matters. I need to know about my parents. I need to belong somewhere for real – and I'm not going to stop trying because you – you want to turn me into a *ghost*.'

'Aliya.' Geddo frowned. 'It's not what you—'

'Infernal menace!' Mr Kamel lunged forward towards the doorway.

Aliya turned and ran.

'*Catch her*,' she heard Geddo cry behind her. '*But don't hurt her!*'

Aliya ran, and as she ran, she groped for the necklace. Behind her something approached, quickly – something that did not walk, but swooped across the ground and then above her, like an angry cloud. Mr Kamel, or some form of him, descended on her – all sharp teeth and claws and tweed and red, glowing eyes.

'I would kill you,' the disembodied form whispered in her ear. 'If it was up to me.'

Darkness wrapped around her, tight, like a wet towel. Grappling furiously for the necklace, she found the diamond deep in her pocket.

'Help me,' she whispered, gracing it with her fingertips. '*Help.*'

The dark cloud dissolved in a red haze.

Aliya hit the ground softly and rolled on to her back, looking up at the sky.

She remained still as the world settled into a recognizable order around her, then sat up and looked around. Next to her was a slow-running stream. In the distance were the same huts and temples she had just passed with Miss Prim.

Everything was quiet.

There was no sign of either Geddo or Mr Kamel.

The necklace lay in her lap, glinting in the sunlight. She slipped it around her neck and closed the clasp. As she did so, a strangeness came over her, a feeling like a shadow settling. For a moment unease tugged at her, and she almost regretted having put it on, but then she chased the notion away. She was past that now. This was her parents' way, and she would follow it. She was *done* hesitating.

As if responding to her thoughts, the chain links sprang to life under her fingertips, whirring against her touch. She could feel the necklace merging with her skin – smoothly, painlessly.

Aliya got up and walked over to the water on shaky legs. The reflection showed nothing, yet she felt the necklace hanging against her collarbone. It was *there*. A twinge of worry mingled with excitement went through her. An invisible necklace? What was the meaning of such a thing?

Then a voice close to her ear said:

'Aliya Sultan, I presume.'

Chapter 17
ZIL

Aliya spun round, and found herself looking into a pair of blue eyes. Before her stood a thin man in a pair of purple harem pants. He had blonde, close-cropped hair and round glasses and stood barefoot in the mud. His hairless chest peeked out of a silk shirt, embroidered with gold.

Aliya blinked in surprise. He looked like he didn't belong in Ancient Egypt, but more like an English tourist on his way to a yoga class, or perhaps a bank employee on the way to an Aladdin-themed costume party, only there was nothing in his expression to suggest he was lost or confused. He was actually smiling at her now. Was he old, young? She couldn't quite tell.

Behind him on a flying carpet lay Miss Prim, who appeared to be asleep.

'I took the liberty of fixing a few things,' the man said with a smile. 'She won't remember any of this. If she did, our plan would be quite ruined, wouldn't it?'

'Who are you? Are you with the time-travel academy? I mean, are you a minder?'

The man shrugged.

'Where's my grandfather?' Aliya frowned in confusion. 'He's – he's not hurt, is he?'

'I did to him and his awful genie servant what they were planning to do to you. I blotted them.'

The man was rocking on his heels and puffing out his chest, looking pleased.

'Will he remember me?' she asked, with a surge of panic.

'I suppose. Is that what you want?'

Aliya nodded, her heart pinching painfully.

'Well,' the man said. 'I'm sure it'll come right. Now, just hold on for a moment while I fix our last piece of trickery.'

She saw that he was holding Miss Prim's tablet. He tossed it over to Aliya who, in a moment of horrified curiosity, looked at the screen where her name sat next to a red, irreversible word: *FAIL*. Aliya stared at it – her head swimming. There it was in black and white and bright red. She had failed. It was over. She would have to go back and admit defeat or maybe, in true Sultan style, blame her ill-luck on a black snake that had appeared out of the blue and gobbled up her tablet.

She stiffened as a thin note grazed her ear – a sound Aliya instantly recognized.

'It's you!' she cried, looking up to see the man playing a flute. 'The shadow . . . the flute. In the park!'

The man paused his playing to smile at her before putting his lips to the flute again.

We meet again, the plaintive note seemed to whisper.

'There.' He pointed to the tablet. 'Take a look.'

Aliya looked down at the screen to find a big, glowing word: *PASS*.

She stared at it in confusion.

'You changed it? With the flute? Wh-what are you? Some kind of wizard?'

'Something like that.' He climbed up on to the carpet and patted a place next to him. 'Jump on. Ready for the second part of your test?'

Aliya clambered aboard.

They flew at a level pace, following the trail of red arrows that soon led to a temple-like building where the guiding marks ended at a closed door.

As the man aimed the tablet at the portal, it clicked open. On the other side was an alleyway, and a mishmash of animals and people. High stone houses reached up so close that they almost touched at the upper storeys. The air was stale and full of dust and contradictory smells: horse dung, spices, sweat and perfume. Aliya looked around, her senses in shock. The alley was full of people – turbans, turbans, turbans everywhere, and some completely cloaked women on the backs of donkeys. There was shouting and braying and chatter. People and animals were pressing through in both directions, vying for space: water-bearers, food-sellers, camels and more donkeys. There were even some bats swooping through overhead.

'Go on,' the man said, gesturing at the chaos.

Aliya tried to find some defining clue. The only way to distinguish the time they were in would be to notice something revealing about the passing people's clothes. But were these Ayyubids or Fatimids or Ottomans? Or Mamluks? She tried to remember the pages she had pored over with Esmat that had compared different turban and dress styles. And the jewellery, and the weapons – but it was no good. She suddenly realized why this assessment was called the *Brain Freeze*.

'I-I think it's Mamluk,' she guessed. 'The time of al-Nasir Muhammad.'

The man looked amused. He shook his head.

'Not the studying type, are you?'

He took the tablet back and began typing something.

'What are you writing?' Aliya craned her neck to see.

'The correct answer, of course. This is a street leading up to Bab Zuweyla, and we are in the year 1470. You can tell by the length of the ladies' sleeves.

'There.' He held up the tablet. Now, next to her name stood that glowing word again: *PASS*.

The man tapped the edge of the carpet and it rose into the air. Below them the city spread out like a sand-coloured spiderweb. Aliya's insides zinged with exhilaration and fear. Dust and wind whipped her face and made her eyes tear. They were so high up, and she was with a person she knew absolutely nothing about.

'My name is Zil,' the man said, as if he had read her mind. He stuck out a hand and Aliya shook it. 'Pleased to meet you.'

'Zil?' she said. 'Like *shadow* in Arabic?'

'That's right, and that's what I am. I'm the companion of the diamond you're wearing around your neck.'

Aliya reached up and touched the invisible necklace.

'But you're a man.'

Zil smiled.

'I look like a man if I want to.'

'You mean you're a . . . genie?'

Zil's eyes glittered. They were bright and blue, like the sky. 'I serve the diamond, and now because you called me, I serve you.'

'But why didn't I see you before? When I used the necklace?'

'I can't reveal myself to the owner of the necklace until they're wearing it.'

Shifting his weight, he steered the carpet downwards towards a grandiose gate, then aimed the tablet at it just as they zoomed through.

The noise of the street died away. Aliya's ears rang with the sudden silence, her eyes struggling to see in the gloom. They swept through a narrow corridor and burst into a wide, circular space skirted by marble pillars. Between them thousands of scrolls were stacked on shelves that seemed to continue forever.

'This,' Aliya breathed, 'is the ancient library of Alexandria! I learnt about this place with Esmat. It's where time-travelling began!'

'Last part of the trial, here we go.' Zil swiped the tablet. 'First question: Explain the library's role in the development of time-travelling.'

Aliya bounced on the carpet, making the sleeping Miss Prim bob where she lay.

'There was this big war at the time of Cleopatra.

The scholars from here were afraid that the library would get destroyed in the crossfire. So, they emptied all the books and stored them away at the Infinitum. They already knew about time-travelling cos they had found a Fortuna grain in a cave and opened portals with it. Are you writing this down?'

Zil grunted. Aliya looked down at a group of scholars in robes and beards, searching among the shelves. The books were all still here. That meant they were in a time *before* the scholars emptied the books and hid them in the travel world!

'Done.' Zil stopped typing. 'Last question: Summarize the travellers' code.' He made a face. '*I vow to collect all Earth's knowledge and hide it away, then do nothing useful with it whatsoever.*'

'That's not it!' Aliya snorted. 'It's *Witness. Record. Reflect.*'

'But what good is having all the knowledge of history if you do nothing with it?'

Aliya shrugged. 'It's forbidden to interfere. That's what they keep telling us. And anyway, the past is fixed.'

'But what if what we love is locked away in the

past, never to return? A child lost to her parents, perhaps. Or a mother and father lost to their child?'

Aliya blinked at Zil, startled. It was almost as if he was talking about her, as if he knew what she had lost. She wanted to search his face, but he was looking at the tablet again.

'So?' she asked. 'What if you lost someone?'

'I might know of a way to retrieve them. But I'm not sure you would have the stomach for it.'

'Why not?'

Ignoring her question, he handed her the tablet.

Aliya watched how the screen lit up with another *PASS!*

A cheerful melody began playing, and the words *YOU HAVE PASSED THE FIRST ASSESSMENT* appeared in neon colours.

Aliya was experiencing a strange mix of emotions: there was relief – she wouldn't have to leave the Citadel, for now at least. But then another stinging feeling came pushing in – she had passed only because she had cheated, and Geddo had been blotted, all because of her. She reached up and touched the invisible necklace, feeling queasy.

'Don't worry.' Zil's voice slipped into her ear, as smooth and silky as a good excuse should be. 'All travellers stretch the rules a little now and then. It's expected.'

Aliya looked up into the genie's blue eyes. She wanted to believe him. It would be very convenient if what he said was true, but then there was something about his smile that did not quite accord with how earnest his eyes looked.

'It helped your mother pass, didn't it? The necklace.' Zil continued. 'And your father . . .' He whistled and shook his head, smiling. 'Wild ones, those.'

'You knew my parents?'

Zil nodded.

'Of course.'

'But . . . you make us sound like a family of crooks.'

'Crooks?' Zil looked amused. 'I meant it as a compliment. You're savvy. Survivors. Improvisers. All the best travellers are. If you stick to the rules you end up in the administration. Or worse, the Council.'

Improvisers. Was that what her parents had been? It certainly seemed like they had played by their own rulebook. So, did this mean that what she had done was OK? She had made sure she passed. She had got a chance and taken it.

'Who sent me the necklace?' she asked. 'And why?'

Zil smiled.

'A family friend felt you were deserving. But like all true good-doers, they prefer to remain anonymous.'

Aliya thought of Mrs Dickens. Had she sent Zil to help her? She *had* said that it was OK to stretch the rules a little.

'So that's why they gave me a necklace, so I could *cheat*?'

'*Magic*,' Zil said, when they came to a hover under the ceiling, 'is not cheating. It's an opening, a promise. It makes us strong where we are weak.' He paused, as if to make her consider. 'It makes the impossible possible – if you have the *guts* to use it.' His eyes widened at 'guts'.

'But isn't magic wrong? Everyone at the Citadel says it is. It's forbidden.'

'Humans always fear what they don't understand. What if we could use magic for good? To right wrongs . . . to stop terrible accidents from happening?'

Aliya thought of the fire that had taken her parents – of the flames that had consumed her life, her chance at a family. A faulty gas boiler had started it. One of those old, rusty things that some Cairo flats still used. Imagine having the power to go back and stop it from exploding . . .

'Now . . . before I take you back, let's have some fun.'

Zil steered them through a passage filled top to bottom with rolled-up scrolls. They entered a hall where scholars in robes were bending over manuscripts or standing together in groups, talking.

Dipping the carpet, Zil snatched a parchment and an inkstand. Using the end of his flute as a pen, he drew a quick ink sketch.

'That's me!' Aliya cried when he held it up. With a couple of strokes, Zil had captured her surprised expression and messy hair.

She watched as Zil dropped the drawing. Before it

reached the floor, he blew a single note on his flute. In response, the image released from the paper and materialized into a figure that expanded and solidified until it stood, monstrous and limp, among the stunned scholars.

'Have some fun!' Zil said. 'Command it!' He leant forward and grazed her necklace with his fingertips. 'Go on.'

Aliya gazed breathlessly at the bizarre version of herself.

'But what if it hurts them?'

Zil shrugged.

The way he was looking at her with his laughing eyes – as if he *knew* she didn't have the guts, as if he had her all figured out – made the blood rise to her cheeks. She was sick of adults tilting their heads or shaking them, feeling sorry for her. Like she was some poor little simpleton.

She rubbed the diamond, summoning the red haze.

'Let it chase them around a bit,' she whispered.

The ink-image of her took one step, then another, then set off at a bumbling lope around the hall, scattering scrolls and panicking scholars. Slippers slid on the smooth marble floor, inkwells and scrolls flew about in the air. Togas tore. Aliya giggled.

'That's more like it,' Zil said, with a satisfied chuckle. 'Isn't it about time for you to *live* a little?'

As the magic swirled in the air, a surge of exhilaration swept through Aliya. Her mind soared. She couldn't stop laughing. She'd felt this giddy once before, in the Citadel library, when she had commanded the necklace to do her bidding. Now the feeling was even stronger, tearing at her like a whirlwind.

'My turn.' Zil sketched another image, himself this time, but before they could drop it, Aliya's tablet sounded an alarm.

'Ah, too bad.' Zil pushed the image into Aliya's hand and picked up his flute. The time set aside for the trial would be over in moments.

Zil blew a note and Aliya's ink monster melted away, its body liquidizing and splashing on to the marble tiles like blood. Aliya's ribs were aching from laughing. It was as if the magic had taken over and pushed its way through her.

'Takes some getting used to,' Zil said as they headed towards a side door, which was glowing red in warning. Aliya watched as Zil guided the carpet to the floor and leant over Miss Prim's limp body.

'Aliya Sultan is the best student you have ever come across,' he whispered into her ear. 'You are simply amazed by her performance. And now –' he snapped his fingers – 'you will wake up.'

He stuck the tablet into her hands and then, with a last wink at Aliya, he blew a note on his flute. A moment later he was gone, vanished into thin air, the carpet disappearing with him.

Miss Prim opened her eyes and looked around. Seeing Aliya, her face broke into a wide smile. Her teeth were big and square, like sugar cubes.

'Congratulations, my dear,' she said, sitting up.

Aliya rushed over to steady her and help her to her feet.

'You've had remarkable success.' She patted Aliya on the back and then turned to open the door.

Aliya followed her through it, feeling unreal. On the other side they were met by cheers and raining confetti and teachers and older students who wanted to shake hands and pat her on the back. 'Well done,' someone said. 'Yes,' Miss Prim agreed, next to her. 'She's a remarkable student. The best one I've ever had the pleasure, the *honour*, to accompany on an assessment.'

A moment later, Aliya was lifted off the ground and crushed into an embrace that smelt of perfume and Turkish coffee.

'I knew you could do it,' Great-Aunt Gigi hissed in her ear. 'You are a *Sultan*.'

As Gigi released her, Aliya realized she was holding something: the ink-drawing, Zil's self-portrait. A few lines captured him: his straight back and his cropped hair. The ink eyes looked straight at her, and then one of them winked.

Aliya shivered.

Chapter 18

NOT QUITE A VICTORY CELEBRATION

In celebration of Aliya's success, Mrs Dickens had prepared a feast. The fireplaces at each end of the cavernous mess hall were lit and crackling cheerfully behind their screens. The heat from the fires fogged up the windows and delicious smells hung like a sumptuous veil in the air.

At the head of the table, Mrs Dickens was pouring steaming green molokhiyya into bowls. As Aliya walked in, the others stopped their slurping and chatting to cheer. Taking a seat, she tried to smile. Only Victoria looked unpleasantly surprised. She swallowed the sausage she was chewing and shouted:

'How could you possibly have passed, Sultan? Did you *cheat*?'

Aliya felt a stab between her ribs. *Had* she cheated? The reason she'd initially called on the necklace was to protect herself from Mr Kamel. Then Zil had showed her what *real* travellers were like, real travellers like her parents. They didn't mind bending the rules a little. They didn't mind using a bit of magic. It was a gift, an asset — a misunderstood power of good, just like menacin — if one only had the guts to use it.

She remembered the way it had felt when the magic coursed through her — how she couldn't stop laughing, how out of control she'd felt. And now — exhausted. Still, it had been worth it. She felt closer to her parents now than ever . . . didn't she?

She tried lifting her spoon.

'What's wrong?' Karima whispered next to her. 'You look really pale.'

Aliya swallowed her annoyance. Karima was always there, always noticing things.

'I'm fine,' she said, a bit too abruptly, then quickly smiled. 'It's just . . . it's been a long day, and I'm really—'

'I know.' Karima nodded emphatically. 'Try to eat

something. Here.'

She put a slice of roast beef on Aliya's plate.

I can take care of myself, Aliya wanted to say, but bit her lip before the words escaped. What was happening? Why was she so angry?

The room was warm, the food delicious. She wasn't an outsider any more. Wasn't this what she'd dreamt about? But now there was an invisible veil between her and the others, even between her and Karima. As if she'd travelled and come back . . . different. And then, suddenly, all eyes were on her.

'Well done my dear,' Mrs Dickens told her, with a flourish of her ladle. 'You have shown that hard work and dedication pays off. You should be proud of yourself!'

Aliya thought of the necklace that lay, invisible, around her neck, and a queasy feeling stole over her.

'In two weeks' time you will have to pass the final assessment, which will focus on your resourcefulness—'

'*The Shocker*,' Mustafa whispered into her ear.

'—which you, God willing, will pass in time to be initiated with the rest of your classmates, on the *hundredth* day of the term, according to our great tradition commemorating the days it took our founder, Philadelphus the Intrepid, to open the first portal to the Infinitum.'

Aliya huffed. So, he had founded the Infinitum, but he had sacrificed a whole lot of people *and* pets, sending them through portals to who knew where. But maybe he was just a *real* traveller, like Zil had described them: an improvisor who didn't care about the rules? Was she like that too?

So, I urge you to make the most of the time you have here, to prepare,' Mrs Dickens continued. 'I was particularly pleased to hear what your minder had to say about you. I couldn't be prouder. Now, before we carve the roast, I just want to make a few—'

The door of the hall slammed open. Everyone turned to see a man in a black suit and a bowler hat stride in with a face like thunder.

'Inspector Prickly!' Mrs Dickens exclaimed.

'Papa!' Victoria half stood from her seat.

'Sit down, Victoria, this does not concern you,' Prickly said with a dismissive wave as he passed her, making a beeline towards Matron, who was stoking the fire at the far end of the room.

Aliya tensed in her chair as she watched them talking in hushed tones. Something was wrong. This was it. They knew. They had somehow found out what she had done, how she had cheated, and now Prickly was here to take her away—

'Novices,' Matron barked. 'Inspector Prickly wants a word.'

'There's no point in mincing my words,' Prickly began, stepping up to the table. As if making up for being petite, he had a large moustache that was waxed into sharp points. 'Our city is under attack! Another elder has been poisoned.'

An astonished murmur went through the gathering. Karima yelped and squeezed Aliya's hand.

'The victim is Mrs Baheyya Adil, Ottoman member of the Council. You've all heard of the poisonings, I presume.' Prickly cast a sour glance around the table. 'We've discovered why we can't cure the victims. The poison is not natural, it's *magic*.'

As the room broke out in chatter, Aliya exhaled

in relief. If this was about poison, it at least had nothing to do with her.

A chill went through her as her eyes met Prickly's.

'Starting tomorrow, there will be a curfew starting at six p.m. and ending at seven a.m.,' he said, turning to Mrs Dickens.

There was a joint groan from the students, which Prickly ignored.

'Anyone found outside after nightfall will be arrested.'

He turned on his heel and, after a curt nod to Mrs Dickens and Matron Olfat, he strode out.

'Well, dears,' Mrs Dickens said, sitting down. She exhaled slowly. 'Not quite the party I expected. All the same, we mustn't lose heart.'

Someone muttered something about Matron Olfat's dungeon lab.

'I heard she cooks up all kinds of creepy things down there,' Victoria said in a whisper, echoing Aliya's thoughts.

She thought of the poison she had seen in Matron's office. Victoria threw a glance over her shoulder at two maids who stood talking by the kitchen door.

'Or it could be one of them. Mythicals used to do magic, didn't they? It's just a matter of time until they slip back into their old habits. Then no one will be safe.'

'Holy chronometers! Take it easy with the accusations.' Mustafa frowned. 'Why don't you just tie them up at the stake and burn them?'

'We all know *you* love mythicals,' Victoria snapped. 'But that doesn't make them any less dangerous.'

Aliya frowned at Victoria's prejudice, but then again, there *was* someone else using magic in the Citadel . . . She looked at the maids, who stood mumbling among each other. Could it have been them?

'That's enough!' Mrs Dickens tapped her soup bowl with a spoon so hard she startled herself. 'We must remember that we're all travelling kin. That means we don't go around carrying suspicions about each other.'

She let her gaze move from student to student

until everyone understood that she meant them too. 'Apparently, there are many unanswered questions here, but not all of them are yours to answer. For now, you must all live with the uncertainty, and hope for the best.'

That night Aliya lay awake, thinking. Should she take the necklace off and go bury it in the park under a tree? She touched the invisible chain and felt its cool, sleek surface under her fingertips. She fiddled with it, searching for the clasp – but as she touched it, panic surged up.

No, she couldn't. How would she manage without it? She had one more assessment to pass.

She thought of Geddo. In the past, she wouldn't have thought twice about asking him for advice. But now . . . where was he? And – she swallowed painfully – did he even remember her, since Zil blotted him?

Getting up on her elbows, she peeked through the dark towards Karima's bed. The soft symphony of the bedpost guardians' and Karima's snores told her the coast was clear. Getting out of bed, she slipped into the bathroom and locked the door.

'Show me Geddo,' she whispered to the necklace, rubbing the gem.

Through the red haze, a window appeared. Geddo was sitting in an armchair in front of a fireplace, but she didn't recognize the room. It had to be a new hiding place.

Geddo had nodded off to sleep. There was a quilt covering his legs. A plate of half-eaten sausages stood on a table next to him. Good, he was eating. But wait – something wasn't right. There, around his waist – a bandage! He had been hurt somehow!

Had something happened when she called the necklace to help her? Zil had blotted Geddo and Kamel, but what if there was more?

What if something had gone wrong?

Not quite aware of what she was doing, she reached into the vision, but the moment she touched it, the image dissolved.

Chapter 19

THE SMITHY

The next morning, just after the curfew had ended, Aliya left the still-sleeping hostel. She walked through the cold, misty streets towards the Ottoman Quarter. All through the night, the only thing that had kept her calm was the thought of a certain citrusy smoke, wrapping around her shoulders like an embrace.

She would go see Professor Nigm. Maybe he could help her understand how everything made sense . . . the magic and her parents. Still, she couldn't tell him about the necklace. It would be like admitting she had cheated. She would have to get answers without spilling the truth.

When she reached the corniche, she understood

what Inspector Prickly had meant about increasing security in the Citadel. Sleek robots carrying laser guns patrolled the streets. As she approached one, a red laser beam shot out of the robot's eyes and scanned her. A moment later a green checkmark appeared on its chest.

'You are free to pass,' an automated voice declared.

Aliya hugged her coat closer and hurried on, thankful the robot hadn't sensed the necklace which (she figured by now) must have some anti-detection charm on it.

Professor Nigm lived at the end of a long, winding corridor in a building adjoining the Department of Chronology. It was skirted by bookcases and niches full of calligraphy and ornate vases. Aliya hesitated for a moment before knocking at his door. Was it too early to visit? Would he be angry? Perhaps she had better turn on her heel and run away?

Before she could decide, a tentacle of lilac smoke reached out through the keyhole. The door opened and there was Nigm, fully dressed in his embroidered vest and black cloak. Only the white turban was missing. Aliya stared up at his bare head (and his bald spot), then down at her feet in mortification. Why hadn't she looked at his face? Why had she *stared* at his *head*?

'It runs in the family,' Nigm said. 'The baldness.'

'O-oh really,' Aliya stammered. 'I didn't notice. I mean, that's interesting.' What was she saying! Why couldn't she just *shut up*?

'I polish it every Friday.' Nigm leant forward and showed her the bald spot, which did look a bit shiny.

She looked up at him, then exhaled in relief when he smiled. A joke. He had made a joke. So, it was fine. He didn't mind that she was there.

'You're early,' the professor said. 'Or late, depending on how you look at it. I've been expecting you for some time. I even prepared that little joke for you, in case you would show up looking petrified, like you just did.'

Aliya followed him into a sitting room, the smoke tugging at her elbows. She found the professor's pipe waiting in a tray on the table. More smoke curled up in response, as if in greeting.

'Have you had breakfast?' Nigm gestured at a

large brass tray on a wooden stand. It was full of small plates with jams, honey, cheeses, olives and sweetmeats. Sitting down, Aliya tried a very red sausage. The hot taste bloomed in her mouth and made her flush.

They ate in silence, the smoke from the professor's pipe winding its way between them like a third breakfast guest.

The feeling that had been haunting her since last night – of being separated from everyone by an invisible screen – was slowly wearing off now and melting away like the labneh on her hot piece of pitta bread.

'Why were you expecting me?' Aliya asked when they were sipping their tea.

'Because your mother was a locksmith, and because of how my Fortuna grain reacted to you. I expected you would come wanting to know more. Am I wrong?'

She didn't know how to explain what she felt, and why she had come. That he, somehow, felt like her last hope. How could she tell him that he, with his taciturn manner and his serious eyes, reminded her of the person she had loved the best in all her life until she had lost him? Memories of Friday breakfasts with Geddo floated up in her mind – of them sitting together eating pastrami and eggs and spicy pickles, and drinking steaming hot tea, just like this one, and she had to bite down on her lower lip to distract herself from the pain.

Nigm got up and walked across the room. Aliya followed him with her eyes, then started. How had she not noticed that one whole wall was filled with jars? There, neatly arranged on wooden shelves, were a mass of differently sized containers, each one filled with a swirling, different-coloured substance. *Smoke.*

'What are those?' She got up, her eyes riffling through the colourful jumble, some trapped in glass, others in brass lanterns or delicate pots of silver and gold.

'My thoughts, memories.' Nigm stroked the front of his vest. 'I'm not good with words. This is my way of . . . processing.'

'What's that one?' Aliya walked over and pointed at a glass jar filled with bright-green smoke.

'Boat trip on the Azbakeyya lake with my family.'

'And that one?'

'A very embarrassing incident involving a lame horse. Don't open that one.'

Aliya stared at him.

'You mean I can open one?'

'Try the one over there.'

He pointed his pipe shaft at a silver lantern humming with dark-blue smoke. Aliya picked it carefully off the shelf and pried off the lid. Nigm dipped his pipe into the jar and inhaled. As he exhaled again, the smoke billowed out like mist. It gently touched Aliya's face, like soft hands, smelling of sandalwood.

'Open your eyes,' Nigm said.

Aliya hadn't realized she'd closed them.

In front of her the smoke had settled into distinct shapes. There was a woman in a long robe and a sash, and a girl about her age. They were holding hands and gazing upwards, just above Aliya's head, as if they were seeing something amusing.

'Who are they?' she breathed.

'My wife and daughter. They're both gone now.'

He inhaled, and the smoke image vanished into the pipe. He blew it gently back into the jar and closed it.

'That's how I remember them.' He smiled. 'They were looking at a pair of doves nesting in a tree.'

'You mean they . . .' Aliya began.

'Died, yes. Last year. There was an earthquake and the roof of our house . . .' Nigm's voice died away as if he had run out of air.

Aliya felt an urge to reach out and touch his arm. Standing there with the jar, he suddenly looked lost. Losing her nerve, she stuck her hand deeper into her coat pocket. One didn't just reach out and touch people, especially not professors one hardly knew.

'I'm sorry,' she croaked instead.

Nigm nodded.

'One day, when I'm ready to step through the door to the next life, they will be there waiting for me. That's my hope, my faith.' He laid a light hand on Aliya's shoulder. 'Those are important. Make sure you never lose them, or you'll be tempted to do stupid things.'

Nigm had lost his family and yet, here he was . . .

hoping. She looked down at her hands, suddenly ashamed. She was so bad at hope . . . and faith. Yes, she believed, but most of the time whatever else was swirling around inside her drowned it out and she forgot. There was an afterlife where loved ones met again, she sort of knew that, but it felt too intangible to hold on to – too far away to mend the hurts that pulsed in her soul. That's why magic was so tempting. It promised an instant fix . . .

'Is there something you would like to tell me?'

Nigm was giving her an intent look – the kind of look that draws out secrets. For a moment Aliya wished everything hidden could flutter out of her mouth like a flock of wild birds, but she pinched her lips closed and forced her secrets down again.

'No, nothing.' She shook her head.

Nigm regarded her in silence for a moment.

'Well,' Nigm said. 'Then it's time for our second visit of the day. Here –' the professor placed her next to him – 'let us call it.'

He stretched his palms out in front of him and closed his eyes. Aliya stood listening to the stillness around them, and to their joint breaths, until something stirred in the air. A golden door material-ized before them.

'I saw this,' Aliya whispered, taking a step forward to touch the sleek surface. 'In the square.'

'It's the entrance to our workshop, the Smithy.'

Aliya thought she saw a light emanate from his palm as he touched the handle. Then the door opened.

Before them lay a workshop unlike anything Aliya could have possibly imagined. There were walls like ice and marble-topped workbenches over which gleaming gold instruments hung in neat rows. There were silver- and diamond-tipped tools too, and the air was filled with a low hum that seemed strange and familiar to her, all at once. The professor closed the door carefully behind him.

'Welcome to the Smithy.'

Turning right down a corridor, they reached a hall with a myriad of glass cabinets stacked full of boxes, some metal, others brightly polished wood.

'We call this the key nursery,' Nigm said, gestur-ing around the room. To one side, light filtered in through large gold-rimmed bay windows, beyond which lay a landscape of desert.

Aliya walked further into the workshop, marvelling at the beauty of the instruments and then at the large pyramids outside the window.

'Where are we?' She pointed out the window.

'You might add *when* to that as well. The Smithy travels in time and space to protect itself from intruders. I believe we're some time in Ancient Egypt, in Giza, as you can see. From outside, the Smithy will probably look like some locked grain store or the like. It is excellent at disguises. But come, it's time we met the Sublimes.'

Professor Nigm led the way down a marble-tiled corridor that brought them closer to the humming Aliya had heard when they first entered. A tentacle of rose-smoke wrapped around her wrist to pull her along. The walls turned from marble to rock as they moved deeper into the interior of the Smithy. Finally, they were in a cave. Aliya looked up into the endless darkness above. Was it the night sky, or was it shadows and stone?

The professor guided her towards a stone ledge. Then she was gazing down into a great well where a radiant mass was moving slowly around itself in mesmerizing swirls. It was dark blue, then purple, silver, and shimmering. It was like looking into a star being born, like gazing into the heart of the cosmos. This, Aliya realized, was the source of the humming she had heard. It spun and swirled, and the mass sang – a song of Creation, or of Time and Space and Everything. *What could this be*, Aliya thought, *but a drop of God's magnificence?*

'Meet the Sublimes,' Nigm said. 'The mother-substance from which all time keys are made, and the heart of our time-travel world.'

'The Sublimes,' Aliya echoed to herself, her eyes full of their brilliance. 'The Baraka. This is where it comes from. That's what makes the carpets fly. It's not magic.'

'It's so much more than magic.'

Now a wave rose from below, up and up, until it was level with her. It approached slowly, humming and radiance surrounding it like a halo. Aliya felt Nigm tense next to her. Her knees felt weak, as if they would melt and come undone like an avalanche in spring. There was something about the presence in front of her that felt . . . divine.

'Don't be scared,' Nigm whispered. 'This is a great honour. Their greeting will tell us if you're acceptable as a locksmith.'

The wave came closer, so close it almost touched her nose. Then she was seeing things inside it, as if in a mirror. She was a child standing on a stool next to Geddo, helping to fry sausages, reading a story in bed – Geddo's old voice doing the characters' voices. Now they were walking to the corner store together, her small hand disappearing in his grip.

A hot tear trailed down her cheek. *Stop*, she whispered.

The truth stops for no one, a voice said in her mind. She felt a burning under her palm, then an intense pain crumpled her into a heap. Her heart was being squeezed by an invisible hand. The necklace burnt her neck – a sharp sting of fire, like a warning.

The radiance above her died away, the humming grew fainter, and the pain stopped. Her face was wet with tears as she looked up into Professor Nigm's concerned face.

'Are you all right?' he asked, helping her up. She

looked down to where the Sublimes were again swirling around themselves in their endlessness.

Aliya shook her head.

'No,' she said. 'And I don't know how to fix it.'

She accepted a handkerchief and wiped away the tears and the snot from her face.

'They rejected me, right?' She bit back more tears. 'Didn't they? That's what the pain was.'

'No.' Professor Nigm took one of her hands and turned it over. 'It's not that simple. Look at your palm.'

Aliya looked down in astonishment. Every fine trace in her hand was illuminated by a translucent colour – pink, deep blue, silver . . . the colours of the Sublimes, there in her hand.

'What does it mean?' She looked up at Nigm.

'You *are* a locksmith.'

Aliya blinked. 'But the pain?'

Professor Nigm stood silent for some moments.

'You're not entirely acceptable,' he said finally. 'Not yet. There's something unclear about you that holds you back.' He met her eyes. 'You have a gift, but you can't rely on it. It's not what makes you. You need a whole person to carry it.'

A whole person. She felt like a thousand splinters of a jigsaw puzzle that didn't know their way back together.

'I don't know what's bad and what's good,' she whispered. 'I don't know what to choose.'

Aliya looked up at him. Did he somehow know about the necklace?

He took a puff on his pipe and exhaled silver smoke that danced through the air and collected into the shape of an object: a compass.

'We all have one of these within us. It is what helps us make decisions. Once you learn to listen to it, it will always show you what's right.'

Aliya watched the needle of the silvery, smoky compass. It vibrated as it turned and slowly dissipated. Did she really have such a thing inside her, that could show her the way?

'We're all navigators, of sorts. We need to keep steering towards the true north, towards truth. Don't waver, don't fall asleep, or you might find yourself lost.'

Nigm smiled, but she could see that he was deadly serious.

Don't get lost.

Aliya sniffed. A smoke tentacle, pale green now, stroked her cheek. She breathed the fresh smell of grass and earth and relaxed a little. Her palms were still tingling with the Baraka the Sublimes had given her, and the light calmed her. Her chest sparkled within, and she felt alive and a little bit brave.

Chapter 20
PREPARATIONS

'The second assessment is *much* harder than the first,' Victoria said with relish before biting into her cream-slathered scone. Aliya focused on ladling fuul on to her plate. Hopefully Victoria would move on to another subject and let her eat breakfast in peace. It was a few days after Aliya's morning excursion to Professor Nigm's and she had just about digested her meeting with the Sublimes. The mess hall was quiet. Apart from the table where Aliya and her group sat, a few maids were at the back, watching the news on the TV.

'Much, much harder,' Victoria continued, wiping cream off her cheek with the back of her hand. 'Or why else would they call it the *Shocker*?'

Aliya sighed. She knew Victoria well enough by now to know that it wasn't the scone that was making her look so pleased. What Victoria really relished was making her feel like a loser, which wasn't hard.

'It's all about practical abilities and character,' Victoria said. 'My cousin ended up in the middle of a bread riot. Her minder had to push the emergency button to get her evacuated. She needed fifteen stitches.' She traced a line across her cheek with her index finger. 'She lives in Cornwall now, and remembers nothing. Some students aren't even fit to become duds.'

'My cousin's friend's older brother got kidnapped by a group of desert bandits,' Mustafa said, carefully stirring his tea. 'But he managed to escape by triggering a smoking stink bomb in the carriage they'd bundled him into. Nearly asphyxiated himself too, though.'

'Don't listen to them,' said Karima, next to Aliya. 'You'll be fine. You got through the first one, didn't you?'

'What about your assessments?' Aliya looked

around the table, doing her best to avoid Victoria whom she feared might start up again. 'Were they really hard?'

'Mine were a breeze,' Victoria blurted. 'I got three obscure Ottoman periods which I differentiated by measuring the sizes of the men's moustaches – so easy. For my Shocker I was locked up in a medieval prison with nothing but my superior wits and my hairpins to help me break out. But I managed.'

She took a sip of her hibiscus drink, looking smug.

Aliya listened in trepidation as the others related their assessments. Fuad had raced on wild camels and escaped a labyrinth deep in a pyramid, disguised as an Ancient Egyptian priest. Aion had catapulted herself out of a desert well with an invention she had built on the spot out of a broken bucket, a dead snake and a heap of stones. Mustafa had won a trivia competition against a group of Ptolemaic scholars.

'What did you do?' Aliya asked Karima finally.

'I healed a pharaoh.' Karima beamed. Her smile faltered when she saw Aliya's expression. 'His toes did grow a little,' she said apologetically. 'But I think he quite liked it. They had different beauty standards back then.'

Aliya swallowed. She'd got through the first assessment by use of magic, but this time . . . maybe she could manage on her own and let bygones be bygones? Listening to the others was not exactly helping her decide. The idea of taking off the necklace and burying it in the park came back again and again, but a strange, howling feeling came over her each time she touched the invisible clasp, as if the necklace clung to her for dear life. Was Zil in there, waiting for her command? She still didn't understand how genies could fit into small objects. Was he there all the time, listening in on every conversation she had? The thought sent a shiver down her spine.

A voice from the TV pushed into her thoughts:

'*Infinitum Security have yet to make a breakthrough in the mysterious poison case . . .*'

Aliya glanced over just as the screen went black. A chorus of *ouffs* followed. The Infinitum news station was mainly run by genies who often shortcircuited the technical equipment with their sparkly vibes, leading to long pauses in the programming.

The poisonings were not the first thing on Aliya's mind. After visiting Professor Nigm, she had gone right back to studying with Esmat. Since the Shocker focused on practical abilities, Esmat had begun taking her on excursions to different quarters in the city where she, with the help of volunteers, had created 'difficulties' for Aliya to get out of. The first difficulty had not been too bad. Esmat had simply left her, tablet- and carpet-less, in the middle of the Mamluk Quarter with the instruction to find her way back, like a stray cat. Aliya had hitched a ride to the Khedivial Quarter with an incense seller's donkey-cart on his way to the Fishawy Bazaar, a bustling market street not far from the hostel.

For her second difficulty, Esmat had made her play virtual Olympics at Cletus' Internet Cafe in the Ptolemaic Quarter. She had done quite well in the chariot race until Philadelphus, the old tour guide, whose beard was still pink, rammed his virtual horse into hers and pushed her off the track. Fair enough, Aliya had thought. Perhaps the old man had put two and two together and remembered that she had given him the macaron that had for ever changed the tint of his facial hair. But Esmat had not been pleased.

'Had this been the real assessment,' she had scolded, 'you would have failed!'

Two weeks of training had passed in this way, with Aliya failing every other task set up for her. Today was the last chance for her to practise – the second assessment was scheduled for the following day.

Aliya took a shaky breath, wondering why Esmat would let her spend her last day of training with the class. There was apparently some difficulty in store for them that she could benefit from. Aliya swallowed her last piece of bread ruefully. That was just what she needed: to make a fool of herself in front of the whole class . . . especially Victoria. She started as a hoarse voice cut the air.

'*Listen up*,' Matron said from the doorway, glaring at them. 'You'll have a special lesson today. You' – she pointed a crooked finger at Aliya – 'are to attend it too. You will all take the minibus outside and meet Professor Kashmir at the hangar.'

'A hangar?' Aliya turned to Karima in exasperation. 'Like where you store planes? Are we going to fly *planes*?'

Karima shrugged. 'That would be odd.'

'Odd?' Aliya squeaked. 'It would be a *disaster*.'

'It would be so cool.' Fuad brushed past her. 'Let's hope it's planes.'

'You look really pale. Do you want a soothing saltine?' Karima whispered to Aliya, fishing a paper bag out of her satchel and shoving it at her. 'No side effects, hardly . . . at all.'

'No thanks,' Aliya said. She did not need strange physical side effects to add to her list of worries.

The bus took them and a bunch of students from Hippolyta's and Mehmet's hostels to the outskirts of the Ottoman Quarter and dropped them off outside a big building that looked like an oversized barn. As they got off the bus, Victoria stopped and glared at Aliya.

'Maybe it would be better if you got a stomach ache and went home. You've fumbled your way through until now, God knows how, but this isn't something you learn in one day. I should know. I'm literally a master at carpet flying. Didn't you see how I handled the tour carpet? It's part of my skillset as a navigator.'

'Carpet flying?' Aliya looked up at the building.

'Yes, carpet flying *is* very dangerous for amateurs,' said Mustafa next to her. 'You should tell the professor that it's your first time. He can give you a really nice and calm carpet, to start practising on.'

'Well, it's *not* my first time,' Aliya said. 'When I first came here, I actually stopped this speeding carpet that . . .'

But Victoria and Mustafa had already walked off.

'I think they have a point,' Karima said, as they walked up the steps and into the hangar.

'I've got a cousin who ended up on the top of the Muhammed Ali Mosque during his first flying lesson. He was covered in pigeon poo when they found him. Won't go near a carpet these days. You really should be careful.'

The students entered a brightly lit reception area where they were met by an elderly man with a bald head and a red cardigan. As if to make up for his baldness, he had a long white Santa Claus beard.

'That's Professor Kashmir,' Karima whispered.

'Hello novices,' he said, peering at them. 'Last class we tackled the theoretical side of how to get to make a new carpet's acquaintance. Today we will put what we've studied into practice. Now, if you would follow me.'

He swung open a pair of doors and stepped to the side to reveal a wide hall packed full of carpets lying in neat, colourful stacks. The air smelt of dust and wool. At the other end of the hall, older students were flying around a stubby lady in a blue turban who sat cross-legged on a carpet in mid-air. Aliya and her classmates gasped as one of the carpets bucked and sent its rider flying into the sandpit below. The carpet flew low, and stopped teasingly next to the boy, who tried to catch it and haul himself on top once more.

'That won't do,' his teacher yelled. 'You've got to show it who's boss!'

Aliya and the others followed Professor Kashmir up to the first section of stacks, where they were met by a choir of muted snores. Professor Kashmir tickled a carpet playfully on the fringe. It stirred and batted his hand away.

He was about to speak when Victoria piped up.

'Excuse me, professor, Aliya here has no experience *whatsoever* with carpet flying. She hasn't even passed the assessments. I thought you should know. I wouldn't want her to hurt herself or, God forbid, one of your precious carpets.'

She gave him a silky smile – the first and last thing about Victoria that was silky.

'No experience?' Professor Kashmir looked at Aliya in surprise. 'Well, that is most irregular.'

Aliya felt all eyes on her and reddened. She shot Victoria a murderous glare.

'Well, the Isfahanis are out of the question then,' Professor Kashmir muttered, scratching his beard, 'and the Shirazis are not to think of . . . hmm, much too sophisticated for a complete beginner. Well, the rest of you go ahead. You, young lady –' he pointed at Aliya – 'come with me, please.'

'Always happy to help, professor,' Victoria said, and curtsied.

'Never mind,' Karima said, as Aliya passed her. 'It

might be for the best, you know.'

'It's *not* for the best,' Aliya mumbled as she followed Professor Kashmir. 'And it's *not* my first time.' Behind her, Fuad was already airborne, sitting cross-legged on a beautiful red carpet that hovered a couple of metres above ground.

'It just said *salaam*,' he cried, with a victorious smile. 'The next thing I knew it was offering me a ride.'

Aliya followed Professor Kashmir through a door into another, smaller room. Here the carpets were thicker, and less colourful. Most of them were off-white, with thick, woolly textures. The snoring in here was much louder. It sounded like a whole battery of lazy loafs were having a snooze.

'You should be able to find a carpet fit to your, eh, abilities in here,' Professor Kashmir said, making a sweeping gesture. 'They were made by a group of Mongolian weight-watchers. The weaving keeps them from nibbling between meals. Well . . .' He considered Aliya as though she was a problem that he had finally solved. 'Just don't wander off, and especially not in there.' He pointed to a door at the end of the room.

'Why? What's in there?'

'Oh, that's quite besides the point as far as you're concerned. Now, if you'll excuse me, my dear, I must see how the other students are getting on.'

The professor left Aliya standing there. She listened, with rising annoyance, to the snoring around her, remembering the beautiful carpet that had carried Fuad away. Sleek and swift, like red lightning. Her fellow students were probably all airborne by now.

She moved through the stacks, looking at the woven images on the carpets. There were fat cows and square men holding hands with what looked like upside-down birds. Another one showed a goat surrounded by teacups. She'd never seen uglier carpets in her life.

The door that Professor Kashmir had pointed out as off limits had a sign reading, 'REHABILITATION'. What could that mean? Aliya tried the handle and found the door open. Her heart fluttered. One little peek wouldn't hurt.

In the next room she found more carpets, but these were laid out on tables, one by one. Around each were all kinds of lamps, for heating and hot air, and brushes and oils. There were also instructions taped to the tables, saying things like: '*Suffers from careless dust-whipping trauma. To be brushed twice daily – gentle strokes*', or '*Clawed by pet cats. To be massaged with healing balm, once daily.*' At the end of the room Aliya stopped in awe next to a beautiful dark-blue carpet. It looked so smooth and silky that she couldn't resist touching it. When she did, it stirred under her, and then – a sound. She leant in closer – but this carpet wasn't snoring, it was growling.

'*Hot coffee spill trauma,*' the label read. '*To be sung to, twice daily, preferably in Uzbek.*'

'So you like music, eh?' Aliya asked, stroking the silky threads. She watched the intricate pattern flow under her hand. 'You're a real beauty, aren't you?'

The carpet rose a little under her hand in response, like a cat arching its back to be stroked.

'I don't know any songs in Uzbek, but I could sing a song in Arabic if you like? My grandpa used to sing it to me when I was little. It's quite idiotic, sorry, but it's the only one that comes to mind. OK, here goes.'

Aliya began to sing an Egyptian children's song about the importance of drinking milk. She had not reached the end of the first verse before the carpet rose from the table and slipped off it. Before she understood what was happening, it had slid underneath her and pushed her off balance so that she was sitting on it. A moment later she was several metres up in the air, holding on for dear life as the carpet swept around the room.

'Please, *pleaaase*,' she cried. 'Put me down!'

But the carpet answered by rising higher until Aliya could touch the ceiling. Should she cling to one of the thick roof beams? Before she could make her mind up a door opened, and the carpet set off towards it like greased lightning.

A little old lady stood in the doorway, peering up at them.

'Inferno, is that you, you naughty boy? Come down here at once, or I'll rethread you!'

But Inferno only sped on faster, and Aliya, who was certain that they were going to crash, threw herself flat on her stomach and closed her eyes. For a moment she felt the carpet's edges fold over her, rolled up like a flying sausage – and out they shot through the door and into the main hangar where she narrowly avoided a collision with a pillar.

Inferno made a wide circle just under the roof. Aliya closed her eyes. The carpet dipped, her stomach exploded with twinkles. Should she use the necklace? She reached for the gem and was about to rub it but then – no. Why not try to do it on her own for once? The image of her father came to her. He was sitting behind her mother on a carpet, zooming through the room with the wind in his hair. He had looked so cool, so in control. She bent over and stroked the carpet along its edge, the way she'd seen him do in her bedroom vision.

'Slow,' she said, making her tone deep. 'Down.'

Inferno twitched and slowed a little, still no nearer the ground. Below her she could see the others. They had got off their carpets and were watching her, even the teacher in the blue turban.

'Slow,' Aliya repeated, stroking the edge again. 'Dooown.'

From somewhere within she suddenly knew how to do this. She put her weight on her right hip and tapped Inferno on the right fringe and he veered right, making a smooth sweep. Below her the students had begun cheering.

Aliya leant to the left and Inferno obeyed, making a beautiful low swoop that forced Victoria to duck.

Then she was on the ground again. The others were around her, helping her up.

'That was amazing!' Mustafa cried. 'You flew and landed a rogue carpet! How'd you do that?'

'I don't know,' Aliya said truthfully. She had just acted on instinct.

'I thought you couldn't fly?' Professor Kashmir said as he helped her up. 'Inferno is one of our more difficult carpets. Well done, Miss Sultan.'

Aliya blushed. No one had said 'well done' to her for as long as she could remember.

'Might be a gift you've inherited from your father,' Professor Kashmir continued.

Aliya's eyes widened.

'My father?'

'Won the Great Race several times.'

'That's a flying carpet competition,' Fuad butted

in. 'Goes through different times through moving portals. It's *very* cool.'

'Very *dangerous*,' Mustafa added. 'Didn't I tell you? You Sultans have adventure in your blood.'

A warm feeling bloomed in Aliya's chest. She'd got something from her mother – the gift of being a locksmith, and now here was something from her father. She had a way with carpets!

'Beginner's luck,' Victoria said, scowling. 'You're going to need more than that to pass tomorrow.'

But nothing Victoria said could darken Aliya's mood – not today. She'd stopped a wild carpet all by herself, without even magic to help. She had actually been *good* at something.

That evening, Aliya locked herself in the bathroom and stood in front of the mirror. The girl that looked back had the same bushy hair and almond-shaped eyes and slightly crooked nose, but she felt different. Maybe she was more like her father than her mother? Maybe she was better at carpet flying than magic? She looked down at her palms. Since her meeting with the Sublimes they had felt different too, as if they were alight somehow. At night she had thought she'd seen the creases in her hands light up with different colours: blue, purple and silver. She had changed since her meeting with Nigm and the Sublimes, and now she was finally realizing how she really felt about magic.

'I'm sorry, Mum,' she whispered, touching the necklace. 'But I can't use this any more. I'll take care of it, and it'll always remind me of you, but I've got to try to do things on my own from now on. Maybe it served you well, but me – I guess I'm different. I'm not very clever, I know, but I might be good at other things and magic just isn't for me.' She didn't want to mention how queasy it made her feel, not out loud at least.

The necklace was so feather-light that she often forgot that she was wearing it. As she tried grasping it, it evaded the grip of her fingers. *Strange*.

She tried again, lodging her nails under the chain, but it would not be caught. It slipped and slithered under her touch, like something living – a thing determined to evade her. She grasped at it again, with a sudden sting of worry. With each touch the diamond sank away, as if it were bobbing on the surface of a pond.

She finally got a hold of the necklace and quickly rubbed the diamond.

'*Let go of me*,' she whispered. 'Zil! Get out here!' Nothing happened. She tried again. *Let go.* Nothing. It was doing that thing again, ignoring her requests . . . or he was, if Zil was in there.

'Get me that book – *The Surreptitious Power of Magic Objects*,' she told it. 'But don't let Karima notice.'

The air in front of her shifted. *Oh, so now he chooses to obey!* A moment later she was holding the book she'd nicked from the library. Maybe there would be some answers in here about how to get the necklace off?

'*Removing and Replacing Magic Substances*,' she read from the contents page. '*Breathing Wishes into Magic Objects.*' But there was nothing about removing necklaces that were stuck to a person's throat. A wave of panic surged through her.

How could her mother's friend have sent her this?

She took a deep breath to calm herself. Her

parents wouldn't have wanted her to have something that could hurt her. Of course not. OK, so maybe there was a way of getting it off that she didn't know about? And Zil wouldn't come. Why? What was going on? Was he not always in the necklace? Could it act on its own?

Leaning on the sink, she took more steadying breaths.

'Are you OK in there?' Karima called through the door.

'Yeah, I'm fine.' Aliya splashed water on her face.

'Nerves, right? Don't worry. It'll be fine.'

Aliya looked at herself in the mirror. She nodded.

Yes, that was it. It would be all right somehow. Hope. One had to have hope, Professor Nigm had said. Panicking never helped anybody. She would wait until things, somehow, got clearer. But whatever happened, one thing was certain: she was *not* going to ask the necklace to help her cheat again.

Chapter 21
THE SHOCKER

Aliya wasn't alone with Great-Aunt Gigi and Esmat at Grand Central Station the next morning. Karima, Fuad and Mustafa had come along, and Aliya was grateful for the distraction. The panic of being trapped by the necklace still lay just below the surface, ready to surge up at any moment. Around them, the great station was alive with its usual morning bustle. Aliya distractedly watched a couple of camels amble past at some distance, their stick legs looking too thin for the load of suitcases they were carrying. The air smelt of animal dung, motor oil and Great-Aunt Gigi's flowery perfume. Buzzing through her body was the kind of tension only a mind-bogglingly nerve-wrecking adventure could stir up. Aliya sucked at the air, hoping a deep breath or two would calm her, but her hands wouldn't stop trembling. She felt hot and cold at once, wide awake and about to faint.

'Aliya Sultan. Time to go!'

Miss Prim waved at her, and Aliya gave Karima a last squeeze.

'It'll be fine,' she whispered. 'Keep my seat at dinner.'

'Mrs Dickens is making something special,' Karima said, eyes moist. 'So you better be there.'

Aliya stuck out her hand to Great-Aunt Gigi, who slapped it away and scooped her up in a hug. Aliya was crushed against a row of sharp buttons, but still, it was a hug.

Esmat smiled and squeezed her shoulder, glowing encouragingly.

The boys lifted her up in a heave-ho embrace, then patted her on the back as she walked off towards Miss Prim.

'You know the drill,' the minder said with another toothy smile. Aliya noticed that she had a small flower behind her ear. Maybe Zil had done her a favour when he adjusted her memory, made her happier somehow?

With a last wave at her friends, Aliya stepped into the same anteroom as last time, only now there were different objects on display. Aliya glanced around at shields and – wait, were those swords? The shelves were filled with weapons! Her stomach lurched.

'The second assessment will test your ability to problem-solve,' Miss Prim explained. *Problem-solve?* Aliya thought. *With an axe?*

'Being a traveller isn't just about knowing the facts,' Prim continued. 'You've got to know how to behave in unexpected situations. Improvise. Think on your feet – all without interfering in the timeline.'

Aliya nodded. Be savvy, improvise – *that* she might be able to do. She had always found it easier to do things than to read about them, but now there were weapons involved . . .

Miss Prim took a small golden pyramid off a shelf.

'Your task today is to carry this golden pyramid to a certain point in the city.'

She took out a circular device with a brass lid

that clicked open to display a holographic image of Cairo. Aliya recognized the Muhammed Ali Mosque on its cliff and, beyond that, the Moqattam hills.

'A portable GPS.' Miss Prim attached the device to Aliya's arm. 'This time the red trail will appear there.' She pointed to the holographic map that had appeared, tracing the arrows that showed the route. 'Just follow it to the destination when you fly.'

'Fly?'

'Unless you prefer going through on foot? In that case you should choose some battle implements.' Miss Prim gestured around at the collection of weapons. 'Perhaps a bow and arrow? Or a scimitar?'

'I-I think I'll go with flying.'

'Well, in that case . . .' Miss Prim pointed to a dark-blue carpet that lay snoring on the floor.

'Inferno!'

Aliya knelt on the sleeping carpet and ran her hand over it. It stirred and gave a low growl.

'Professor Kashmir sent him over. Said you two have a connection.'

Aliya smiled. She tickled Inferno on his fringe,

and he began whipping his tassels into the floor, like a dog would wag its tail.

Miss Prim pointed to an X on the map that still hung in the air between them.

'Here's your target. I'll be following your progress from here.' She pointed to a screen on the wall. 'You'll have fifteen minutes.'

She walked up towards the red door that would launch Aliya into the assessment.

'So that's it?' Aliya asked. 'I just fly the pyramid to this point?'

'That's it. And, of course, avoid being injured or killed along the way. Any questions?'

'*Killed?*'

Miss Prim banged the door open. 'Just joking. Or am I?'

Aliya stared at her.

'*What?*'

'Oh, and don't mind the—'

'Whoosh,' Aliya finished. 'I know.'

She dived through the door into the light vacuum, clutching the golden pyramid. This time she was ready and didn't even mind that the

Whoosh nearly sucked her freckles off. Behind her, Inferno twisted in agony as the Whoosh whipped him free of dust and, perhaps, a couple of fleas. But just as before, it left the necklace alone.

She stepped out on to a street in what she guessed was Old Cairo. Before her, a narrow alley led towards a wider space where – Aliya blinked – round things were hurtling through the air.

Flying cannonballs!

A few seconds later a shower of sticks replied, coming from the other direction.

Spears.

Aliya clambered on to Inferno, her mind whizzing with fear. 'Let's get this over with!'

As if he understood, the carpet rose into the air with a growl, then shot out through the alley.

Stone walls and archways whizzed past Aliya on both sides. Holding the pyramid in a firm grip, she tried to remember how in the world you got a carpet to rise.

The square and the battle were coming steadily closer. Aliya's eyes were tearing, the dust-infused wind slapping her face. She needed to do something fast, or both she and Inferno would be mincemeat and, well, minced fibre.

'Up, Inferno! Up!' She tapped the carpet on the front fringe and, just metres before they entered the square, Inferno thankfully ascended until she could see the Mamluks on the top of the Sultan Hassan Mosque, fiddling with their cannons.

Aliya exhaled in relief. Up here she was safe. Now, come to think of it, this was almost easy. All she had to do was follow the map, avoid the situation down there, and deliver the pyramid. It wouldn't take long. She clicked on the GPS and the map zapped into view in front of her. On the lower right-hand side, the time she had left blinked in red. Ten minutes. She had better get going.

'Go, Inferno!' She brought her body forward – the signal for the carpet to speed up. Inferno responded, hurtling through the air. A jubilant feeling soared in her chest.

'Wheee!' she yelled, flailing her arms out and feeling the wind gather in her palms, the pyramid safely pinched between her knees.

They were halfway across the square below when

Inferno gave a violent twitch and collapsed to the side. Aliya slid sideways and nearly slipped off. At the last moment, she righted herself and regained her balance, heart beating like a war drum in her throat.

What was happening? Another twitch. Inferno folded up like an accordion. A moment later she was falling helplessly through the air. Next to her Inferno was plunging, like a colourful rag, all scrunched up.

A cannonball swished past them. Below her, the sounds of battle were coming closer. She grabbed the invisible gem above her collarbone.

'Save me!'

She was in the middle of the fight when arms caught her. Against a backdrop of whizzing arrows and blood-smeared Mamluks, Zil was smiling at her – his eyes bluer than the sky behind his glasses.

Aliya was speechless until they reached a safe distance above the battle again, sitting on Zil's carpet, floating high above the city.

'Where's Inferno?' she cried, looking down at the mess below.

'I wouldn't worry. He's no doubt wearing a

tracker. Your friends at the Citadel will get him back and fix him.'

He reached out and touched the device on Aliya's arm. It buzzed, then sucked the holographic map into itself and fell silent.

'Let's put them on hold. We'll blame it on temporal disturbances.'

'What happened?' Aliya said. 'He just collapsed.'

Zil met her eyes and for a moment Aliya thought he looked smug.

'Lucky you had the necklace, aren't you?'

Aliya felt the diamond, so light against her skin, yet heavy on her heart.

'I would've managed fine without it this time if Inferno hadn't collapsed like that. It was almost like . . .' She frowned. 'As if someone had *sabotaged* him.'

Zil arched his eyebrows.

'Sabotaged? There's a big word. We're finding creative ways to cover up our incompetence, aren't we?'

'You mean it was me who did that to Inferno?' Aliya felt anger bubble up. How could she have been responsible for making a carpet collapse?

'It's OK.' Zil raised his palms in a placating gesture. He was wearing a flowing gold kaftan today with a matching scarf and was still barefoot, as if he'd dressed up for yet another Aladdin-themed costume party. His flute rested behind one ear like a pen.

Aliya thought of how white he was, and how British he sounded. Who had ever heard of a British genie? Well, there was Margaret from the library, she supposed, but still – there was something off about him. She hadn't been certain before, but now she could *feel* it. Was it because her meeting with the Sublimes had somehow made her more aware?

'We all have our strengths and weaknesses,' Zil continued, sitting cross-legged, his kaftan sparkling. 'Didn't I tell you that magic is a gift, to make you strong where you are weak?'

'Who said I'm weak?' Aliya glared at him. 'And this necklace, it weighs on me.' She gestured at her throat. 'I want it off! *Now*, please.'

With a fluid movement, Zil lifted his flute and blew a thin, hoarse note. The sun darkened and left them floating in a sea of blackness.

'What's going on?' Aliya whispered, sudden fear turning her skin to ice.

It was so dark now that she couldn't see her hand in front of her. Another note, closer now, cut through the gloom and then – a warmly glowing vision bloomed in the dark. There was a window, framing a most familiar sight: a threadbare green sofa, an old lamp with a carved wooden elephant at the foot.

Her childhood home. And there, seated at the dining table, were her mum and dad. The world paused, and Aliya was floating, captured by the moments played out before her.

'Wouldn't it be wonderful if we could turn back time?'

Zil was next to her in the dark, whispering into her ear. Aliya nodded, watching her mother lean forward to put a slice of mango into a little girl's mouth.

That was her. This glowing piece of life had been hers before the fire tore everything apart.

'What if I told you that it was possible to have it all back?'

The dark cleared, the vision dissolving. Aliya reached out as if to catch it, but she was again sitting in mid-air in front of Zil. The glow of the vision was still in her eyes, the rest of her shivering in the moist, cold air.

'What do you mean?' she asked. 'How would that be possible?'

'All we need is a very special key. It's called the Darkling, and it is kept in a secret place.'

'The Smithy,' Aliya mumbled. 'I've been there.'

'Once we have the Darkling we can go back in time and change it. We can stop the fire! You could have your family back!'

Zil was close to her now, so close his breath touched her face. Aliya saw that there was a spider-web crack in one of the lenses of his glasses.

'You mean that?' she breathed. 'You mean, really . . . no tricks?'

'No tricks.'

She looked down at the intricate patterns on the carpet. This thing that Zil was proposing seemed just like the design – a puzzle she couldn't quite figure out.

'But it would be stealing,' she said.

'It would be returning the Darkling to its rightful owner.'

Aliya frowned.

'How? That's Dorian Darke. He's dead. He's . . .' She grasped at something just beyond reach – an impossible thought just made possible, as if part of the puzzle had laid itself out for her.

Zil smiled.

Aliya felt light-headed. Around her the night pressed in.

The man in front of her was no genie. He looked different now with his cropped hair, but it was him. She'd seen him on the poster in the exhibition of Unforgivable Crimes Against the Code of Time-Travelling. Aliya felt his hand fish for hers. It felt cold. Colder than ice.

'Dorian Darke,' he said, squeezing her limp hand. 'Pleased to meet you.'

Chapter 22
A RIFT IN TIME

'How could you be Dorian Darke?' Aliya shook her head in disbelief. 'He's dead. There was a funeral.'

'Magic.' The man who wasn't Zil, but the locksmith called Dorian, smiled. 'I created a chimera – an illusion of the mind – to take my place. Quite a basic spell, but very useful. The Council wanted to exile me or destroy my life's work. I couldn't allow that. My key is a work of genius. With it, we'll go back and make things right again.'

'But wouldn't it be dangerous? Professor Nigm said—'

Dorian gave an impatient huff. 'Don't live like a mouse, Aliya! We can't sit around and wait for life to give us what we want.' He bared his teeth in a smile, incisors glinting. Reaching out, he touched her neck in a sudden movement that sent icy chills down her spine.

'Your mother would have understood. We developed the Darkling together. I need you to carry on where she left off. *That's* why I sent you the necklace. That's why I've been helping you!'

Her mother . . . the Darkling. Was this what her mother had wanted all along? Was this her legacy? To help Dorian with this impossible time key? *He* had been the secret benefactor. The family friend who had sent her the necklace, the smouldering letters . . .

'Does it have magic? The Darkling?' she asked, hugging herself to stop her body shaking. 'Is that what makes it different?'

Dorian prodded her in the chest with a thin white finger.

'Smart. The answer is yes.'

Aliya's heart was aching, her head swelling with impossible thoughts. Get her parents back? Was it possible?

'Once we stop that boiler from exploding, there will be a recalibration of events,' Dorian continued, his voice soft now – slipping into her ears, enchanting her mind. As she looked up at him his skin glowed, his eyes shone. There was a shimmer in the air around him.

'You'll fall into a deep sleep and when you wake up – your life will be different. You won't be an orphan any longer. Your grandfather won't be a heartbroken wreck. Everyone will be safe and well, and your life will be whole.'

Whole. The word blossomed in Aliya's mind, like a flower suddenly bursting open in sunlight.

'Here!' Dorian held something up: a time key with a handle in the shape of a peacock. It looked like the ones Aliya had seen before, except its Fortuna grain wasn't white and shining. It was black.

The key crackled in his hand. When he held it out, Aliya realized that she had seen this exact one before. It belonged to Nortia Zenith, the traveller who had been found unconscious by her portal, her key stolen. It had been all over the news when she first got to the Citadel.

'Did you steal that?' she whispered.

Dorian gave her a terse smile. 'I've just borrowed and upgraded it a bit.'

With magic, Aliya thought, as the peacock spread its wings and rose in the air before them. *He's used magic to make it come alive!* The bird-key's eyes were trained on Dorian, hanging on every movement of his hands.

And now – Dorian stabbed the air. The peacock followed the motion, its beak slicing open a rift of pure darkness. Dropping to the surface of the carpet, the bird became a key again. Dorian picked it up and slid it into a pocket of his golden kaftan.

'Come on.' Dorian grasped her by the elbow, pulling her towards the rift.

'I can't go in there!' Aliya hung back, tugging her arm free.

Dorian took off his glasses. He rubbed them thoughtfully with his silk scarf.

'You don't trust me yet.'

No, she didn't. In fact, there was a howling uncertainty inside her that was steadily tilting towards definite distrust . . .

Dorian drew his flute from behind his ear. With a hoarse note, the scene around them melted away and a street took shape in its place.

'Where are we?'

She jerked in fright as a volley of gunshots crashed through the air.

'Cairo. First day of the 1919 Revolution. The Egyptian revolt against the British protectorate.'

A young, European-looking woman – a few years older than Aliya – appeared around a corner, heading straight for them. She was carrying a boy in her arms, and there was panic in her face. Parts of her long, auburn hair had come undone and there was a rip in her skirt. As she approached, Aliya saw she was crying. The boy she carried clung to her front, clutching at her lacy shirt, his skinny legs dangling down her sides.

'Don't fret, Dory.' The girl threw a fearful look over her shoulder. 'We're just going to hurry home now. Everything will be all right.'

'My sister,' Dorian pointed, 'Cassandra.'

Another volley of shots rang out, making Aliya cower where she stood – a reflection of Cassandra's movement. She dropped the boy, who tumbled into the dust of the street.

'That's you?' Aliya asked Dorian, but before he could answer a mob of people rounded the corner – a mass of men, young and old, faces contorted in anger, moving forward like one body. More gunshots cracked through the air, then soldiers in dust-coloured uniforms rounded another corner. Suddenly the street was thick with people and sounds. Shouting, gunshots, stomping feet.

'Run!' Aliya shouted at the girl who stood, frozen, looking around at the approaching mayhem. As if in a trance, she began tugging at the boy on the ground.

'Hurry!' Aliya shouted. 'Get up!'

'They can't hear you.' Dorian made a sweeping gesture with one hand, and the scene around them melted away. They were again sitting on the floating carpet, high above a medieval city, the black rift that the peacock had opened hanging in the air above them.

'She was fifteen. Killed in the crossfire. I was seven.' He wiped a palm over his face. 'I need her back.' His tone was light, but Aliya could hear an undertow of pain in his voice.

Dorian cleared his throat and put his glasses back on.

'So, you see, we both have matters to set right. Persons in need of retrieving from the past.' Standing, he offered her his hand. 'That makes us companions. Now come. I've got something else to show you.'

The rift Dorian had opened had begun blossoming with colour. Clambering through it after him, she found herself standing in her parents' old flat. Aliya winced at the sight of an old teddy bear, and there was her old stroller, and her shiny, red jelly sandals.

Smoke was curling and creeping across the floor. Aliya stepped through it, towards her parents' bedroom. Stopping on the threshold, she saw the outlines of their bodies under the covers, rising and falling ever so slightly as they breathed. Soon they would stop breathing, stop being alive.

'The fire has just started,' Dorian said, behind her.

Smoke crawled between her legs, making its way

into the room. It stayed close to the floor, sneaking forwards like a thief.

'The boiler,' Dorian said. 'Your parents won't wake up. They've already inhaled too much toxic gas. Don't you want to stop it?'

Aliya nodded, throat tight.

'*Then save them,*' Dorian whispered, close to her ear. He laid the peacock key in her hand. Cupping it, Aliya felt the bird stir and come alive again – a fluttering mass of blues and greens. Its ebony eye trained on her. She was in charge now – she could feel it.

'There.' Dorian pointed to the fire that had begun creeping up the walls, spreading like infernal wallpaper. Directing her hands, Dorian pointed the tip of the key at the smoke. A blast rang through the apartment – spewing out flames and debris. It rained over them in plumes of angry smoke, like a demon released from hell. Aliya cowered, then realized that nothing was touching her.

'Another perk of magic,' Dorian said, gesturing at the radiating dome around them that he, somehow, had magicked out of his hands. 'Very Dumbledore, don't you think? Oh yes, I'm old.' He smiled. 'But I've read your classics.'

Aliya spun around towards her parents' bedroom door.

'What do I do?' she screeched, her hands shaking around the fluttering peacock. Aliya winced as Dorian laid his cold hands over hers.

'Here, we'll cut the fire out. Send it somewhere else – into a void that we can open with the key.'

They aimed the peacock's beak at the flames, drawing a large circle around it, encapsulating it in another bubble that hung above them in the air.

'Cut . . .' Dorian mumbled. He moved the peacock's beak and sliced open another rift in the air. The bubble of fire floated into the darkness.

'. . . and paste.'

The air sealed. They had cut the explosion out! Sent it into a void in space and time!

But now new smoke was curling along the skirting board. She recoiled as the peacock crackled between her palms.

Something was wrong with the bird. Flashes were erupting through its body, tearing through its metallic feathers, as if it was about to come apart. Aliya stumbled backwards, jerking her hands away from Dorian's.

'Borrowed keys tend to fault after a little use,' Dorian breathed, sparks raining over his palms.

Behind them, the rift they had come through was closing again.

'Quick!' Dorian shoved Aliya forwards with his elbow. 'Go through!'

'But my parents!' Aliya tried to turn back. 'We've got to save them!'

Behind her a new explosion rattled the walls. She ducked as projectiles of flame raged at them. Then she climbed through the rift.

On the other side they clambered on to Dorian's carpet again. With a final squawk, the peacock sealed the rift and the flat disappeared, as if it had never been.

Aliya sank down on her knees, watching the peacock as it fizzled and convulsed like a dying creature.

'We failed.' She drew a shaky breath.

Dorian sank down next to her, but as she turned

to him, there was no sympathy in his face. He was smiling.

'This is just the beginning,' he said. 'A demonstration, if you will.'

'What do you mean?'

'I told you that borrowed keys tend to corrupt after a while. They can't carry the impact of what we're doing.'

'What *are* we doing?' Aliya cried, horrified at the mess they had left behind, at how they had accomplished nothing – nothing except her witnessing the fire *before* it killed her parents.

'Cutting and pasting in time. We took the badness, or part of it, and sent it away somewhere else.'

'But we *failed*. My parents are still going to *die*.'

'Next time we'll have a stronger key – a key that won't let us down. We'll save them. My sister, your parents. Only magic can give us that.'

Their eyes met.

'The Darkling,' Aliya whispered.

Dorian nodded. 'And you will get it for us.'

Chapter 23
GOLDEN THOUGHTS

Once again, the spartan hall had been transformed into a festive extravaganza of sumptuous food and decorations. The cobwebs in the steep windows glittered in the light from the chandeliers. From where she sat, Aliya could see several fat spiders the ghoul maids had attached to them, like ominous baubles. Despite the ghoul maids' attempts at decorations, the hall felt cosy. Both fireplaces were ablaze, keeping the winter chill out of the hall. Several lengths of colourful bunting hung suspended in the air over the richly laid table – an addition provided by Mrs Dickens who stood beaming at the head of the table in a bright-yellow dress with a sunflower pattern and a hat to match. But the festive mood wasn't only because Aliya had passed – it was tonight that the Initiation Ceremony would be held, when the new students would be shown their future career paths. Since the morning, at the hostel there had been talk of little else other than something called the Opening of the Door Ceremony.

'As I was saying, we'll each take turns to open this wooden door on a platform,' Karima told Aliya, continuing the informative monologue she, with many interruptions, had kept up since the night before when Aliya had returned victorious from the Shocker. 'It looks just like any old door, but it's a portal and it *knows*, the moment you touch its handle, which department you belong with – what you're supposed to be! And it's never wrong. Well, except that one time when it opened to a black void and a student nearly fell through it into the space-time glitch. Turned out he'd cheated on his assessments and didn't deserve to be there. Another cheater got catapulted into a Mongolian raid on medieval Baghdad. Lucky for him they could get him out of there before he turned to mince.'

'That sounds pretty harsh,' Aliya said.

'I know, doesn't it? Think it's to deter anyone from cheating. Anyway, you're so lucky to have passed the Shocker, and only yesterday! Talk about cutting it close!'

Aliya stared into her soup. She had, to all appearances, passed the Shocker, but what would happen when she opened the Door? Would she fall into the mysterious nothingness that somehow existed between time and space? She was a cheater after all, wasn't she? Not just that – she'd been the reason that Inferno got partially unravelled. That morning, before breakfast, she had visited him back at Professor Kashmir's. He was back in his spot in the carpet rehabilitation room – partly dissolved into threads. Aliya's heart sank as she thought of how he'd flicked her hand away when she'd tried to stroke him.

She glanced over at Fuad, who was almost unrecognizable with a sleek, combed-back hairdo and a tuxedo. That, she noted, didn't stop him from wolfing down baby potatoes as if he were getting paid.

Mustafa looked even neater than usual, his gold-trimmed kaftan and embroidered vest fitting like a second skin. Aion had shed her biodegradable hold-it-all vest for a silvery dress that lit up like a Christmas tree whenever she laughed.

Karima looked radiant in a green velvet gown with puffed sleeves. Even Victoria looked different tonight, in a pale-yellow dress with a wide skirt that took up two seats at the table.

The long table was laden with all of Mrs Dickens's specialities: roast quail with gravy and baby potatoes, fresh hot rolls, squash fritters, stuffed artichokes, and mounds of jelly, lemon sherbet and creamy chocolate pudding. In the middle of the table stood an apparatus that Mrs Dickens saved for special occasions: a gently bubbling chocolate fountain. Over the table suspended silver letters spelt out: 'Well Done Aliya!' and 'Happy Initiation Day!'

And yes, Aliya's second assessment had been a success. Not only had she finished in record time, but she had carried the golden pyramid through medieval Cairo in an incredible feat of navigation and carpet manoeuvring. Only, it hadn't been her doing, but Dorian's. It was time-meddling and magic that had turned her into the hero of the hour.

She glanced down at her right hand, which at

that moment was being squeezed by her great-aunt. Every so often, she would bend down and wipe some non-existent stain off Aliya's collar, or fuss with her hair. On her other side sat Esmat in a silver dress with matching glasses — a combination that made her shine like a star.

Aliya tried to look happy as she slurped her soup and did her best not to look over at Professor Nigm, who sat a few seats away, sipping something out of a goblet. She felt his eyes on her now and then, and felt her cheeks heat up in response.

Every time she thought of her lost family, pain seared through her heart, and she realized she didn't *care* if her inner compass pointed straight to hell. The image of her parents lived in her mind. She had to save them. There was no other way.

With the hand Gigi wasn't clutching, Aliya squeezed Dorian's parting gift: a skeleton key made of bone. It would take her straight to him, through any portal, once she had got hold of the Darkling — the key that could change the past.

'Dearly assembled.' Professor Nigm had stood up and was looking around at the gathering. As his gaze reached her, Aliya pretended to be engrossed in her soup. 'Tonight is special for many reasons. You will be fully initiated into the time-travel academy. But also, through the Opening of the Door ceremony, you will be shown your future paths.'

Aliya met Karima's eyes across the table and knew exactly what she was thinking. Once she opened the Door tonight, Karima would be officially initiated into the Medic Department. After that, her parents would have to drop the idea of bringing her home. She'd be safe.

'For some of you, the Door will confirm what you already know about your unique talents. For others, the Door's choice might come as a surprise. But rest assured, the Door never makes mistakes. Whatever path you are shown tonight is yours.'

'Just don't open the Door to the Maintenance Department,' Gigi hissed in Aliya's ear. 'No Sultan has ever been a . . . maintenance person.'

'She means people who change lightbulbs and fix clogged toilets,' Esmat explained.

'Or that department that nurses sick sphinxes and wood nymphs with colds,' Gigi added.

'That's the Care of Mythical Beings with Slight Ailments Department,' Esmat said.

'Absolutely not.' Gigi adjusted the collar on Aliya's dark-blue velvet dress. 'Sultans do not unclog toilets or wipe vomit. Sultan Junior, I hope you'll remember this.'

Aliya nodded. How was she meant to influence what some fate-revealing door was deciding *for* her? Great-Aunt Gigi looked satisfied, though. It always relaxed her to give orders.

Aliya focused on her own thoughts. In her mind's eye the image of her family still glowed. Even now, as she tried to be part of the celebration, it was there, absorbing her – like a living thing.

Another thought tried to push its way in: one about how changing the past could have unknown consequences, about how someone like Dorian Darke, with his intense blue eyes, might wreak havoc on the Citadel with that kind of power. Yet she would pay any price to stop what she had seen, to stop the fire. She would give Dorian the key and she would have her family back.

*

It was the news that first alerted the party guests that something was amiss. Mrs Dickens had just cut into the three-tiered mound of jelly when Matron appeared and roared for silence before turning up the volume on the flatscreen. The TV showed a genie newscaster standing outside a burning building. Behind her the fire brigade were already fighting the flames.

'That's Mrs Dashings's haberdashery!' someone cried. 'Another crack! Just three streets away!'

'A fire is just now raging in the Khedivial Quarter,' the reporter announced. 'It is reported to have appeared out of a crack in the sky.'

Aliya stared at the burning shop. Only hours ago, she and Dorian had opened a rift and sent a piece of fire into the void. But . . . what if it hadn't really been a void?

'Excuse me.' Professor Nigm stood up. After a curt bow he made a swift exit, a plume of red smoke trailing him like a tail. Aliya felt a stab of guilt as she watched him leave. What if this fire had been sent by *her*?

In a cacophony of scraping chairs, everyone stood

up and hurried out into the square outside. Smoke was billowing over the housetops. In the distance, the sky was an angry red. But that wasn't the most alarming sight; a huge rift ran a jagged course over the burning housetops, and . . .

'It's pointing straight at us!' Mustafa cried.

The crack, through which nothing but pitch-dark showed, pointed like an accusing finger straight at the hostel roof.

'Nobody move!' It was Inspector Prickly, pointing the tip of his cane at them, his waxed moustache glinting in the dying light.

He stood at the main gate, his voice echoing towards them over the cobblestones. With him were Nitzi and Hosneyya, the hostel sphinxes, and a gaggle of robot cops, their electric-blue eyes sending laser scanning beams across the square.

'What's the meaning of this, Peter?' Gigi cried as the inspector, with the help of the robots, herded the party of adults and students into a cluster outside the hostel gate.

Inspector Prickly slammed his cane into the ground.

'Magic!' he cried. 'That's the meaning of this. The poisonings, the cracks in the sky – every clue leads straight here to this hostel.'

A hush went through the crowd, along with some disbelieving scoffs. Karima exchanged a worried glance with Aliya.

'This is outrageous.' Gigi stepped out of the crowd and stood towering above Prickly. 'The Council has assured us, repeatedly, that all talk of magic is nothing but silly rumours. You can't really expect us to believe—'

'I have the facts of the case.' Prickly twirled the edge of his moustache triumphantly. 'And truth offers no compromises.' He pointed past them through the hostel gate. 'The poisoner resides here!'

Another agitated hum went through the crowd. Aliya nearly lost her balance as one of Aion's holographic cats swept past her legs. She wasn't the poisoner . . . So, who was using magic at the hostel except her? She glanced over at Matron, who looked a shade paler than usual.

'You will all remain here while the premises are searched!' Prickly commanded.

'I can help you, Papa.' Victoria tugged at her father's sleeve. 'I knew there was something fishy going on right from the start when—'

'Stay out of this, Victoria.' He shook her off. 'This is not the time for your fancies.'

'Fancies?' Victoria howled. 'Papa! I *want* to *help*!'

'This is *my* hostel!' Matron placed herself squarely before Prickly, blocking the hostel gate.

'Then your rooms will be the first ones we search.' Prickly pushed past her. For the next few moments there was pandemonium as adults, sphinxes, robots and students pressed into the hostel. Aliya arrived at the kitchen door just in time to see Prickly disappear down to the dungeons. Matron flew after him, her maids following in a panicky throng.

A tense couple of minutes followed. The children, Mrs Dickens, Gigi and Esmat stood looking over at the door where the inspector and the matron had disappeared.

'You need not look so worried, my dear,' Gigi said to Aliya, who stood frozen to the spot, her head burning with horrible possibilities. 'You haven't done anything wrong.'

When Prickly appeared again he was flushed.

'It was as I thought,' he said, dabbing his moustache, which was now glistening with sweat. 'Her lab's full of poison. Blasted mythicals. Should've left them all where they belong, *outside* the Infinitum.'

'I will have you mind your language in front of the children,' Gigi cried, then clapped a hand over her mouth as Matron appeared in chains, grasped by two robots.

'I was trying to develop an antidote!' Matron cried, struggling in their grip. 'They were samples from the crime site, you blistering fool, not *my* poison.'

'Insulting the head of security,' Prickly said, puffing his chest out. 'That's an additional offence.' He waved his napkin in a nonchalant gesture at the robots. 'Take her away.'

'It's true!' Karima piped up. 'She saved my life. She's not a poisoner.'

Prickly ignored her and the robots zoomed away, a struggling Matron between them, shouting about boiling livers and brains. The maids were led out after her, also in chains, by more robots.

'You're a nasty piece of work, aren't you?' Sawsan, the ghoul maid, snapped at Prickly as she was dragged past him. 'Same as your daughter.' She stuck out her tongue.

'I told you it was the mythicals.' Victoria sidled up to her father. 'I knew it, Papa. It was obvious to someone as perceptive as me.'

'Search the rooms upstairs!' Prickly said, waving to the sphinxes and ignoring his daughter.

Immediately, the sphinxes headed towards the stairs.

Aliya exchanged a horrified look with Karima. They both had things to hide. From the upper storeys, they could hear the older students being hounded out of their rooms.

Halfway up the stairs, Nitzi the sphinx stopped, sneezed and turned around while Hosneyya continued up to the first floor. She sniffed the air.

'There's something else.'

Then, as she turned back down towards the students, her eyes lit up.

'There!' She sniffed the air again, then looked straight at Aliya. Time seemed to slow as the sphinx padded towards her, eyes half-closed in concentration, pointy nose raised. She was sensing the necklace!

Aliya looked around. Should she run, hide? No, it was too late. The distraction had at least given Karima a chance to slip upstairs.

Inspector Prickly had stopped too and turned around. The sphinx had almost reached her. Nitzi tried to push her way through the throng of students and robots. It would all be over soon. They would find the necklace and . . .

A hand touched her neck. She jerked in shock as she realized it was holding one of the snapping flowers that grew on the banister.

'Shh,' Mrs Dickens whispered in her ear. She rubbed the flower across Aliya's neck.

Thankfully, it did not try to bite her now that it was broken off its stem.

The sphinx had reached her. She gazed up at Aliya in confusion.

'What is it, Nitzi?' Inspector Prickly demanded.

'I thought . . .' Nitzi began. 'But I must have been mistaken. But this smell is . . .' She sniffed Aliya and a quiver went through her feline body. 'Sausage.'

Before Aliya realized what had happened, the sphinx had given her a wet lick across her torso.

She screamed, backing away.

'Sausage,' the sphinx whispered, apologetically.

Inspector Prickly heaved a huge sigh and marched upstairs. Aliya turned to Mrs Dickens, but she had slipped away. Aliya saw her disappearing into the kitchen.

Why had she protected her? She'd thought Dorian was the secret mastermind behind all that was happening. How did Mrs Dickens fit into it all?

A scream cut through the air. It was coming from the first floor, where the first-year girls' rooms were. As Aliya reached the landing she realized, to her horror, that something was happening in her and Karima's room.

She slid to a stop in the doorway just in time to see a robot put Karima into a pair of handcuffs.

'What are they *doing*?' Aliya screamed at yet another robot whizzing past her, knocking her into the doorframe. She desperately tried to catch Karima's eye, but she wouldn't look up. Fuad was suddenly at her side.

'They're saying Karima helped Matron with the poisonings,' he said. 'That she's got an illegal *lab* in here.' He pointed towards the bathroom. 'That there's magic everywhere in this room. Did you know about this?'

'No!' Aliya cried. 'I mean, that's not true!'

She opened her mouth to speak, but nothing came out. What she wanted to say was that the sphinxes were sensing the magic traces the necklace had left in the room, and that they were wrong for blaming Karima and her corpseweed! Yet she just stood there staring, her mouth opening and closing like a fish on dry land.

'This girl is clearly the culprit,' said Inspector Prickly, pointing at Karima, who stood dejectedly looking at the floor. 'We found traces of poison in her homespun lab, along with this.'

Aliya nearly screamed when she saw what it was Prickly was holding up. It was *The Surreptitious Power of Magic Objects* – the treatise she had stolen from the library!

'This work on magic is clear evidence,' Prickly

continued. 'And what's more – she's been poisoning the food she's delivering. This is not the first time we've heard of Miss Mandil's so-called accidents. Two months ago, she turned Mr Pondiberry yellow, and before that she made Mrs Hanafy's nose grow five centimetres! I have a list of complaints against her in my office as long as my arm! Now, out of the way, young man.'

Prickly barked these last words at Fuad, who was trying to hold on to his sister. Karima was marched out of the room between two robots, the sphinxes and Prickly bringing up the rear.

As Karima passed by Aliya on the way out, their eyes met. The question in Karima's eyes was like a stab in her heart. Why had there been a book on magic in their room? But Karima still did not speak and neither, to her shame, did Aliya.

When Aliya was finally alone, the silence throbbed in her ears. The intoxicating feeling that had captured her when she thought of saving her parents was losing its hold, and now – it was like waking from a dream. What had she done?

On the bathroom floor, in a heap of smashed experiments, Aliya found the corpseweed plant. She carefully fished it up and hid it in the window niche behind a curtain. The plant's tentacles were a bit crooked, but he smelt just as bad as before . . . a bit like unwashed socks now.

She'd saved Karima's plant, but what about Karima herself? She should act – go down and run after Inspector Prickly and explain everything. Confess.

She took out the strange bone key Dorian had given her and turned it over between her fingers, over and over, as if there was something there, on its pale surface, that would help her decide.

Chapter 24

MRS DICKENS

She didn't know how long she had sat staring into space before there was a knock on the door. Mrs Dickens stood there, looking in at the devastation. After a moment she stepped inside and clicked the door shut behind her.

'We need to talk.'

There was something in Mrs Dickens's voice that made Aliya sit up. Something was very wrong with her too. Her usually ruddy cheeks were pale, and her eyes were red, as though she'd been crying. She remained standing, wringing her hands.

'What is it?' Aliya asked. 'Do you know something about the magic?'

Mrs Dickens winced.

'It was me,' she whispered. 'I poisoned the elders. Poor Matron . . . she knew nothing about it, and Karima just delivered the food.'

'You?' Aliya looked at her in disbelief. 'What . . . *why?*'

Mrs Dickens took a shallow breath.

'I had no choice. I also have . . . a necklace.' She touched her throat with her fingertips. 'It came in an envelope. I thought it was a birthday gift from my sister, so I put it on . . .' Her voice trailed off. Pulling out a napkin, she dabbed at her eyes.

'We thought it was one of the maids,' Aliya whispered, stunned. 'Or maybe the matron.'

'My dear,' Mrs Dickens sniffed. 'I've been watching you. You haven't been the same ever since you came back from the second assessment. You've met him, haven't you?'

Aliya nodded.

'What did he promise? To bring back your family?'

Aliya started. 'How did you—?'

'That's his way. With me, he said he could bring back my husband. My Reggie. I lost him two years ago. Heart attack. I kept thinking that if I'd only been with him, I could've saved him.' She paused and stared in mid-air. 'You spend a lifetime together and forget what it's like to be one person alone. So when Dorian promised a way to bring Reggie back, I wanted to believe him. But it's all lies, dear. When Death takes us, we pass out of time. No one can be brought back, not even with magic.'

Aliya blinked. 'They can't . . . ever?'

'I know it is hard to accept, but you must understand. They will wait for you in the afterlife. But in this one, we must be patient with our losses.'

Aliya looked up at her, her mind struggling. The golden vision was still there, ensnaring her thoughts. But it was beginning to lose its hold and fade away.

Death, she thought, *cannot be changed. He lied.*

'The necklace,' she said. 'Do you know how to take it off?'

Mrs Dickens pulled an envelope out of her cardigan pocket and handed it to Aliya. 'Read this. It will explain.'

Aliya ripped the envelope open and pulled out a note.

Aliya,

I was hoping it wouldn't come to this, but you will understand that I need a backup plan in case your weaker nature takes over and tries to ruin my plans. The necklace you are wearing will only come off when you fulfil your mission: you need to bring me the Darkling. Use the bone key to deliver it to me at my Shop. I'll be waiting for you. You've got until midnight.

'What does this mean?' Aliya looked up at Mrs Dickens, her chest tightening with panic. 'That it will only come off if I fulfil my mission?'

'It means the necklace will strangle you unless you do what he says.'

Aliya's hand went to her throat. For a moment the room around her went fuzzy. Her temples throbbed.

'I thought it was my mother's,' she whispered.

Mrs Dickens sank down in a chair next to her. She caught one of Aliya's hands and patted it gently.

'She *did* own it once, but only because Dorian played the same trick on her as he's played on you. She was his apprentice, and the one who realized that the key she had helped him make – that Darkling – was dangerous. She saw Dorian try it out – how he began meddling with the past. She didn't know about the magic though, or she would have been more on her guard. She told the Council what she *had* seen, and they gave him a choice . . . to destroy the Darkling or choose exile.'

'Then he faked his own death to avoid having to do either.'

Mrs Dickens nodded.

'He's been scheming ever since. His first plan was to make your mother bring him his key. He sent her the very necklace you are wearing now to force her to obey. He never forgave her for telling on him. Your mother, thinking that it was a surprise gift from your father, wore it and was caught.'

Aliya struggled against a sudden surge of nausea. The truth was horrible, but she needed it. She had to understand it all, at last.

'But she never did give him the Darkling,' she said.

'Or else, he wouldn't be after *me* to get it for him.'

'Your mother thought she could reason with Dorian, that he'd give her more time. But, she was wrong. Then the necklace . . . well . . .' Mrs Dickens pinched her eyes closed. 'Oh, dear . . . I can't say it.'

Aliya stared at her – bewildered. 'But the fire?'

Mrs Dickens shook her head, dabbing at her eyes. 'He set that to cover his tracks and get the necklace back. He turned your parents' boiler into a ticking time bomb.'

Aliya looked unseeingly at the floor. A faulty boiler. That's what Geddo had told her, and what Darke had shown her, when all along . . .

'You mustn't let him tempt you to meddle in time.' Mrs Dickens gripped Aliya's hands firmly. 'The cracks in the sky – it's the magic that's causing them. Attacking the timeline will cause it to recalibrate itself – that means everything in this universe will be rebooted . . . ripped apart at the seams and rebuilt. If he continues, our world will be destroyed.'

'You mean when I cut out that fire . . . it did that?' She pointed out the window, at the smoke still billowing over the housetops.

'When you cut something out of the timeline, it doesn't get erased. It's sent somewhere else. It's all part of the upsetting.' Mrs Dickens shook her head. 'Time must be left alone or it will lash back.'

'Cut and paste,' Aliya mumbled, remembering Dorian's words in her parents' apartment.

Mrs Dickens nodded.

'He said we were sending it into the void,' Aliya said. 'He didn't tell me it would end up in the Infinitum.'

'He wouldn't, would he?'

They sat silent for some moments.

'Geddo was right,' Aliya said at last. 'He said there were traces of magic in my parents' flat after the fire. He knew something was wrong, but when he realized the truth, no one believed him. Not even me!'

'The Council has been so fixated on erasing every trace of magic from the Infinitum that no one here even recognized it when it was right before their eyes. It served Dorian well, didn't it?'

'And you?' Aliya said. 'He made you poison the elders?'

335

Mrs Dickens nodded.

'It became my sorry duty to get rid of them one by one. I had to carry out his revenge. I even tampered with Matron Olfat's remedies to make them useless. He's mad, Aliya. He wants what he wants and will eliminate everyone who stands in his way. My dear, if you try to resist or speak of the necklace or of Dorian's plans, the necklace will kill you. It listens . . .' She brought her hand to her neck. 'It will only allow you to do what it thinks serves his, its master's, interests. Each of our necklaces carries a wish that needs fulfilment. Mine is tied to yours and yours to mine. Unless we both complete the wishes, we will die.'

Aliya looked out the window, at the square bathed in moonlight.

'He's making sure we don't try to be heroes, like my mother.'

'I don't have much to live for any more.' Mrs Dickens's voice quaked. 'Since my Reggie died, it's just been me and Betty, my sister. But you, my dear.' She cupped Aliya's hands in hers and held them to her heart. 'You have got your whole life ahead of you. You must do as he says. You must.'

Aliya threw her arms around Mrs Dickens and hugged her, sobbing into her vanilla-scented cardigan.

She accepted a handkerchief and wiped her tears and blew her nose. Mrs Dickens grasped hold of her again and rocked her lightly from side to side.

'I'm so sorry.'

Aliya nodded and sniffed.

'Me too.'

Chapter 25
THE INITIATION

The door to Karima and Aliya's room banged open and Great-Aunt Gigi tumbled in. Mrs Dickens quickly wiped her eyes and got up, helping Aliya to her feet.

'The Initiation Ceremony begins in fifteen minutes!' Gigi shouted, grabbing Aliya by the arm.

Aliya winced. The shock of Mrs Dickens's revelation still stormed in her mind, with one inevitable thought piercing through the shockwaves: unless she did what Dorian wanted, both she and Mrs Dickens would be strangled by their necklaces.

She exchanged a last look with the cook before she was swept off by her great-aunt. At Gigi's command, Aliya quickly dressed in a silky party dress and a warm winter coat before rushing downstairs to the waiting cab.

After a hurried ride, during which Gigi tried to make something presentable with Aliya's hair, they pulled to a stop outside the Victorian Quarter, where the Initiation Ceremony was being held. Aliya followed her great-aunt through the massive gate and on to the Victorian town square, where the house fronts had been dressed in lights, bathing the wide space in a soft glow. She stopped and gazed at the long dinner tables with white linen tablecloths, glinting glasses and bowls of fresh flowers and candles. The Victorian Quarter's clock towered above them on its thick stone pillar, illuminated from within by a yellow light. 'Little Ben', as the Victorian travellers affectionately called it. At its foot, a stage had been erected. On it stood a simple wooden door.

There it was: the Door that would reveal hers and the others' fates. Groups of dressed-up students stood milling about around the stage. Aliya spotted some of the girls from Hippolyta's Hostel in rich furs and sparkling jewel diadems. Next to them stood a group of boys from Mehmet's looking grandly medieval in white turbans, boldly coloured sashes and glinting weapon belts.

Under different circumstances, Aliya would have been enthralled. The mystery of the Door, the soft music, the twinkling lights, the magnificent outfits, and the sumptuous smells wafting on the air – but all she could think about was the necklace, and that she was four hours away from getting strangled.

Great-Aunt Gigi waved to a group of elegant people sipping drinks next to the decked-out stage. 'My Council colleagues,' she explained in a low voice. Aliya noticed a familiar figure among them in a glimmering suit: Neon Ticker. He was the one on the news who had insisted that all talk of magic at the Infinitum was nothing but superstition and old wives' tales. How wrong he had been!

'Just in time.' Gigi clicked her handbag open and found a golden watch. 'Eight o'clock sharp.'

A microphone crackled. A spotlight searched the square and came to rest on a figure climbing the stage. Neon Ticker again. Aliya bit down on her lip as Neon exchanged a greeting with Inspector Prickly, a fresh wave of anger and guilt riding over her rough-shod. What had they done with Karima?

'She's locked up in his attic,' someone said behind her. 'I can't believe that ruddy fool wouldn't even let her attend the Initiation.' Aliya wheeled around to find Fuad. He gave her a curt nod. 'She was looking forward to this.'

'I know,' Aliya whispered.

'Mum and Dad will bring her home tonight.' Fuad pointed at a serious-looking man with sideburns and a woman in a red cloche hat. 'They'll blot her instead of charging her, cos she's a minor.'

Aliya stared blankly into the crowd in front of her. After all the work Karima had done to be allowed to stay. Was it really going to end like this?

She noticed Aion a little way off, standing next to a man in a silver suit who looked semi-transparent. Aliya winced as a waiter carrying a tray of glasses passed right through him – a bearded man with glinting ear studs.

'That's a hologram of her father,' Fuad explained. He nodded at the bearded man. 'People from Aion's time prefer attending remotely. They call it *sustainable socializing*.'

'Esteemed guests. Students. The moment of truth has arrived.' Neon gestured at the Door, then tipped his head at Prickly and the horde of robots that stood motionless and watchful behind him. Aliya recalled the image of Matron Olfat being led away in chains. What had happened to her?

'It's been an eventful evening,' Neon continued. 'But I am pleased to announce that the fire in the Khedivial Quarter has been put out.' There was scattered applause. 'I am also happy to announce that the Infinitum, and our Citadel, is a safe place once more. The culprits who caused the disturbances to our world have been apprehended. Their crimes will not be taken lightly. Mark my words.'

'Expulsion,' Fuad said. 'That's the best Matron can hope for.'

'What's the worst?' Aliya asked.

'Death by impaling. That's what they do to mythicals they feel are unsafe.'

Now Neon Ticker raised his hand for quiet.

'On behalf of the Council,' he said as he stroked his algae-green hair out of his eyes, 'I would like to inform you all that we, of course, knew about the

342

magic. We just didn't want to tell you, to avoid any panic.' He smiled. 'You can always trust us, the Council, to do what's best for our travelling community.' More scattered applause followed, uncertain this time. It was drowned out by the metallic clatter of Prickly's robots clapping.

'They knew about the magic?' Fuad scoffed. 'Yeah, right.'

'But now to the main event of the evening. The Opening of the Door ceremony is about to begin. When the novices open the Door, their fate will be revealed, their paths laid open to them.'

Neon stepped to the side and made way for the first student – a girl with a hat full of pears and feathers who Aliya recognized from Chronology class. She was from Hippolyta's hostel and a Victorian like Victoria.

'Our first student has stepped up to find out what the future holds for her!' Neon announced. 'Now concentrate, Edith. Take hold of the handle and when you feel a tingle pass through your hand, you open it. Understood?'

Edith nodded. The audience went quiet as she

grasped the handle. She pulled the Door open to the view of an apparently endless corridor lined on both sides by cabinets. There was a film of dust in the air. Wild heaps of books and precarious stacks of files lay on the floor, looking as if the cabinets had burped them out. A wooden cabinet creaked open, and a balding man appeared, wielding a duster. It was hard to tell what colour his suit was supposed to be – it was so covered in dust. Edith backed away in dismay as he approached the doorway where she stood.

'Apologies, apologies.' The man coughed and proceeded to shake Edith's limp hand. 'Welcome to the Infinitum Archives. Got a bit stuck back there.' He pointed with the duster at the wooden cabinet he had just emerged out of. 'Many of the old cabinets still contain unregistered portals from before our administration got organized. Just spent the last half an hour dodging yatagan swords at the Ottoman invasion of Otranto – that's a town somewhere in southern Italy.' He held up one side of his blazer to show a large stab hole in the fabric.

'A round of applause for our first student,' Neon announced, closing the Door, and ushering a pale

Edith off the stage.

At least the Door hadn't opened to the blackness of a space-time glitch, Aliya reflected, as she watched the next student step up on the platform – a cocky boy with a budding moustache from Mehmet's Hostel who, without much ado, opened the Door to the Irregular Time-Practices Department. After him came a string of students whom Aliya had seen in passing but knew next to nothing about. Then, suddenly, it was Mustafa's turn.

'That's my son!' A brawny man in a white turban flashed a wide smile as Mustafa made his way on to the stage. He gave his father a panicked look, then stepped up to the door, wiping his palms on his trousers. As he pulled the Door open, a majestic sphinx came into view. Mustafa stumbled backwards, eyes wide with shock.

'Welcome to the Care of Mythical Creatures Department,' the sphinx said, a little drily. 'I don't bite, you know. I'm not an animal.'

'I'm sorry . . . I'm— This can't be right,' Mustafa stammered, eyes darting from his father to the sphinx. 'I'm supposed to be— I thought I'd be something else.'

'You're a carer,' the sphinx said. 'Not all Mamluks are fighters.'

'That's right.' Mustafa's father had come up to the platform. Reaching out, he laid a large hand on Mustafa's thigh. 'I always knew you were different from me, son. That's why I sent you to this school.'

'But I don't want to be different.' Mustafa's voice quavered. 'I'm a Mamluk. I've got to be—'

'Mamluk means *the one who is owned*,' his father cut him off. He shook his head. 'I was sold into slavery and forced to be a warrior. But you – it's the privilege of a Mamluk's son to be born free. That means you are free to follow a different path.' He gestured at the Door.

Mustafa wiped his eyes.

'Really?'

His father nodded.

Mustafa looked back at the sphinx, who had stepped aside to reveal a great hall where a large, hawk-like bird with reddish feathers hung upside down from a glittering chandelier.

'Is that . . .' Mustafa took a step towards the door, eyes widening. 'A *Roc bird*?'

'A young one.' The sphinx nodded. 'Nearly ate my assistant yesterday. Not quite civilized yet.'

'Have you tried feeding him sugarcane?' Mustafa asked. 'Fills up the stomach and—'

'Another novice has been shown his path,' Neon interrupted. 'Mustafa Sirry will join the Care of Mythical Creatures Department next year as a part-time apprentice while continuing his wider studies.'

The audience applauded as a relieved Mustafa stepped down to join his father.

Then it was Fuad's turn. The Door revealed an office, but there was nothing in sight but a gold reading lamp with a hairy black lampshade. Neon shuffled through his papers.

'Professor Abdel Batin?' he called through the door. 'Are you there?'

Suddenly the lamp moved, and then it spoke: 'Nothing to worry about, son. Just a little joke.'

The lamp unfolded and became a lady in a gold suit. The lampshade transformed into a head of black hair.

'Ah,' she said and stretched. 'Haven't done that since I was forty-five.' She held her hand out to

Fuad. 'Welcome to the Incognito Department.'

Fuad gave her a tight smile, clearly too worried about his sister to enjoy himself.

A knot in Aliya's stomach began to tighten. It would be her turn soon.

'Aion Verge!'

Aion climbed on to the platform. Before opening the door, she cast a gloomy look at her father, whose image was glitching and kept winking on and off. She looked a little happier when the door opened to the Travel-Inventions Department, and she was greeted by a whole team of inventors in white lab coats.

'Victoria Prickly!'

Victoria bounded up the stage.

'Easy,' Neon cried, as Victoria nearly pushed him off the platform with her wide skirt.

Without further ado, Victoria banged the Door open. An old man in a green turban looked out at them with a dignified expression. He stood in a room full of glinting instruments – telescopes, astrolabes, and sundials. The walls were covered with maps, some of which moved.

'Dash my wig, I knew it!' Victoria shouted with a triumphant look at her father below.

'Welcome to the Navigation Department,' said the old man. 'I am Professor Qamar, Senior Navigator.'

'I know who you are, you old duffer,' Victoria said, looking happy. 'I mean, I am so happy to be chosen for your department, professor.'

'The Door does the choosing, not me,' the professor said drily. With a nod, he carefully closed the Door again.

'We'll see about this,' Inspector Prickly muttered, ushering his daughter off the platform.

'No, we won't.' Victoria turned on him with an ugly grimace. 'If you don't let me be a proper traveller, I'll send a chrono-capsule through to Mama. She'll cut her mission short and come back to set things right. She might chase you with the knitting needles again!'

Inspector Prickly dabbed his forehead with a napkin.

'There's really no need to bother her with this. But, pumpkin, won't you settle for minding a nice portal like your cousin Charlotte? She's such a calm, well-mannered girl . . . a proper young lady.'

'She's a *dud*!' Victoria screeched. 'There's absolutely nothing similar about us.'

She charged off through the crowd, Inspector Prickly following, the horde of robots bringing up the rear.

And then it happened. Aliya's name was called. She walked towards the platform and the Door that stood there, like a mysterious veil between her and the future. She hardly heard what Inspector Prickly told her, or the shrill voice of her great-aunt shouting advice. All she could think of was what would appear when she opened the Door. Infinite darkness? Or would she be sucked into some Mongolian raid like that other cheater? Her mind buzzed, her heart galloped. She clasped the handle and closed her eyes . . . and pulled. The Door swung open.

At first, there was nothing but lights and shadows. Next to her, Neon Ticker gasped.

'It's the Smithy!' someone shouted. 'She's opened the Smithy!' An astonished murmur rippled through the crowd. Aliya stared. In front of her was the workshop she had visited before. There were the desks of marble and walls that looked like ice, the rows and rows of beautiful instruments, shiny and gleaming. Somewhere from within, the Sublimes hummed. How had this happened? The Door hadn't flung her into the glitch . . . It had forgiven her.

Professor Nigm stepped into the light and smiled down at her.

'Welcome back,' he said.

'Professor Nigm,' Aliya breathed. 'I-I can't be a locksmith.'

'Of course you can. This is a special moment.'

Professor Nigm reached out for her hand.

'This is an honour reserved for locksmiths only. The touch of Initiation will temper your innate powers and—'

'*No.*' She backed away from him. 'No, you don't understand.'

Aliya looked out at the sea of expectant faces. They all thought she was deserving, that she had done outstanding things to be where she was. And now, they were ready to initiate her into what was perhaps the most important department in the Infinitum, performing some of the most dangerous tasks. And they were going to hand over that immense trust, not knowing that she was a curse in disguise – a curse wrought upon them by their enemy. She closed her eyes, and yelled:

'I can't be a locksmith! *I cheated on the assessments!*'

The necklace tightened around her neck, harder and harder until her vision blurred, and she collapsed to her knees. Aliya clasped a hand around her throat . . . the necklace was punishing her for resisting Dorian's plan.

Behind her, Professor Nigm said something, but she couldn't hear what it was. As if in a dream she heard Neon ask for calm. Her great-aunt stood at the edge of the square, petrified. People were pointing and shouting.

After a few horrifying airless moments, the necklace loosened a little and she drew a shallow breath.

She stood up.

Making her way down from the stage on shaky legs, she set off at a run across the square and disappeared into the cold evening.

Chapter 26

RUNNING ON EMPTY

When she couldn't run any more, Aliya sat down on an abandoned camel saddle. Around her, what she guessed was the Ottoman Quarter lay silent, its ornate wooden shutters closed tight against the wintry night. The cold air smelt faintly of incense. Her feet were aching, and her heart was sick. She took a deep breath, just to make sure she could. The necklace was uncomfortably tight around her neck. She pushed down the fear that wanted to shoot up and paralyse her. She had panicked. Running away had seemed like the only way forward, but now – where would she go? Escaping the Infinitum would only seal her own death sentence, and Mrs Dickens's. What about the elders? Dorian would continue until he had poisoned them all. And Karima . . .

Aliya pulled off her satchel and rummaged around for her tablet. Great-Aunt Gigi had refused when she had wanted to bring the now quite stained and worn bag with her to the party. It did not match the dark-blue velvet dress with the ruffled collar that she had made Aliya wear. In the end, Aliya had smuggled the bag along, hidden under her black winter coat. In it lay the bone key Dorian had given her, and the tablet that she needed to keep track of time. Aliya clicked it on now, squinting as the blue light hit her eyes. It was ten thirty – one and a half hours until midnight. That was the time she had left until the necklace would strangle her unless she delivered the Darkling . . . but to where? She unfolded Dorian's note again. *Use the bone key to deliver it to me at my Shop.*

The Shop . . . Geddo had spoken of one, as had Sawsan, the ghoul maid. The whole Citadel had been whispering about it – the Devil's Thrift Shop, the Old Evil, the Shop of Second Chances. Could this be the place Dorian meant? A magic shop created by a traveller gone bad, which fed its magic by preying on life . . . on souls?

A siren cut through the night. She stood up and listened. Another wailing call joined the first. Running back to the corniche and the river, she reached the main thoroughfare just in time to see a third ambulance roar past, heading for the Victorian Quarter.

The party. Something had happened at the party!

She ran back – ran until there was a taste of blood in her mouth and a stitch in her ribs made her fold over in pain. Limping through the gate to the Victorian Quarter, she saw that the beautiful tables had been pushed to the side to make room for the ambulances. Flowers and candles lay strewn on the ground, mixed with confetti and streamers. It was oddly quiet. Older students and staff were crowding around the entrance to the dancehall, where one of the ambulances was parked.

She weaved through the crowd, her heart hammering.

'What happened?' she asked a lady in a face veil.

'More poisonings.'

'Who? Who got poisoned?'

She got her answer when Inspector Prickly was carried past her on a stretcher. He had already shrunk to three-quarters of his normal size. Victoria was clinging to his hand.

'Victoria.' Aliya jumped forward and touched her arm. Their eyes met for a moment. All the cockiness had melted off Victoria's face. She looked like a small child now, clinging to her father's shrunken hand.

Aliya watched as the Pricklys were settled into the ambulance and driven away.

Then, looking down, she saw a dark-blue smoke tentacle curl around her wrist. Pushing through the crowd, following the smoke like a trail, she spotted Professor Nigm on an approaching stretcher. She was shoved out of the way again as a new ambulance approached.

'Professor!' Aliya tried to get through, but only caught a glimpse of him being lifted into the ambulance. The smoke lingered for a moment, wrapped around her wrist like words he couldn't speak to her.

'There was a lot of them tonight,' a turbaned man next to Aliya said. 'They think it was the punch.

Only the elders drank from that. But it's funny, isn't it? The girl they say did it has already been arrested. The mythical too. So, who did it? That's what I want to know.'

Just when Aliya was going to look around for Mrs Dickens, she came towards her, carried on yet another stretcher. She, too, had shrunk. She had poisoned the punch, like her necklace had forced her to . . . but why had she drunk from it herself?

Another ambulance was roaring into the square, sirens blasting.

Aliya caught Mrs Dickens's hand. 'Why?' she whispered wildly into the cook's ear. 'Why did you drink from it?'

Mrs Dickens shook her head. 'I couldn't stand by and see them get poisoned . . . by my hand.'

'That's just your guilt talking!' Aliya cried. 'You didn't do anything wrong. You had no choice!'

Aliya could feel Mrs Dickens's hand shrinking in her grip.

'I know, dear.' Mrs Dickens closed her eyes. 'I felt so ashamed, standing there, serving up the punch. Then something came over me and I had a sip.' She sobbed. 'I don't deserve any better!'

'No, that's not fair. That's not—' Aliya tried to hold on to Mrs Dickens's hand, but she was carried away. A moment later she had disappeared into the ambulance.

Aliya covered her face in her hands and screamed: a short, panicked roar. The world was crumbling around her, and it was her fault.

She had only thought about herself, about how she could get what she wanted: a home, belonging, how she would make her parents proud, how she'd make herself count. But the magic, hiding and cheating, it had ruined everything, and now everyone was in trouble. Even Karima – Karima, who had done all that she could to make Aliya feel at home, who had been a real friend.

A surge of anger went through her – anger at herself, and at Dorian. No, things could not end like this. She had to *do* something! Looking up at Little Ben, she felt the necklace tighten around her neck. She had one hour left until midnight; one hour before it would strangle her.

Chapter 27
FLYING RESCUE

Aliya found the carpet airing in a backyard a couple of blocks away from where Inspector Prickly lived, and where Karima was held prisoner in the attic. It was a battered thing with faded patterns in red and blue, and stirred when she tickled it on the fringe. Aliya pulled it carefully off its rail, hoping that the family whose yard she was in was sound asleep, or out with everyone else on the corniche watching the ambulances rush past on their way to the sanatorium.

'I'll bring you right back,' Aliya told the carpet as she spread it out on the gravel. 'I just need you to help me find Karima.'

A few taps on the fringe was all it took, and they

rose into the air. Aliya steered the carpet round the yard once, then headed up and over the rooftops. In the scramble to find a carpet she had thought up a plan. It was half-cooked at most, and full of holes, but it was a start. She'd have to make up the rest as she went along. Think on her feet. Improvise. And the first thing she needed to do was to save her best friend.

Inspector Prickly's building wasn't difficult to spot from the air. Her tablet's GPS quickly located it. Also, it was the only house with bars on the windows.

As Aliya slid up to an attic window, she spotted Karima through the glass, cross-legged on the floor, staring into space. She jumped up when Aliya reached through the bars and knocked on the glass, but her red-rimmed eyes were guarded as she opened the window.

'I didn't keep secrets from you,' Karima said, leaning on the windowsill. 'Why didn't you tell me about that book? And about the magic? Have you got something to do with the things that have been going on?'

Aliya nodded. Her heart pinched painfully as Karima's eyes widened in disbelief.

'But it's really complicated,' she said. 'I wanted to tell you so many times and I will, but right now I can't. I'm trying to make things right again but it's going to be dangerous and I don't have much time, so will you please just trust me?'

Karima stood silent.

'Why are you here?' she asked after a moment.

Aliya gestured at the carpet. 'Your parents are coming to bring you home, aren't they?'

'So you heard?'

'I-I couldn't just let them take you home,' Aliya faltered. 'Not without you even having a chance to clear your name.'

'Oh, so now you want to help me?' Karima's eyes flashed with anger. 'You weren't so talkative back at the hostel when they arrested me, were you? *Were you?*'

'You're my best friend,' Aliya stammered. 'I've never meant to—'

'Really? But best friends don't leave each other to be arrested *instead* of them, do they?'

'OK!' Aliya cried, desperately. 'I know . . . I blew it. But I just want to help you now, OK? At least let me do that. Then you won't have to talk to me again, ever. I promise.'

Karima stared at her. Aliya could almost hear her mind churning with thoughts.

'Are you really in a lot of danger?' she asked at last.

Aliya wiped her dribbling nose on her sleeve and nodded. She couldn't bring herself to speak or she would blubber all over the stolen carpet.

'OK, well.' Karima gave a curt nod. 'Still, there's no way I can get out of here.' She rattled the bars. 'Prickly thought of that. These are super-strong. I mean, really, who turns their attic into a prison?'

Aliya looked down at her palms. Ever since she'd met the Sublimes, they had been tingling as if something had been awoken within her. What if the whole attracting-metal thing worked this time, for real, just like the book for apprentice locksmiths had said?

She closed her eyes and concentrated. When she opened them again, the fine traces in the skin of her palms were glowing – blue, purple, silver – the colours of the Sublimes. She held them up to show Karima, whose eyes widened in astonishment.

'You're – you're *glowing*!'

'It's been like that ever since I met the Sublimes and—'

'You *met* the Sublimes?' Karima's eyes widened, with awe this time.

Suddenly a look of terror came over her face.

'That's my parents.' She pointed through the bars towards a couple who had just turned the street corner. 'Whatever it is you're doing – hurry!'

Aliya took a deep breath and remembered the passage in *The Apprentice Locksmith*:

Place your object in front of you and position your palm directly over it, then slowly attract the object until it touches your skin.

Aliya glanced down. Karima's parents were walking towards the house at a brisk pace, followed by Fuad, who suddenly looked up and saw them. He set off at a run towards the building.

'Fuad's coming.' Karima began bouncing with nerves. 'If he gets in the way of this I'll—'

'Stay back!' Aliya held her hands to the bars. 'I'm

not sure what's gonna happen.'

She closed her eyes and thought of the Sublimes, of their power and how alive she had felt when she had stood in front of them. Her hands heated up, but it didn't hurt, it felt . . . natural. Something was flowing out of her as naturally as wind breezes through trees. In front of her, Karima screamed. Her voice sounded far away, as if she were shouting through water.

Aliya jerked backwards. Most of the bars on the window had melted and hung off the window ledge like metal icicles. The necklace squeezed around her neck, as if in warning, but it didn't cut off her air supply. Dorian still needed her, after all.

'What was that?' Karima was staring at her as if seeing her for the first time.

Aliya stared at her glowing palms. The colours were steadily fading.

'It's a locksmith thing.'

Karima looked awed. 'I *told* you, you were one! How'd you do this, though? Who taught you?'

'I'll tell you later. Would you please get on the carpet?'

The door behind Karima slammed open.

'Hey!' Fuad stood in the doorway, his dark hair wild in the cross-draught. 'Are you OK?' He looked drawn and worried. 'What's going on?'

'Don't you *dare* tell Mum and Dad!' Karima took an angry step towards him. 'I'm not gonna stay here and rot. I didn't poison the elders, and I've got a way to prove it.'

Voices were drifting towards them from the stairs. Fuad slammed the door shut behind him.

'That'll be them. If you're doing this, you better be quick.'

Karima stared at him.

'You're not going to stop me?'

'Does that look like what I'm doing? Go!'

'Come on!' Aliya cried, reaching for Karima over the melted iron mess.

'Mum always lets you get away with things,' Karima continued, rooted to the spot, staring at Fuad. 'She still cuts your chicken, for God's sake, and you never make your own bed. And when Aunt Marwa visited in the summer *I* had to go with her on those slow-motion walks every day while *you* played cricket at the club!'

'I had to dance the cha-cha-cha with her!' Fuad cried. 'And eat her fried-brain sandwiches. She thinks all *men* like fried brain – well, I don't! And she never gets tired of telling me what my *duty* is. You think my life's all hunky-dory, but I've got all Mum and Dad's expectations to live up to! It's like they're setting me up to fail!'

They stood quiet for some moments. Aliya sat motionless, hovering just outside the window, watching Fuad, who had gone all red. She'd only ever seen him gobble down food or wear disguises. Who'd have thought there were so many feelings inside him.

'You never told me.' Karima looked as surprised as Aliya felt.

'You didn't ask.'

Fuad led Karima to the window and held the carpet still as she sat down behind Aliya.

'Maybe you're not such a spoilt brat, then,' Karima gave her brother a nod.

Fuad combed his hair out of his eyes.

'Thanks . . . I think.' He let go of the carpet and it

drifted away into the air. 'Let me know that you're safe!'

The door behind him slammed open. Aliya and Karima just got a glimpse of Karima and Fuad's stunned parents before they took off, soaring into the night sky.

They flew over the Victorian Quarter, sweeping over the main square with its chaos of agitated travellers and ambulances, then hovered for a moment next to Little Ben's steeple to let Karima take in what had happened to the elders.

'I hid Corpsy in our room,' Aliya said, when Karima looked like she was about to burst into tears. 'In the window niche, behind the curtain. I'm-I'm so sorry I didn't say anything when—'

'That's it! Take me to the hostel.' Karima gripped her shoulders, eyes alight. 'Corpsy smelt like old socks two days ago. I think that's the final stage before the cabbage smell sets in, which means he's ready!'

Aliya recoiled. She'd told Karima about Corpsy to relieve her own guilt, not to encourage her to race to the sanatorium and get caught all over again.

'I think you should hide somewhere,' she said. 'Until we find out how to prove you're innocent. You could hide in the hostel attic—'

'I can't hide when there's a chance that Corpsy might work!' Karima stared at her, her cheeks blooming.

'Well, I've got something really important to do!' Aliya snapped. The night's heady mix of fear and exhaustion was beginning to take its toll. She felt just about ready to crack. 'You're just going to get yourself arrested again!'

'What I need to do is important too!' Karima was yelling too now, a hurt look on her soft face.

'I'm sorry,' Aliya said, trying to ignore the panic that lay just below the surface, ready to bubble up and paralyse her.

'What's wrong?' Karima caught her hands. Aliya shook her head furiously. The necklace had allowed her to rescue Karima, but she knew it wouldn't allow her to tell anyone what was really happening.

'I can't say.' She looked up at Karima. 'I want to, but I can't. If I did, I'd be in a lot of danger – like, deadly danger.' She stroked away a tear.

'OK.' Karima nodded.

She hauled something out from under her coat and dropped it in Aliya's lap. It was *The Surreptitious Power of Magic Objects*.

'I managed to snatch this when they were carrying me off to Prickly's. I just had to know what it was you'd been hiding from me.'

Aliya shoved the book in her satchel.

'It's not what it looks like.' She gave Karima an anxious look. 'I mean, I—'

'It's OK.' Karima squeezed her hand. 'I mean, I don't understand what's going on, but I believe you. We made a pact, remember? We'll keep each other's secrets and we'll do our darnedest to stay here.'

'Uh-huh.' Aliya wiped her nose on her sleeve. Suddenly the tears wouldn't stop streaming. She caught Karima in a tight embrace. 'Thanks.'

Chapter 28
THE DARKLING

Once Karima had entered the hostel, Aliya knew she had to hurry. The clock that hung on Mr Taxidioti's grocery across the street showed that there was only half an hour left until midnight.

She slipped into a shadowy alley next to the hostel. Buttoning her coat up, she took a deep breath. The bone key Dorian had given her still lay in one of her pockets, ready to be used when the time came. But first, she had to steal the Darkling.

Raising her hands in the air the way she'd seen Professor Nigm do when he'd summoned the door, she mumbled a silent prayer that ended with: *Please take me to the Smithy!*

Her palms throbbed for a moment and a faint

light pulsed from them into the dark. For a couple of breathless moments she thought it hadn't worked. Then a golden door materialized before her. The entrance to the Smithy.

Aliya grabbed the handle and pulled it open. She was met by the bright workshop, with its desks of marble and walls like ice. Stepping in, she carefully closed the door behind her, then walked along a marble corridor on shaky legs, gazing up at the countless glass cabinets, full of shimmering boxes of different-coloured metals or brightly polished wood. She opened one of the boxes – inside was a time key.

But where among these hundreds of keys would she find the Darkling? They were several more corridors branching off this one! She took a few tentative steps down one, then stopped – had she heard something? For a moment, she could have sworn . . .

'Yes, you,' a small voice said. Aliya whipped around but found no one – only a brass table.

'I *said*, name please,' the voice snapped. Then she saw it. On the table sat a small . . . mouse? Hamster? It looked like something in between the two with its fluffy white fur and sleek little face. It had small, human-like hands and a tweed vest. Aliya blinked. Tweed vest?

'What are you staring at?' the little creature said, sounding miffed. 'Why are you looking at my vest? You never seen a vest before?'

'No, I just—'

'There's a matching cap too. It's being dry-cleaned.'

'I-I was just . . . looking around.'

She tried to look innocent while the little creature sized her up.

'I can tell from your expression that it's your first time. You're a novice, walking around in a daze *ooh-ing* and *aah-ing*. You're the new apprentice I suppose? I got the memo.' It pointed to a nest of papers that looked like they had been slept on.

'Yes, I—'

'So, to cut the tedium short I will tell you a little bit about myself,' the creature charged on. 'My name is Salman bin Adeem bin Ghassan, but the girl-child I once lived with called me Sweetcheeks. Cheeks, for short. I'm a *grump*, from the family *Grumpiphalus Flexibus*, originating from northern

Iraq and parts of southern Turkey. My main occupation is keeping this key nursery in order and delivering keys through the pipes.'

It tapped a brass pipe running from the centre of the desk up towards the ceiling with a small paw. Aliya followed the pipe with her eyes and saw how it divided and shot off into an intricate system that somehow connected to the glass cabinets.

'In my spare time I like to burrow, preferably in heaps of soft earth. Worms are a bonus.'

'Oh,' Aliya said, quite lost for words.

'Oh?' Cheeks huffed. 'Is that all you have to say? The likes of you usually have a sea of questions.' It looked around. 'But where is your mentor? The mentor always attends the orientation. That's the way it's been for the last hundred and fifty years.'

A light flicked on in Aliya's mind. The grump was under the impression that she was on an orientation with Professor Nigm. It had no idea that it was the middle of the night.

'Yes, my mentor,' she said. 'He just sent me to get something, actually . . . I'm supposed to fetch a special key. I think it was called the Darkling?'

The grump's eyes popped.

'The *Darkling?*'

'Um, yes, the professor needs it for a . . . routine inspection. To, um, install some extra security around it, or something like that. And I was told to ask only you for it.' She smiled.

Cheeks stood up and stretched itself to its full height, which was about as tall as Aliya's hand.

'The Darkling is kept in a high-security vault at the very end of that corridor,' the grump said, gesturing grandly to a passage full of doors. 'No one goes in there.'

'Yes, I understand, but the professor asked me to—'

'No one.'

'Yes, you said that, but—'

'Unless the professor comes here himself, the key to the Darkling vault is going nowhere.'

For someone so little, the grump sure could look mean, and the way he kept biting off Aliya's sentences – she understood why he was called a 'grump'. That was a whole lot of attitude for someone the size of a grapefruit.

'Um, actually,' she began, groping for an idea.

Sticking her hand in her satchel, she rummaged for something – anything – that could help. Her hand found the box of macarons from Karima, the ones that had knocked out Mr Philadelphus during their orientation tour. *Perfect.*

'The professor didn't really ask me to get the key,' she said, slapping the desk with what she hoped was a carefree air. 'That was just a joke.'

Cheeks gave her a dead-eyed stare. 'I'm in stitches.'

'Yes, well . . . he's on his way just now to collect it himself. He wanted me to tell you to get the vault key *ready*, and . . . to deliver these.'

She fished out the macarons. The grump gave the box a suspicious side-eye.

'It's a new thing,' Aliya improvised. 'They give it to the . . . eh . . . best worker of the month.' It had been a thing in her old school – student of the month.

'Do you mean that I—' Cheeks finally looked a bit baffled.

'Congratulations!' Aliya flipped open the box. 'Ta-daa!'

'Sweets aren't really my thing,' the grump said, stroking its little belly. 'If they had really cared they could have sent a worm or two.'

'Well, what I have *looks* like a sweet but is actually . . . worm-flavoured. Yes! Worm-flavoured.'

Cheeks stuck out a paw for the box, but Aliya quickly withdrew it.

'Imagine how pleased the professor would be if the key was already waiting for him when he arrived. Which is what he is about to do at any moment. You know how busy professors are . . .'

The grump looked unconvinced.

'I won't touch the key. Promise.'

The grump eyed the box again, then got down on all fours.

'All right. Wait here.'

In a flash, the grump had scurried into the pipe and disappeared. There was some rumbling inside the wall. A few minutes later it was back, carrying a thin wooden box attached to its back by a rubber band fastened like a belt around its belly. He unloaded the box on to the table.

'So, where's the professor?' The grump gave Aliya

a suspicious look. 'You're not touching this until he arrives.' He patted the key box. 'And not even then – he can unlock the vault, not an apprentice.'

'Just called to say he's on his way.' Aliya pushed the macarons towards him. 'In the meantime, here you go.'

She opened the box, broke off a piece and handed it to the grump, who sniffed the crumb once and then swallowed it in one bite.

'I don't know what kind of worms you usually eat, but this . . . tastes nothing like . . .'

The creature smacked its mouth and swayed a little. A moment later it plopped down on his little bottom with a dazed expression. The grump stared into space for a while, yawned loudly, then looked up at Aliya as if it had just seen her standing there. A moment later, it was curled up into a fluffy ball, fast asleep.

'Thank you,' Aliya whispered, grabbing the key box. The little creature was turning steadily pink. Oh well, it was hopefully reversible. Although she had seen Mr Philadelphus showing off his still-pink beard at the Initiation Ceremony.

She'd done it: she had the key to the vault where the Darkling was stored. Now she needed to find the vault. Fast.

She started running down the corridor the grump had pointed out.

And then, there it was: a door at the very end that was, unmistakably, the vault. The door was even thicker than the one to the Volatile Volumes section, and next to it there was—

Aliya skidded to a stop and ducked into a nearby doorway, a new fear tightening her chest. The vault was guarded by an enormous hieracosphinx! She peeked out at the massive creature – all bluish black feathers and massive claws. And that great, curved beak!

OK, she thought, heaving a breath. *I've got the key. All I need to do is show it.* Never mind that it was an enormous mythical being with a lion body and falcon head. She had the key.

Aliya stepped out from the doorway, the creature's eyes flicking up to meet hers, a growl rumbling in its chest.

It's civilized, she reminded herself as she held out

the key for inspection. *It's clearly not going to snap my arms off with that razor-sharp beak. Or maul me to death with those very long claws.*

For a few breathless seconds all was still and then – magically – the beast backed away, leaving her passage to the vault door free. Sweat slipped down Aliya's neck as she moved up to the door. She felt the sphinx's eyes on her as she inserted the heavy key and turned.

Click.

The vault slid open.

'I'll-I'll just be a second,' Aliya mumbled, slipping inside. She pushed the heavy door shut behind her with a *clang*.

Aliya took a steadying breath. Around her lay another workshop with rows upon rows of shelves with key boxes. Glinting silver and gold instruments hung from the walls. The room was plastered with alarming signs: *Danger!* and *Don't touch the glass! Keep away!* and, even more alarmingly: *Will Kill!* This last sign was stuck on a glass-topped cabinet in the very centre of the room.

Quaking, Aliya remembered Professor Nigm

telling her about locksmiths who had died trying to study the Darkling – left breathing but blank, empty. She stepped closer and gazed through the glass top of the cabinet . . .

The Darkling was the most beautiful and terrifying thing she had ever seen. The photo she'd seen at the exhibition hadn't – couldn't have – captured its true likeness. It was shaped like a black snake biting its own tail, and just like the peacock key Dorian had used, its Fortuna grain was pitch-black. Lodged in the snake's eye, it seemed to watch her.

This was danger incarnate, full of pulsing, potent magic. Yet she knew she had to pick it up.

She brought her hand up to the necklace.

Make this safe.

Red haze streamed out and, slipping through the tiniest of cracks between two panes in the cabinet, it grazed the Darkling where it lay, gleaming.

Aliya stood still. Was it safe now?

Gently lifting the glass top open, she stretched out her fingers towards the key. A strange aura hung in the air around it, as if it was surrounded by a radiance of power. This, Professor Nigm had told her, was the most powerful and dangerous key in the history of the Infinitum . . . and she was about to touch it.

As her fingertips landed on the glittering scales, a shock went through her that almost swept her off her feet. She had done it. She had touched the Darkling and she wasn't dead. The key felt as if it contained an atom bomb of impatient power just waiting to blow something – everything – up. So much power . . . and right now it was all in *her* hands. A feeling of exhilaration bubbled through her, and as she met the Darkling's pitch-black eye . . . the image of her sleeping parents was back. It floated before her inner vision – those arrested moments before it all ended.

She weighed the key in her hands. What if she were to go back, just one last time? It was just one boiler explosion. Sending it somewhere else wouldn't be the end of the world, would it?

Mrs Dickens had said she mustn't meddle, that death couldn't be reversed. Yet why would Dorian go through all this trouble if it wasn't possible?

The golden thoughts were back. The temptation to just make a little cut . . . a little paste.

She held out the Darkling, then closed her eyes and visualized the moment she wanted to reach, her parents sleeping in their beds, the boiler fire not yet irreversible.

When she opened her eyes the key had – mind-bendingly – come to life. A large black snake – big as a fire hose – writhed in the air between her outstretched palms. Aliya nearly fell backwards in shock. The snake's gleaming body left gilded traces in the air as it circled between her palms, its forked tongue flicking.

And now the snake lunged and sliced the air. A rift of pure darkness appeared, quickly filling in with colour – there it was: a portal to her own past. She could see her childhood home as clear as day, her parents, the slow line of smoke from the boiler cupboard. This was her chance!

The air above her quaked – a crack appeared that ran through the workshop like a wound. The floor shook. The world around her trembled, as if the Infinitum heaved a sigh. And then – the Darkling lunged through the portal. Aliya, who was pulled along, flapped through the air behind it like a superfluous attachment.

But instead of stopping, they whipped past her flat – colours and scenes streaking past too fast to register, her sleeping parents fading in a flash.

'Wait!' Aliya said. 'Go back!'

As they flew, a long hiss rose from the snake. *So hungry.* Soundless words echoed through Aliya's mind. The Darkling's voice. *Hunt. Hunt.*

Aliya tried to orient herself but before she understood what was happening, the snake opened its great mouth and began to swallow parts of the scenes they were passing – leaving black rips of nothingness in its wake.

'Stop!' she screamed, tears running down her wind-lashed cheeks. 'Go back!'

But her hands were glued to the Darkling, caught in its magnetic field. The snake slowed down. The images around them staggered and she began to discern the scenes they were slicing through.

A bearded man in a red tarboosh was flying through a desert. There was something distinctly familiar about him, Aliya thought, right before the Darkling gulped a great rip in the air and sent the man tumbling towards the ground. A Sultan! She had seen him in the clipbook Esmat showed her, commemorating their family's greatness – unmistakable with his messy hair and slightly crooked nose, just like hers and Geddo's.

She looked back in horror, but the snake had already sped on. That had been one of her ancestors and she, and this horrid beast of a key, had ripped a moment out of his life and sent him falling to God knew what fate!

More familiar faces met her as the Darkling continued its gobbling of her ancestral past. There was a big-nosed lady on a desert expedition who got knocked off her camel, and then a muscular Sultan caught mid-fight, wrestling a nasty-looking genie. Aliya screamed as the Darkling circled back and gobbled the moment when her ancestor sliced off the monster's head with a silver scimitar. What would happen to him now? When his moment of triumph disappeared?

Sultan after Sultan had moments stolen and gobbled by the Darkling, which swelled and blackened with each mouthful of their lives. The

Darkling tore straight through a family gathering, gobbling their laughter. Only, unlike the peacock key, which had opened another rift and pasted the moments it had cut out, the Darkling was just swallowing. It was *feeding*, Aliya realized, on her past – on her ancestry. Magic was a parasite. That was what she had heard, over and over. It fed on Life, and now it was feeding on her family's.

And then, as the Darkling slowed down and began steering back towards the present, whipping past her history again as quick as light, Aliya had yet another horrid insight. Esmat had said that her ancestors had believed they were cursed. Many of them had died mysterious deaths and the family blamed it on a mythical black snake. Now she understood. *She* was the curse! It hadn't just been an excuse her ancestors had made up to cover up their failings. It had been real – and her fault!

They were back at the rift where they had begun. The Darkling, engorged on her ancestors' lives, slid back through the opening and into the workshop. With a flick of its glimmering tail, the rift closed behind them. Aliya still hung from its great black body, like a paperclip stuck to a giant magnet.

The room shook. Was there an earthquake? Another rumble went through the air and Aliya realized the Infinitum was breaking apart. *The meddling*, she thought, breathlessly. The Darkling had set more than one catastrophe in motion.

Now the Darkling rose before her like a cobra, all blackish gold – beautiful and terrible. It began to encircle her in its massive body, her hands slipping against its smooth sides. The scales felt like fire under her palms. It ensnared her until only her head emerged above its coiled body. Then, she was looking into its glowing eyes. *You*, it hissed, flicking its forked tongue at her. *You must*. The coil squeezed Aliya until her lungs couldn't expand enough to draw in any more air.

Release me, she thought, a desperate plea rather than a command. But was it hers or the Darkling's – or both?

But then, without warning, the Darkling let go. The great snake shrank, hardening from organic to metallic, its undulating body stiffening until it was an object again – a key lying on the floor.

Aliya was shaking from head to toe with fear and exhaustion and shock. What had happened? What had she done?

A rumbling growl reached her from behind, followed by a heavy thump. Aliya whipped around, heart in throat. The door was open and the hieracosphinx glared in at her.

'There she is!' screamed a small but shrill voice. On the floor, not reaching above the sphinx's paw, was the grump. He was awake, furious and bright pink. Karima's macarons were for power naps, Aliya suddenly remembered.

The hieracosphinx cawed – an ear-splitting sound – and took a heavy, thundering step towards her.

'CAW!'

Glass smashed to smithereens as it unfolded its wings and swept them across the shelves. Aliya hunched into a ball behind a display cabinet, covering her face as shards rained over her.

'CAW!'

Think! She rummaged through the satchel. Should she try the macarons again? No, hieracosphinxes only ate raw meat. Besides, the grump had probably told it what she had done.

Something thin and sleek grazed her fingers. Aion's cat hologram stick! Aliya fished it out. It was worth a try.

The sphinx swung its massive head to the side, searching for her. Aliya fumbled with the holo-stick, found the button and . . . *zap!* A fat ginger cat leapt into the air.

The sphinx clucked in surprise.

For a few blissful moments, all was quiet as the beast followed the holographic shenanigans of the cat as it leapt and shimmied between the remnants of the shelf units.

'*Caw?*' The sphinx was tilting its head this way and that, looking like a befuddled chicken.

Aliya rummaged through her satchel again. The cat would only be a temporary distraction. She'd have to think of something else if she was to escape this in one piece. But what?

'CAW!'

As expected, the sphinx was losing interest in the cat. Ruffling its feathers, it whipped its head in annoyance, slipping back into fearsome guard mode.

The floor shook as the sphinx padded closer to where Aliya had slid under a workbench. She pressed herself to the wall as a large paw came probing.

Suddenly she knew exactly what to do.

She pulled out her tablet and swiped the screen with trembling fingers. Only 5 per cent battery left! How could she have forgotten to charge it?

With trembling fingers, she typed words she needed into the search bar.

'CAW!'

A massive beak felt around for her, snapping menacingly in the air. She could imagine the crunch her bones would make if it reached her and then . . .

The sound of trumpets rang through the air. The sphinx froze, then withdrew. Aliya clicked the volume up. A choir of men and women rang out in proud song:

'*Biladi, biladi, bilaaaadi. Laki hubbihi wa fouaaadi. My country, my country. I give you my love and my heart.*'

Aliya dared a glimpse. The sphinx was standing

in salute, its wings spread wide, its falcon beak lifted proudly – just like during the orientation, when Mustafa had saved them from being mauled in the air-traffic jam. The Egyptian national anthem had saved her once again.

Crawling out of her hiding place, she searched for the Darkling on the floor. Her hands trembled as she grasped it. She had to get it to Dorian, fast, or it would be over for both Mrs Dickens and her, but . . . she couldn't let him use it ever again. He would destroy the Infinitum without blinking. He would let the Darkling gobble up people's lives without a second thought, as long as he got what he wanted.

If Dorian got the Darkling, no one would be safe.

What could she do? As the national anthem reached its second verse, she pulled out the book on magic objects that Karima had returned to her.

Kneeling on the floor, she flipped through the pages until she came to an entry that read: *Infusing magic into an object*. A series of holographic photos showed a witchy-looking lady using a set of pincers to lift a black blob of magic out of a cursed teapot and dropping it on to a photograph of a Victorian lady who, as the magic touched her, began to splutter and scowl as if she had come alive. For this operation to work, the treatise explained, one needed to utter the incantations listed below on the page. Aliya scanned through the words – they were written in a language she didn't know. She'd need pincers, and an object to transfer the magic to – she knew just what to use. Riffling through her satchel, she found the self-portrait Dorian had made her during the first assessment. She unrolled it carefully. The thin, elegant man looked out at her with that same expression. She could see what it was now – anger mixed with despair, with hate. Dorian didn't believe in goodness. He had no hope. Not like Professor Nigm. Sneaking past the sphinx, who still stood in salute, she grabbed a pair of long pincers from among the instruments on the wall. She probed the black pearl in the Darkling's eye with the pincer tips, then took a deep breath and began to read the strange words. This was improvising. This was thinking on her feet. *This* was being a real traveller. *Please work*, she thought, as she read to the end. Sweat was beading on her brow. *Please, please work.*

The Fortuna grain shuddered in relief as the magic lifted, slipping off the grain and leaving it a brilliant, luminous white. A cursed, pulsating blob now hung off the pincer tip. She dropped it on the sketch of Dorian. The image stretched and began to develop. The thin face loosened and grew sagging cheeks, the back arching into a hunch. Dorian's eyes found hers and he roared a soundless roar. Careful not to touch the paper, she used the pincers to pick the image up and slip it into an ebony box she found on a shelf. She snapped the lid shut and closed the little clasp. Her hands were shaking. So far so good — the necklace had not reacted. Now the magic was taken care of, but what about the Darkling itself? She studied the Fortuna grain that now, released from the magic, glowed like a captured star. It radiated warmly against her skin as she picked it out of the snake's eye and slipped it into her pocket. Without the Fortuna grain, the Darkling looked blind. She rummaged for another empty box among the ones on the shelf nearest to her, then slid the grain-less key into it and snapped the lid shut. It was done. She would deliver the Darkling, but Dorian wouldn't be travelling anywhere with it.

But wait, why had the room gone quiet? She looked down at the tablet that lay on top of her satchel. It was dark. The battery had died! The sphinx whipped its large head to the side and blinked at her, as if waking up from a trance.

'CAW!'

Aliya glanced around in panic. She was trapped.

The hieracosphinx was so close now that she could feel its rancid breath on her neck.

A couple of steps more and it would snap her like a pretzel in its powerful beak. With trembling hands, she reached for the bone key in her other pocket. *Snap!* A heavy beak caught the hood on her coat, dragging her backwards. Aliya screamed, clinging to the desk. The hieracosphinx tugged at her – she pulled the other way . . . *Rip!* The hood tore right off. While the eagle head was still tossing the hood about, Aliya threw herself towards a cupboard behind her. She stuck the bone key into the lock and flung the door open. It was dark inside . . . very dark, and the cupboard seemed bottomless. She hesitated for a moment.

'CAW!'

The hieracosphinx thrust itself towards her, eagle beak gaping. Aliya plunged into the darkness, slamming the door shut behind her as she went. Whatever was coming couldn't be worse than being mauled to mince. Or could it?

Chapter 29

THE SHOP OF SECOND CHANCES

She fell. Down and down she went, tumbling through the darkness until – *thud* – she hit a sloping pane, and began sliding downwards. Her speed slowed, thankfully, and finally she slid to a halt in a cloud of black ashes. There was light coming from an opening in front of her. Crawling forwards, she realized that she was sitting in a fireplace. She'd descended through a chimney, like Santa Claus.

Aliya checked her pockets. The box with the grain-less Darkling lay in one. In the other, the Fortuna grain glowed warmly against her fingers. Its warmth spread through her and for a moment she felt less alone and a little less scared. She peeked out into a shop. The air was musty and close, with shelves full of odd, dusty objects: old clocks, ugly dolls, books, and stuffed animals contorted into strange poses. She guessed it was a second-hand shop, although some of the items (a basket of mismatched socks, a stand full of old toilet brushes) seemed senseless. She jumped as a black teapot next to her sneezed. So that's what it was: a shop for magic things. This had to be it. The cursed place her grandfather had told her of: The Shop of Second Chances. But where was Dorian Darke?

Peering through the dirty window, she saw there were other, dark shopfronts on the opposite side of the street. This had to be back in the Earthly Dimension, somewhere in Old Cairo.

A grandfather clock stood in a corner. The time was one minute to midnight.

'Hello?' she called. A hush answered her and for a moment she imagined that the objects in the shop all *tensed*, as if they had heard her. 'Hello?' she called again. 'Dorian Darke?'

She stood still, breathing in the silence. Where was he? For a moment, the whole world was frozen and waiting. The clock stood opposite her, its face chalk-white in the dark, its iron arms counting the minutes, the seconds before it would be over. Panic crept through her, freezing her body rigid. Her breath came in shallow bursts. Which one would be the last?

Then came the metal clang as the clock struck midnight. Aliya stood frozen until the last chime echoed through the dark shop. She closed her eyes. She knelt on the floor and cupped her hands in prayer.

Nothing happened.

For a breathless moment, she thought she had made it. Heaving a great sigh of relief, she was about to stand up when the necklace tightened over her windpipe, crushing it closed. She fell over, clawing at her neck, panic raging through every cell of her body.

Then he came, walking towards her across the floor, rolling his flute between his thin fingers. In the gloom he was ghost-like, his hairless chest shining white through his open shirt.

He stopped and looked down at her with an

unreadable expression. Aliya pushed the key box containing the Darkling towards him, writhing with pain and panic: *Take it!* He crouched in front of her and picked it up. Aliya watched him through a blur of tears. There was no air. Black shapes appeared in her mind's eye – they were flowing out of the diamond in the necklace and surrounding her in a ghostly dance.

Then, the pressure released.

Aliya sucked air into her lungs as though she had never breathed before. Dorian Darke's blue eyes were watching her.

'You fulfilled my wish.' His voice came from far away. 'So, you get to live.'

She felt for the necklace. It had materialized against her skin and hung loose around her throat. Pulling herself up, she heaved breath after breath, panic still raging in her chest. She ripped the necklace off and threw it away across the floor, her eyes streaming. She wasn't dead! She could breathe!

But any moment now Dorian would realize what she had done. She needed to get out of here . . . fast. Scanning the room, she located the door as Dorian lifted the lid off the key box.

Now.

She pushed off the floor and darted in among the dusty shelves. Reaching a door, she clasped the knob and turned, then shook it, then banged at the dusty wood to open. The knob grew warm in her hand – then it grasped her! Dizzy with disgust and fear, she saw that it had turned into a gnarled hand that was gripping hers in a monstrous handshake. She screamed. Tugging herself free, she stumbled backwards into Dorian, who caught her hard by the neck.

'My key,' he hissed into her ear, showing her the now grain-less Darkling. 'What have you *done* to my key? *Where is the Fortuna grain?*'

He hurled her down. She fell, hitting her brow against the floorboards. A lightning flash of pain seared through her head, and something warm ran down the side of her face. When she touched her temple, her hand came away smeared with blood.

He was going to kill her.

Her scalp stung with pain as Dorian lifted her by the hair. Then she was standing again, blood trickling into her eyes.

'You think you're clever, don't you?' Dorian's face was close to hers – his blue eyes bloodshot, his breath foul, his skin yellowed and sagging. Up close she could see what he really was: a crumbling shell of a man, inflated by magic – like hot air in a balloon.

'They took everything from me,' he wheezed. 'My status, my dignity . . . and made me choose.' He grimaced. 'Your people. Your fellow travellers made me choose – to destroy my key or myself.' He gave a mirthless chuckle. 'What would *you* have chosen?' He pulled her closer until their eyes were level. Aliya held her breath in disgust as the tip of his yellow nose touched her skin. 'You know what it's like to lose everything. I thought you'd understand. You saw what happened to my sister.'

He sobbed suddenly – a cracked, ravaged sound.

'Cassandra wouldn't have wanted this,' Aliya whispered. 'She wouldn't have wanted you to hurt others.'

Dorian's eyes widened, and Aliya could see the madness in them glimmering like a faraway light.

'Don't speak of my sister! She was killed by *your* sort.'

Aliya stared at him, speechless. He meant Egyptians, Arabs – not time-travellers.

'If you people had known your place, it wouldn't have happened. Cassandra would have lived.'

'What about *my* parents?' Aliya whispered through gritted teeth. 'They would have lived too if you hadn't killed them!'

'Traitors!' Dorian roared suddenly. 'All of them. Scheming behind my back. Just like you.' He gave her a violent shake. *'Where's the Fortuna grain? What have you done with the magic?'* Aliya winced as a light spray of saliva hit her in the face – but again, she didn't answer. 'Do you think you've won? Do you think you've saved your precious friends?' His fingers closed around her neck. 'Oh Aliya, this is just the beginning . . .'

Aliya tried to gasp but couldn't; he was holding her too tightly. Her feet were dangling off the ground, Dorian's bony fingers squeezing painfully into her flesh.

'Now, tell me where you've hidden the grain, or I'll finish what the necklace started. Why do you think I saved you from the fire that killed your parents?' He shook her. 'Only so you could finish what your mother didn't. She created the Darkling with me. That's why, apart from me, only someone of her bloodline can touch the key without getting killed. That's why I needed you. That's why I bided my time and waited for you to grow, why I took the pains to get you to the Infinitum, to turn you into a student, to pass the assessments . . . All that effort to make you what your mother was – a locksmith with access to the Smithy, who could access the place I was exiled from. A locksmith that could handle my Darkling, who could finish what she didn't. But if you don't . . . what use are you to me then?'

Dorian's face swam before her eyes. A wave of nausea surged. She couldn't breathe. She would die like this, and the last thing she would see was the manic eyes of the man that had killed her mum and dad.

Something warm and quick slipped into her hand. A sudden glow tingled through her fingers and made them feel alight – the Fortuna grain! Her palm buzzed with energy, just like when she had melted the window bars and got Karima out.

She made a fist inside her pocket with her pulsating hand, a sudden hope stirring. She would give this maniac something else to scream about. As she removed her hand from her pocket, it was radiating with silvers, blues and purples. The Fortuna grain had somehow turned itself into a ring that glowed on her finger. Reaching up, she touched the frame of Dorian's glasses and they melted under her touch. He howled and let go. Aliya drew a ragged breath, her throat throbbing with pain. She watched as Dorian clutched at his face where the molten metal had scorched his skin. There was no time to lose. She set off as fast as she could make her shocked body move, heading for the shadows and somewhere to hide, but Dorian caught her by the back of her coat. He lifted her up, howling with fury, and threw her backwards across the floor.

She crashed into an old chest which shuddered and bucked at her back. Aliya fished the ebony box from her satchel and threw it with a clatter to the floor. Dorian stopped.

'Is this it?' He picked up the box. 'Is this where you've hidden the grain?'

Aliya sat still, in silence. She had no idea what would happen if Dorian touched what was inside, but it was her last chance . . .

'No, please,' she cried, feigning terror. 'Please give that back!'

Dorian swallowed the bait, snapping the lid open. He drew out the self-portrait he had sketched during the second assessment, in the Alexandria library.

Aliya caught a glimpse of how the enchanted image writhed as Dorian brought it closer to his swollen face, examining it in confusion. That had been her impromptu plan: to remove the magic from the Fortuna grain to stop Dorian from using the Darkling. If only the sketch would distract him long enough for her to make an escape . . .

'Hello, Dorian,' a soft voice sounded from the portrait. An inky hand rose out of the paper and touched his face. He flinched. 'We meet at last.'

'I don't know you.' Dorian inhaled a panicked breath, jerking backwards to detach the hand that was pawing at his neck.

'But you do,' the voice said, more insistent. 'You *made* me.'

The hand grasped him by the throat – a fierce, decisive tug.

Dorian howled, a strangled croak. He clawed at the hand, but it grew into a body that stood tall and shadowy, hovering over him like an inky mirror image, grinning – a monstrous version of himself.

They grappled. For a moment, Aliya met Dorian's eyes, brimming with fear and hate. He struggled and thrashed, but the image was stronger. It scooped him up into a tight embrace, melting the two figures together.

Aliya glimpsed the last of Dorian's eyes. The blues were all white now, like on a panicked horse.

He collapsed. The two bodies on the floor dissolved until there was nothing but a black shadow hovering over the space where they had lain.

Aliya was trembling and her cheeks were wet. She must have been crying without noticing. Taking a deep breath, she wiped her face with her sleeve. She had done it. She had escaped from Dorian and the necklace – but only within an inch of her life. Her whole body was sore, her head throbbed. She sat still for some moments, just taking breath after breath.

Click!

Next to her a lamp turned on, bathing the shop in a green, eerie light. The hairs on Aliya's neck stood up, and a chill of goosebumps spread along her arms. Around her the shop felt different, alert.

Next to her, a porcelain cat turned on its table and looked at her.

'Welcome to the Shop of Second Chances,' it said. Aliya jerked backwards, then forwards again as she realized that the stuffed beaver behind her was speaking too.

So this was it. This was the place the myths had told about: the Old Evil, the Black Market, the Devil's Thrift Shop . . . the Shop of Second Chances, pulsing with cursed, stolen life.

'Look behind you!' the cat cried peevishly. A pair of carved monkeys on a lamp cackled with laughter. In the corner of her eye, Aliya saw that the shadowy shape on the floor had begun to rise.

'Dorian! Dorian! Dorian!' an accordion whined, sending a cloud of dust into the air.

'Just choose an object to bring with you out into the world,' a stuffed beaver said. 'It will grant you all your wishes.'

'Never,' Aliya whispered, stumbling through the jam-packed tables, eyes darting left and right in search of an escape. Meanwhile, the shadow had taken the shape of a man – a man with long, trailing arms and shadowy claws.

'People wander in here,' said a pair of ceramic frogs. 'They might not know what they're looking for. They might be down on their luck. We provide them with a solution, a second chance. It's so easy. Just choose something.'

'Over my dead body.'

'Oooh,' said a pair of porcelain shepherds. 'We could work with that.' They blinked at her, their eyes black and expressionless. 'Give your soul to us and we'll use it to create yet another part of ourselves, another piece of our shop. We all live in symbiosis here.'

'Symbiosis! Symbiosis!' the accordion whined.

'All for one and one for all!' cried the shepherds.

Aliya ducked through a doorway that led down a dark corridor and ran.

From the wall, a portrait of a lady with large hair

in a lacy dress hissed at her. Other portraits joined in. Aliya ran, a taste of blood in her mouth, further and further down corridors that twisted and turned to no end. Behind her doors and walls shifted. As she stopped to catch her breath, she saw the tip of the shadow just rounding a corner. And then, a voice she would have recognized anywhere:

'So, you thought you could kill me, did you?' Dorian screeched.

Throwing a look behind, she saw him coming – a shadow picking up objects as it went, objects that stuck to one another to make a strange, man-shaped heap of paraphernalia. Panic zapped before her eyes like lightning. How could he be alive?

'This is what magic can do!' Dorian cried, his voice echoing through the old pot that sat where his face should be. His windpipe was made of the flute he had used to cast spells.

'It lives on, even after the death of the body!'

A new surge of panic swelled in her head, and she ran on, casting glances backwards while objects and portraits hissed:

'Choose an object and we'll let you go.'

The corridor finally ended in a small, windowless room. Aliya scanned it in panic, but there was nowhere to go, only a wooden cabinet in a corner.

'He's coming. He's coming,' the lock on the cabinet clattered out.

She saw Dorian now, rattling his way towards her. Something warm slipped over Aliya's hand. Looking down she saw the Fortuna grain, slipping through her fingers like a luminous worm. Oh yes! That was it! If only it would work!

She groped in her battered coat for the bone key. It was still there.

'Will you help me?' Aliya whispered to the glowing grain, her voice cracking.

She attached it to the end of the bone key. The grain seemed to know what she was asking, because it shaped itself into a pearl and became solid, the way it was when attached to a key.

Behind Aliya, Dorian appeared, a mountain of cursed objects now, turning the room dark. She fumbled for the cabinet's keyhole, then heard the lock spluttering as she forced in the key. *Oh God*, she prayed. *Let this work.*

Click. A flash of light, and Aliya pulled the door open and jumped. A hand made of porcelain figurines grazed her cheek as she turned to close the door and, for a split second, she was looking into the pits of his eyes – black as death.

This is not over, the shadow that was Dorian whispered, then she fell helplessly backwards.

Chapter 30

THE POWER OF CORPSEWEED

Aliya fell through the dark. Towards what, she didn't know. The Fortuna grain had wrapped itself around her index finger and was shedding a warm glow into the blackness. Images of Dorian as a shadow with his pitch-dark eyes raged in her mind and at times she thought she saw his smoky hands reaching for her through the dark.

Then, something was approaching from below – a surface divided by thick wooden beams. She hit it softly with her feet and squatted, catching a beam to balance herself. Suddenly there was a hatch with a handle in front of her. Pushing it open, she was met by rain, falling softly on her face. She inhaled deeply, a wave of relief washing over her. She was outside and there was light and space. She was *alive*.

Crawling out of the hatch, she found she was on a roof. She heaved herself on to the wet tiles. Her body felt like a sack of stone, her head throbbed, but her heart sang with joy at the familiar view that spread out around her in all its patchwork glory. She knew these housetops and pillars of smoke rising in the night air. There in the distance – Little Ben! She was back in the Citadel. She was on the hostel roof!

The rain was steadily growing stronger, pelting her, but she didn't mind. She brought the Fortuna grain to her lips and kissed it. *Thank you*, she whispered to it. The grain glowed. Then, it transformed into a light-worm again, scurrying up her arm. Tickling her neck, it climbed until it reached her ear, where it lodged itself on the lobe like an earring, solidifying again like a pearl. Aliya touched it tenderly.

They had made it. But the Shop and Dorian – or whatever he had become – hovered in her mind. The thought of them made her feel the cold of the rain, and she shivered. She had seen the real face of magic, now. Dorian was like the beautiful prince in Geddo's fairy tale, who had traded his soul for power.

Far below, the hostel gates opened and closed with a slam. Looking down, she saw a figure stumbling out into the rain. Aliya sat up. She would have known that curly hair anywhere!

'Karima!' She flailed both arms in the air.

Karima looked up, peering at her, her face marbled in the rain.

'Aliya?'

Karima paced around, cradling a bundle in her arms.

'What are you doing on the roof?' she shouted.

Aliya waved. No point in trying to explain. Instead, she yelled, 'Wait for me!'

Aliya lifted the roof hatch open again. The hostel attic was below her, now – thank goodness. Skidding down to the floor, she hurried down the spiral staircase that led to the lower floors. By the time she burst outside and through the gates, Karima had taken shelter under a piece of protruding roof.

'You're bleeding!' Karima cried, stepping into the light. 'What *happened*?'

'What happened to *you*?' Aliya pointed at Karima's nose. It had grown to the size of a small cucumber, and her skin was light purple.

Karima uncovered Corpsy and stuck him under Aliya's nose. 'Do you smell that? *Cabbage*. Means he's ready.' She drew a small vial out of her pocket. 'I took some of the poisoned punch and drank it. Then I cured myself, and it worked!'

'That's amazing, but . . . that was *really* dangerous!'

Karima shrugged.

'I did pass out for about an hour, and I got some slight side effects.' She boinged her nose, making it wobble. 'But it's better than shrinking! Come on. We've got to get Corpsy to the elders.'

On the way towards the sanatorium, Aliya breathlessly narrated everything that had happened to her, only stopping when Karima shouted out her surprise or horror.

Splashing through puddles, they made their way through the sleeping city. Flushed and soaked to the bone, they arrived at the grand staircase of the sanatorium, where a new problem presented itself.

'How do we get to the elders?' Aliya asked as they stood looking in at the brightly lit reception area.

'They'll take one look at us and throw us out again.'

Karima puffed in frustration. 'I've not come this far to be put off by some nurses.'

They ran up the stairs and pushed through the doors, carrying Corpsy before them like a battering ram.

'Karima Mandil, medic in residence,' Karima told the receptionist as they stood, dripping, on the shiny tiled floor. The receptionist was a slick-haired man in a white kaftan with a lot of small buttons. He gave them a vague smile.

'I've got to get this antidote to the elders, quickly.' Karima waved the bundled-up Corpsy to show him.

'Are you a mythical?' The receptionist pointed at her nose with his pen. 'You're purple.'

'What has that got to do with anything?' Aliya blurted. 'This is a matter of life and death!'

The receptionist picked up a receiver and dialled a short number.

'We've got a situation here,' he said in a conversational tone. 'Please hurry.'

He put the receiver down with a click and gave them another vague smile. The girls exchanged a glance, then charged towards a pair of white doors.

'H-hello!' the receptionist called after them. 'You really shouldn't do that.'

'Mythical, my bum,' Karima panted as they bounded down a white-walled corridor. They skidded around a corner, then broke into a brisk walk, leaving a trail of wet marks behind them. A nurse in white scrubs was coming towards them, rolling a trolley and checking something off a list on his clipboard.

'Dr Mandil, mythical guest clinician,' Karima called out. 'Which way to the poisoned elders?'

'Second floor, door to the right.' The nurse didn't lift his eyes from his list.

'Thank you,' Aliya said, just as the sound of loud voices began echoing through the corridor.

They ran. Up the stairs they went through the first door on the right and then – *smack* – into a broad back in a black dress studded with sequins as big as coins. Aliya bounced sideways into Karima, who in turn tripped forward. Corpsy slipped out of her arms and landed on the floor with a crash that sent earth spraying in all directions. For a couple of breathless moments they stared in horror at the mess of earth and tentacles on the floor. Corpsy's bright-pink roots were exposed, looking fragile and helpless.

'Is that corpseweed?' a gruff voice said. The person in the black dress turned around. Matron Olfat looked down at them from over her crooked nose.

'It's a disaster,' Karima breathed.

The matron's beady eyes fixed on Karima for a moment, before she bent down and picked up the corpseweed. She sniffed it.

'Cabbage.'

Karima nodded.

'You stole this plant from my hothouse,' the matron continued, brow furrowing dangerously.

'Yes, ma'am,' Karima whispered. 'Only . . . it was for the love of science.'

Matron Olfat grunted. Behind them a security guard had appeared and stood shuffling in the door-way. Matron Olfat held out a hand to pause him.

'Corpseweed is misunderstood,' Karima said, getting up and taking a tentative step closer to the matron. 'It's not just a pesky weed, or just to make compost. If you feed it poison through the small mouth here' – she pointed to an opening between the tentacles – 'and care for it while it matures, it can produce an antidote to that poison. I know it works! I tested it on myself!'

'Has some side effects, I see.' Matron Olfat reached out and pinched Karima's nose.

'I took the poison and I didn't shrink,' Karima cried. 'Corpsy saved my life, just as you did once when I had TB. I will never forget that.'

Matron grumbled something inaudible.

'I did it for both of us, ma'am,' Karima pressed on. 'To show them what menacin can do!'

Matron scratched her nose and for once in her life, Aliya thought, she seemed lost for words. Then her heavy, bejewelled hand came down and patted Karima clumsily on the head.

'Well, I know something about being misunderstood. Had to capture Prickly and hang him upside down in the dungeons before he agreed to listen to my side of the story. He tried to arrest me for the mass poisoning, remember?'

Aliya suddenly remembered how the matron had been handcuffed and hauled off by Prickly's robots – the suspected poisoner.

'And did he listen?' Karima asked, eyes wide.

Matron Olfat scoffed.

'Only after I fed him some flies.'

'What about the robots?' Aliya blurted, forgetting how afraid she was of the matron. 'How'd you manage them?'

'Stink bomb. Now come along.'

She turned to the guards who stood hunched together in the doorway, watching them uncertainly. With a sudden movement she lunged towards them, black-nailed hands outstretched like monster claws.

'*Boo!*'

One of the younger-looking guards fell backwards on his bottom. The others pulled him up and scrambled off the way they had come.

'Do you really think she fed Prickly flies?' Aliya whispered to Karima as they followed Matron through the corridor. 'And hung him upside down? I saw him at the party . . . unless it happened before it started, just after the arrest?'

'Well, Prickly's not likely to tell us if she did. She's done worse things in shorter time . . . Or so the rumours say.' Karima grinned. 'That's just the thing with Matron. You'll never know for sure which stories are true. Maybe that's the way she likes it.'

They entered a brightly lit room that looked like a maternity ward. There were cots on wheels everywhere, only they weren't filled with babies.

'Inspector Prickly!' Aliya cried, stopping at the first one and looking down at a small version of Victoria's father, snoring into his moustache.

'I've tried everything I've got,' Matron Olfat said. 'Nothing will work.'

'This will.' Karima reached out and broke a piece off Corpsy's tentacle. She stuck it into Inspector Prickly's mouth. 'Do the same with all of them.' She broke off more pieces and gave them to Aliya and Matron Olfat.

Aliya scurried between the beds, sticking bits of corpseweed into the mouths of the baby-sized adults, cringing a little every time. Why had Dorian chosen this poison to get back at them? He could have given them something that killed them instantly, or turned them to ash. Maybe it was because he wanted to humiliate them, to make them feel small and helpless, like babies?

She stopped to look down at Professor Nigm. He too was asleep. With his aquiline nose and his neatly trimmed beard, he managed to look distinguished even in miniature. She gingerly pushed a bit of corpseweed into his mouth.

'It's working!' Karima yelled behind her.

Aliya whipped around to find Inspector Prickly sitting up in his crib. He was much bigger now, and purple. His nose also seemed to be growing at a faster rate than the rest of him.

'What the blazes happened here?' Prickly looked around in befuddlement, then looked down at his purple hands and shrieked. Matron Olfat lumbered over to pacify him.

In the other beds, the elders were slowly undergoing the same restorative transformation, turning bigger and purple and big-nosed. Soon it looked like a whole tribe of mysterious mythicals had congregated.

'Mrs Dickens,' Aliya cried, running up to the cook, who had just sat up in her cot and was looking around with a dazed expression. Aliya grabbed her by her purple hands, and for a moment everything swayed out of focus. Her head felt light, and like it didn't belong to her body.

'Everything's come right, Mrs Dickens. See?' she mumbled, gesturing at the room, which was filling with staff and happy shouts and clamour.

'The necklace.' Mrs Dickens brought a quick hand to her throat, relief lighting up her eyes. 'It's disappeared! Thank God, it's gone.' She gave a quaking sob.

Aliya smiled, then cradled her head. Her legs felt like jelly.

'Oh my dear, you're bleeding.' Mrs Dickens reached out and touched Aliya's forehead, then tried to hold her up, but too late. The world melted away.

Chapter 31
GEDDO

Aliya opened her eyes to a familiar sight. Geddo was sitting on the edge of her bed, holding her hand in his, as if it were a wounded bird. His eyes were red, and his hair was longer than she remembered. But no matter. Aliya dived into his arms and cried, long and hard, until she felt like a wrung dishcloth. The world disappeared and the only thing that was real was Geddo — his old voice, and the smell of him, of sandalwood and lemon aftershave, and his wizened hand patting her gently on the back.

It was only when she'd had her fill of crying that she realized her head was in a bandage and that she was in one of the sanatorium rooms, in a bed with a yellow bedspread and matching curtains. Through the window she could see trees and bits of blue sky. It was bright and sunny. How long had she slept?

'You've got a concussion.' Geddo motioned her to lie down again and made her blow her nose.

'What's wrong?' she asked, noticing the bandage around his waist, just like the one she'd seen in the vision the necklace had showed her. 'Why do you have a bandage? Are you OK? Are you *hurt*?' More tears erupted and dribbled down her cheeks. She clung to Geddo again. When she finally let go, Geddo gave her a tired smile.

'During the assessment, when I tried to stop you, Dorian stabbed me.' He indicated the bandage. 'Nothing the nurses here can't fix.'

'But if you're all right, why do you look like that?' She indicated his walrus moustache, which had grown long and blended with a wild beard. He looked like he needed a hedge-trimmer, not a barber.

'This is what worrying about you looks like. For days and weeks on end.'

'Worrying? I thought you . . .' Aliya's voice trailed off. She had been so busy surviving that she hadn't had the time to recalibrate how what had happened affected Geddo. He had never been mad, that was for sure, because all of what he had tried to warn her and the Council about had been real. And now – she understood why he had tried to keep her away from the time-travelling world. He had expected something like this, like Dorian's plan. He'd been trying to keep her safe.

'Did you know I was a locksmith?' she asked.

'Since you were little. There were signs.'

'So when you said that *someone like me* shouldn't be at the Citadel, you didn't mean I was—' She meant to say *an idiot*, but the word got stuck.

'You're a gifted child.' Geddo nodded slowly. 'But your gift is dangerous, or else Dorian wouldn't have come after you. After your parents died, I realized there was something off about their deaths. Your mother had been close to Dorian Darke – he was her mentor – and when he died mysteriously too . . . well, it seemed so odd. And then there was the fact that you, a child of five, had somehow escaped the fire. I found you on the steps outside, asleep. Someone had put you there.' He sniffed. 'But no one would listen to talk of magic, to my *"outlandish suspicions"*. So, I retired and began my own investigations.' He stroked Aliya gently over her bandaged head. 'And I became your guardian.'

Aliya nodded.

'What happened then? Where did you find him – Dorian?'

'Six years later, in Old Cairo, in a magic shop.'

The Shop of Second Chances, thought Aliya.

'In the end, he confessed. He told me how he had been hiding out in the Shop and plotting his next move – a move that involved you getting initiated as a locksmith and bringing him his key. I think he enjoyed seeing my pain. He told me he would come after you next, then he hexed me so that I would appear mad whenever I spoke of him. And you know the rest, habibty.'

Aliya remembered how Geddo's face had convulsed whenever he'd talked about Dorian or the Shop, making him look mad. That's what she thought had happened to him at the time. But it had been because of a curse. Dorian had made Geddo look mad to anyone he tried to warn.

'Once I realized the danger you were in, I tried to lock you up. I even destroyed our family portal, thinking you'd be safer. But look where it's got us.'

'So you remember?' Aliya felt a new lump in her throat. She'd been so afraid that he wouldn't. 'I thought you had been—'

'Blotted. Yes, I was.' Geddo sighed. 'I still am, but I'm recovering. Matron Olfat's remedies are helping. They're disgusting, and I think my ears have got bigger, but I'm remembering again.'

'What about Mr Kamel?' Aliya asked, remembering how terrified she'd been of the genie – he was the stuff of nightmares.

'He's outside.' Geddo gestured at the door. 'He's rough around the edges, I know,' he said when Aliya frowned. 'He's not been through the Reform and Civilization programme yet. I've homeschooled him.' He smiled. 'After Dorian revealed his plans, I tried to return to his shop, to raid it. I found Kamel trapped in an old tin. He was very grateful to be set free. If not for him, I wouldn't have escaped that hellish place.'

So that was why he was so obedient to her grandfather – Geddo had set him free.

'The shop you're talking about is the Shop of Second Chances, right?' Aliya asked. 'I've been there.'

Geddo's eyes widened.

'Kamel!' he called over his shoulder. 'Get in here!'

Now it was Aliya's turn, and she told Geddo and Mr Kamel everything that had happened to her, from beginning to end – about the necklace, the smouldering letters, about the genie, Zil, who had turned out to be Dorian Darke and lastly, about what had happened in the Shop of Second Chances. She left out the part about how she had tried to use the Darkling, and what it had done to the Sultans' ancestors. That guilt was too fresh to be shared. She would have to find a way to set things right, somehow. If the Darkling had swallowed those stolen moments, maybe there would be a way of making it spit them out again?

Mr Kamel stood in a corner with his arms crossed

and listened, his yellow eyes glowing. When she had finished he walked up to her and stretched out a pale hand. He squeezed Aliya's in a firm and quite *civilized* handshake.

'That shop is a hell on Earth, and I'm amazed you escaped from there, and from him. But he didn't die, did he?'

'I don't think so,' Aliya said, her voice small. 'He's different, but he's still alive.'

Mr Kamel nodded gravely.

'Isn't there a way to destroy the Shop?' Aliya looked from Mr Kamel to her grandfather. 'Couldn't you assemble your old SWAT team and go and burn it down or something?'

'The Shop travels around in the world through its magic,' Kamel said. 'And takes on all kinds of disguises. Same goes for the owner. It would be a hard fight, very dangerous and difficult.'

Geddo hummed in agreement.

'That's a fight for another day.' He patted Aliya's hand.

The three of them were silent for a moment, what had been said still hanging in the air between them.

Aliya's head was heavy, and she closed her eyes, relishing the snugness of the room, of Geddo's warm hand on hers.

The peace was broken by Gigi, who swept in with a partly visible Esmat in tow. Behind them trailed a long line of Matron's maids carrying trays with treats, flowers and, Aliya noticed, a potpourri of paper bats and spiders.

'Sultan Junior.' Gigi sank down at Aliya's bedside, plonking her lacquered handbag into Mr Kamel's hands. 'I've got everything in hand. Anything you need – *anything*, you tell me.' She sighed heavily, then dabbed her forehead with a handkerchief.

'It's been a most trying twenty-four hours. Esmat kept disappearing.'

'Since you vanished from the ceremony, I've been a bundle of nerves,' Esmat's disembodied head explained. She gave Aliya a tender look. 'Couldn't help it.'

'But you're well now – oh.' Gigi grabbed Aliya by the hands and brought them to her chest. 'Our youngest Sultan, our hope, our—'

'Gigi,' Geddo interrupted. 'You promised.'

'What!' Gigi gave him an indignant look. 'I'm calm.' She fanned herself. 'But you're right. Our hope for the future needs to rest, needs to gather her strength.' She patted Aliya's cheek, who stretched her arms out and drew her into a hug.

'Thank you,' Aliya whispered. 'For everything.'

Gigi sniffed in surprise.

'You're very welcome, dear. We're family, aren't we?'

Family, Aliya thought as she lay back against the pillows with Geddo's hand still safely clasped in hers. *That's worth fighting for.*

Chapter 32
A PROPER CELEBRATION

Mrs Dickens had outdone herself: the long table in the dining hall was heaped with so much food that the plates nearly slid into the guests' laps. She was probably still feeling guilty, Aliya thought as she helped herself to more chocolate pudding.

As she glanced around at the assembled guests (some of whom were still slightly purple from the poisoning), a warm feeling spread until every part of her was tingling with happiness. Everything was perfect. The two fireplaces were lit, and the cavernous room was filled with talk and laughter.

More importantly, everyone who mattered to Aliya was here. Geddo was cutting his steak and laughing with Great-Aunt Gigi, who looked relaxed, for once. She had continued to visit Aliya at the sanatorium, each time giving a heart-quaking speech about how she'd saved the Sultan family honour. Next to her, Esmat was smiling too, deep in conversation with Mr Kamel who, for once, had left his horrid pipe at home.

At each end of the table sat Matron Olfat and Mrs Dickens, watching over the students. Matron Olfat was dolled up in a dress with lots of sequins that blinded the guests when the light from the chandelier hit them. Her lips were a glaring red – perhaps she was wearing the lipstick Great-Aunt Gigi had given her on that first day, Blood Bath Number Seven. What was more, she had not spoken about turning anyone into intestinal delicacies or feeding them to the rats in the dungeons – not once. Perhaps it was because ghoulish medicine had been vindicated, and the bans against it lifted.

To complete the picture, there were her excited classmates and friends. Victoria was helping herself to more jelly, talking at full speed while she ate it. Inspector Prickly had finally allowed her to go on with her navigation studies. Getting shrunk to the size of a baby might have helped him recalibrate his priorities. Not that any of that had done anything for Victoria's attitude.

'I knew who the real villian was all the time, of course,' Aliya heard her tell Aion. 'But Papa forbade me from saying. He confides all matters of importance to me, you know, because I'm so trustworthy.'

Aion didn't seem to be listening. She was busy stroking a (very real) ginger tabby that sat on her knee, swiping at the flower and fruit centrepiece – an initiation gift from her father.

Next to her, Mustafa was looking neat as usual in a spotless white turban, while Fuad had combed his hair and was doing his best to eat slowly. And Karima – Aliya watched as she ladled more greens on to her brother's plate – she was a hero. After saving the elders, she had been apprenticed to Matron Olfat. Her food delivery days were over, and she was to learn real menacin . . . in a dungeon, with the matron. Aliya smiled. *Oh well, as long as she's happy about it.*

Aliya sipped her strawberry cordial, her chest glowing with the warmest feeling. She could finally tell herself the words that she'd longed to say for so many years – these people were family, Infinitum style. She was home.

Except . . . where was Professor Nigm?

Aliya found the professor on the balcony off the novices' common room, looking out over the Citadel where Little Ben was just visible in the twilight. The golden tips of faraway pyramids glinted in the dying light. The crack that the magic had opened was barely visible now, thanks to the locksmiths – all was well in the travel world again.

'I'm not much of a party-goer,' Professor Nigm said before Aliya could speak. 'But I'm glad you found me. There's something unfinished between us.'

Aliya stepped out and stood next to him, breathing in the smoke from his pipe, pale purple and lavender-scented tonight.

'I heard of what you did to the window bars on Inspector Prickly's house,' Nigm said. 'You used your powers.'

Aliya nodded, unsure whether this was a reprimand or praise.

'They became activated when you met the Sublimes,' Nigm continued. 'But not controlled. That takes training. Now, you're like a ticking time-bomb. We must teach you to keep yourself and others safe.' He gave her a searching look. 'Do you agree?'

Aliya looked down at her palms. None of the brilliant, ethereal colours were showing now.

'Yes,' she said. 'I don't want to hurt anyone.' *Never again*, she added to herself.

Professor Nigm nodded. 'Good. Then let's do this.'

He took her hand in his. First nothing happened, then she felt a deep tingling in her palm. A rush of warmth swept through her before Nigm let go again. When Aliya looked down, the image of a radiant key was glowing from her palm.

'Your initiation,' Nigm said. 'You are now my apprentice.' He smiled.

'Holy chronometers!' Aliya whispered in awe.

'You did well. You chose right, even when it was difficult. That's following your compass.' He tapped his chest, just above his heart.

Aliya nodded, although, regardless of how happy she was, there was still a piece missing. It probably always would be. How could she ever be a whole person without her parents? It was loss, and that was how it felt – like a missing piece. But it didn't hurt as much now, and that was a start.

'Professor, I have this.'

She fished out the Fortuna grain from where it had hidden in her pocket, and showed him.

If the professor was surprised, he didn't show it. 'A Fortuna grain?'

'I took it from the Darkling . . . so that Dorian wouldn't be able to use it to travel.'

'I see.'

She stretched the grain towards him, but as she did so it liquidized into a small, glowing worm that quickly slipped on to her fingers, transforming into a radiant ring.

'That's pretty clear, I think,' Nigm said. 'It belongs with you now. It'll be your companion in what lies ahead.'

'What lies ahead?'

'You took the Fortuna grain, but Dorian still has the key.'

Aliya froze.

'What does that mean?'

'The Darkling is a powerful tool, even without the grain. It's incapacitated at the moment, but knowing Dorian, he won't stop until he finds a way of using it.'

Aliya bit down hard on her lip.

'It's my fault,' she said. 'I brought him the key. I *left* it there.'

Nigm frowned. 'You did something terribly brave. If not for you, this whole world might be crumbling around us.'

'But the Darkling?'

Nigm took a puff on his pipe. 'That's a fight for another day.'

She looked up at him in surprise. 'How can you be so cool about it all?'

'I had a good dinner. The night is beautiful.'

'But—'

'Another day, Aliya. Right now, we need to digest.'

She shook her head in exasperation. Digestion? *What?* Was he talking about digesting, like, *the dinner*?

'You can't fight a battle of this magnitude in one day. You need patience.'

Aliya shook her head, unconvinced.

'And' – he pointed at her with the pipe shaft – 'you're *not alone*.' Nigm gave her a sideways glance. 'What's happened is not your burden to carry. We all play a part, we all carry responsibility. Try to remember that.'

Aliya exhaled slowly.

Professor Nigm reignited his pipe with a light touch of his index finger. He exhaled a smoke cloud that formed into a ring in front of them.

'Oh,' Aliya breathed. 'Cool. Will I have a pipe too, now that I'm your apprentice?'

'I don't think so.'

They stood side by side, watching darkness fall. Around them the city was preparing for sleep. Shops were closing. Vendors were packing up their curious displays. Over the rooftops, pillars of smoke were still rising from chimneys. Tomorrow there was more to come, more challenges, more danger.

Aliya took it all in – the sights, the smells – all of it. This was her home now, and she was responsible for it. She had to set things right, whatever it took, and she was ready.

ACKNOWLEDGEMENTS

This book is my apprentice novel. As such, many generous and insightful people helped it take shape. My gratitude and thanks to:

Lucy Irvine, my wonderful agent who, Professor Higgins-like, pulled this book out of the slush pile, harnessed my runaway imagination, and taught it to tell *one* story at a time – not five.

Kesia Lupo, who like Lucy, has been the biggest champion for this story. The two of you have really made all the difference for me as a writer.

Barry Cunningham, who took a chance on me, and who confirmed my notion that the people in children's publishing are some of the nicest you can meet . . . and that they all have small dogs.

To everyone at Chicken House, who have made me feel safe and supported while finishing this book.

Fraser Crichton, for editing with such insight and tact.

Imogen Cooper (who also has small dogs) and her Golden Egg Club, who helped me understand what it is to write for children, and who, again, helped give my story *one* spine – not five.

To Gaia Alessi, for the brilliant artwork.

To critique partners Dimitri Verikio, Lisa Varchol Perron, Jen Malia, Megan Clendenan, Mandi Rusher-Haqq, Mayken Bruenings, Hannah Hanson, Kimberly Mach, Roni Carr. I learnt so much from you.

To readers Rhonda Roumani, Christian Todd, Anna-Marie Krahn. Thank you for taking the time to read and comment.

To writing buddies for sharing the journey: Carolyn Brougham, NT Hong, Katja Kayne, Davina Bennett, Nicola Tams, Suzie Pascoe.

To my friends and cheerleaders: Lamya Taher, Ghada Shawki, Sabrine Rushdy, Nehal Hammouda. Sisters forever. You make Cairo feel like home.

Thanks to my wonderful parents (yes, that includes you too, Helge and Anita) for never pulling the breaks on my creativity, and for trying to make me read more. I do – now.

At last, thanks to my beloved children, Luli, Nusha, Sunsun and Safy. Everything that I write, I write with you in mind (and heart).

Ahmed, beloved husband, you are my best friend and companion in this life and the next, inshallah. Thank you for being there, always.